I0671799

THE WARRIORS' DEADLY SHADOW

Hector A. Sectzer

ALBION
PUBLICATIONS
&
CBS PRODUCTIONS
Publishing

i

Albion Publications
A division of Albion Global Marketing Limited
Printed in the United States of America
First Edition 2017

For inquiries, contact: Inquiries@CBSproductionsInc.com
                or use: reply@CBSproductionsInc.com

Library of Congress Catalogue-in-Publication data
Sectzer, Hector A.
    The Warriors' Deadly Shadow / Hector A. Sectzer
    Includes bibliographical references
    ISBN: 978-0-9817290-0-8 (paper)

Cover and Interior Design by Hector A. Sectzer

Reviewed by Robert Wagner

14 13 12 11 10 / 10 9 8 7 6 5 4 3 2 1

THE WARRIORS' DEADLY SHADOW

PREFACE

Over 10 years ago, after I finished co-writing my first ever script (a comedy about bumbling secret agents), I was approached by an individual who claimed to be connected with a group of elite fighters that train the "Black Ops" and other undercover USA agents in an obscure form of martial arts. He went on to say that the main focus of this operation was to form several groups of nine individuals each and train each group as lethal counter-assassins that could infiltrate any subversive government, group, or entity whose objective was to harm the United States of America.

He assured me that these so-called "counter assassins" main objective was to only "defend" – never attack, however when threatened they could kill an enemy in three seconds or less. He asked me to write a script for the making of a major motion picture based on these real life teams, which I did at the time.

While in the beginning I wasn't sure of the validity of what this gentleman that approached me was describing, through years of research I found several articles about a US undercover military group called "Shadow Warriors" that actually fit the stranger's claims. Upon further research and substantial effort, I got to meet the actual group that trained these undercover US agents – the SOG's, the NOC's, the Black Ops, etc.

Through the years that followed, I gathered information about some of their missions and the goals determined by the US Government, and **compiled enough information to put together nine separate books about the clandestine, "dark cover" missions of these "Shadow Warriors"**. The first book titled *"The Warriors Deadly Shadow"* starts from the inception of this obscure, surreptitious organization and the initial battles they fought against crime organizations to protect and save the freedom and way of life of the United States of America.

This book will open the eyes of the American people to the sacrifices of a few for the freedom of us all. These Counter-Assassins for the good of America have ingrained in their being from the inception of their training that they are the protecting angels of justice.

So, two questions often arise in the "Warrior's" mind: (1) "When Fighting Evil, can a Government send an Angel to do The Devil's Work?" or must that Angel be prepared to be as much of a Devil as Evil itself?; and (2) Can the "Angels of Justice" follow the rules, while "Evil" doesn't and still be able to protect the free world?" My initial unwilling participation became less and less reluctant as my research uncovered the work of these unsung heroes "The Shadow Warriors".

I don't know why I was chosen for this task and I had over ten years to think about it, but I am glad that I can be part of telling their incredible story that every American deserves to know. This is the first time ever that the true story of the "Shadow Warriors" ever gets publicized in any book or story form. Needless to say, names and exact developments were changed to protect the secrecy and identities of everyone involved.

> *"Beware Evil, for out of the shadows of injustice*
> *and wickedness rises the all mighty sword of*
> *the Shadow warriors"*

INTRODUCTION

"This Book Is Compiled From Actual Events"

A group of extremely skillful and ruthless criminals from all over the world are summoned by a former director of the USA "Black Ops" operatives with the goal of forming a worldwide alliance to overtake the free world. Led by one of the most dangerous female criminals of our day, Gina Venezie, (FBI code name "The Panther") and her cutthroat comrade, Tex, attempt to compromise the Worlds' banking system for the International Organized Crime Syndicate, "UNITY".

Their plan is two-fold: 1) to kidnap the 'Master Technology Geek' of an underground group formed by a college fraternity, known as "Hackers, Inc.", a college band of notorious black-hat computer hackers who invent a "Sniffer" program, capable of piggybacking on every financial transaction executed over the internet and the banking networks; and

2) Create a virus program that freezes every deposit made in every bank, for a period of 48 hours, long enough to take that money and collect high interest in short term notes ready to mature and collect billions in interest. The principal is then unfrozen making their heist almost "bulletproof". The monies made from the virus program are then used to unbalance the US banking system. UNITY's goal is to maintain total control over the world's banking system through the virus program.

The only real threat to UNITY's plan is a highly trained group of NSA special agents, known as SI-9, the "Shadow Warriors" trained in the discipline of "Lin Kuei", a sect of

Ninja warriors secretly led by Xavier Crown, a mysterious government agent code name "Shadow 6".

After the sudden demise of the active "Senior Shadow Warriors" team, the only option left to the government is to use the group of 'still wet behind the ears', young NSA agent trainees, whose capabilities and strengths have yet to be tested on the field. Crown's entourage of nine teenagers trained in Lin Kuei, each with the skills of nine ferocious animal fighting systems and the power and strength to match were to be the upcoming replacement to the senior "Shadow Warriors" twelve months from their demise. This special team was bred to honor and uphold respect for the law from childhood. The question is, are they up to the task?

The secret knowledge of centuries of training in the Lin Kuei discipline is embedded into a bracelet handed over to Shadow 6 by his mentor. Shadow 6 and the Young Shadow Warriors vow to avenge their mentor's death, the murder of the senior Shadow Warrior's team and circumvent UNITY's plans at all cost.

The young have always fought for our freedom. The average age of the soldiers in The American Civil war was 25.8 years old, with 20% younger than 18 years of age. The average age of an infantryman that fought in Vietnam was 22 years old. Over 250,000 boys under the age of 18 served in the British Army during World War I.

ABOUT THE AUTHOR

Mr. Sectzer has over 35 years' experience in the marketing, advertising, and News arena. He is been involved with Radio, Television, Newspaper, Social Media, and other outlets of the mainstream media for a great part of his life.

He has formed strategic alliances with many of the world's leading media organizations to help his companies achieve the success and credibility to move forward in the field of Media and Marketing.

In cooperation of his business contacts he created several companies that encompassed medical, fitness clubs, financing, social media, and wellness facilities.

On the non-profit side, Mr. Sectzer was involved in several projects that raised money for children afflicted with fatal diseases. These Projects attracted the attention of people like Jennie White, the mother of "Ryan White" the first child to die of Aids due to a transfusion, as well as Elton John and former president Ronald Regan.

He was also partner and organizer of several food drives that fed thousands of people in Southern California, as well as programs that raised hundreds of thousands of dollars to fight breast cancer.

Mr. Sectzer participated as a moderator for NCCJ; an organization to teach young adults about the negative repercussions of prejudice against color, creed, religion, and sex. This organization was funded by Herb Albert.

As part of his efforts to halt human trafficking, Mr. Sectzer traveled to India in 2008, visiting over 12 cities, to meet the Dalai Lama and several of his advisors to put together a project that rescued children from villages in the Himalaya Mountains that get raped and sold into prostitution. The children were brought back to India and placed in an orphanage.

During his research in the past ten years Mr. Sectzer recruited the aid of major political figures as well as government officials that shared in secrecy the content of this very delicate and complex information that went into creating the "Shadow Warrior" series.

THE WARRIORS' DEADLY SHADOW

CHAPTER ONE

THE RISE OF YOUNG XAVIER

"Present Day"

In the thick of the night, blending with the black tar on the deserted road, a phantom car, on a drug run from Mexico races at a demonic speed. There is no sign of the moon or the stars in the jet-black desert night. The outline of the *Matt Black Lamborghini* is barely visible to the eye... the roar is deafening.

The car traveling with its headlights off eats up the road like a hungry tiger after its injured prey. The driver wears night vision goggles. The *Speedometer* reads 220 MPH. The deep throaty humming of the engine intensifies.

As the Lamborghini travels maniacally, swallowing the road at a fierce speed, a *CHP Patrol Car* parked on the dirt part of the road, with its wheels slightly touching the paved road comes into vision. Crickets break the night's silence.

The CHP officer sits in his patrol car, attacking the remains of a half-eaten hamburger, his breathing labored, his eyes bulging as he slurps the remains of the hamburger down his overgrown belly. Loud Country music plays on his radio. French fries hang from his shirt as if they were "free rock climbing" to the mouth of a volcano. Empty bags from a fast food drive-through and dirty napkins can be spotted on the floor and in the seat next to him

In the pitch-black night where the moon is nowhere to be found in the vast and desolated sky, the roaring of the Lamborghini engine continues getting louder and louder and closer and closer to the CHP patrol car. As the phantom car crushes the road, crickets go silent, birds fly away in panic and desperation.

The CHP officer takes one last huge bite off the hamburger, holding a large cup of hot coffee with his left hand. With a look of curiosity, he puts his ear against his side window, straining to hear something. Remains of saliva-filled food hang from his unshaven face. He finds it difficult to hear over the loud Country and Western music, playing Folsom Prison Blues, by Johnny Cash. The officer brushes off french-fries that are hanging for dear life on his chest as he reaches forward to turn the radio down.

As his hands touch the knob on the radio, WHAM! The Lamborghini, roars past the CHP car at a record-breaking speed of 240 MPH. The CHP car rocks violently from the vacuum. The officer is startled, the coffee lid flies off his cup as the officer squeezes his left hand to find his balance.

Boiling hot coffee spills on his crotch, the French fries that he had brushed off his chest and now lay on his lap swallow part of the coffee and begin to swell and move as if swimming in a murky river. With a look of shock and pain from the burning coffee, the CHP looks down screaming and brushing the hot coffee from his lap. The mountain climbing, backstroke swimming French fries hit the floor with violent force.

The *Radar Detector in the police car* registers -0- MPH.

The lone driver, with night vision goggles and a headset on keeps going without slowing down.

Loud music is heard through his earphones playing "Back in Black" by AC/DC, as the black Lamborghini continues to speed away. His radar beeps, registering another burst of radar jamming, seen on the screen of his dashboard.

The driver bursts into laughter.

NSA SECRET HEADQUARTERS – LOS ANGELES, CA

The National Security Agency (NSA) is an **intelligence organization** *of the United States government, responsible for global monitoring, collection, and processing of information and data for foreign intelligence and* **counterintelligence** *purposes, a discipline known as* **signals intelligence** *(SIGINT).*

Inside a large briefing room of the NSA office, sits a massive conference table, numerous oak and leather chairs circling the table, flags from all around the world, pictures of every USA president and a huge screen viewing satellite coordinates rests front and center on the back wall, completing the décor as a briefing takes place. A large number of photographs are spread throughout the table.

The senior Lin Kuei team, an undercover stealth team of patriotic assassins for the US government, sits around the large conference table. Eric Stone, white, male, 60's, chiseled face, piercing eyes, former senior member of the Lin Kuei and former Chief Operator Of Ground missions as code name "Shadow 6", briefs them on their mission.

Eric Stone: Gentlemen, one of the most notorious groups of criminals to ever form an allegiance stand before you in this photographs. SCS Intel has informed us that within the next 72 hours this group of terrorists with tentacles all over the world are about to congregate somewhere in either Los Angeles or Italy for a meeting with very lethal consequences.

The room sits in silence; the shadowy figures of ten men can be seen sitting around the conference table.

Eric Stone: The group consists of the following: From Tokyo, the Yakuza family led by Mr. Taka Onotsu; from Saudi Arabia the leader of the Alihamad, Sheik Muhammad Ri-Ule; from Beijing, the Kan family dynasty; from the Ukraine the Katstov family; from Israel, Hyman Weiss and his associates; from Belfast Ireland, the O'Roscoe Mob led by the infamous Sean O'Roscoe; and lastly from Sicily and the Americas the "*Il Capo dei Capi*", Don Francesco Cataldo.

Additional pictures flash in sequence on the screen as Eric Stone describes each group of criminals and their background.

The current senior member of the Lin Kuei and Chief Operator of Ground missions, code name "Shadow 6" speaks.

Shadow Six: (Birth name, Xavier Crown, tall, muscular man in his late 40's, dark hair, intense eyes, chiseled face.) And what is such group of caring and peace devoted individuals up to, and when can we get correct Intel on whether the party is in LA or Italy?

Eric Stone: They are uniting... all under one roof, for only one purpose, to destroy the world economy by contaminating every banking institution with one of the most lethal viruses ever devised by anyone to date. Code name – "Candy".

They were set to meet in LA, but all those thugs are wanted and since they were aware that we knew of their meeting, we believe they are changing locations out of the country. We should have confirmation by tonight; our SCS operative on the inside will report with the correct info then.

A very familiar picture of an underworld figure pops on the screen.

Eric Stone: You all know of Gabriel Venezie, ex-Shadow Warrior Leader, notorious criminal, now Leader of "Unity", soon to become the most feared organization of unified criminals in the world. Your job? Find out their plan and stop them.

Shadow Six: We'll need all their files, any research to date – the who, where, and how that you have to date. Also, the info from our undercover operative tonight, please sir.

Eric Stone: Done. And Six...

Shadow Six: Yes, sir?

Eric Stone: At any cost, by any means. No matter what the collateral damage may be... stop them.

Shadow six stares at Stone, looks at his Warriors and slightly motions to them. Everyone gets up and exits the room. Stone is left standing with a look of desperation and anxiety on his face.

THE UNITED STATES 1967

The climax and victory of the Civil Rights Movement resonates throughout America; the escalation of the

Vietnam War is in full force. Young men escape to Canada to avoid the undeclared war, branded as "a police action". Thousands of young men become conscientious objectors.

The drama of a generational revolt with its sexual freedoms and use of drugs threatens America. The raise of the cartels and the influx of drugs from Mexico and overseas, plague the American population. The Cold War continues as the USSR and USA buck heads as two gigantic rams in the midst of a battle for leadership of the pack.

The **Space Race is about** to put a man on the Moon and has the USA spending hundreds of millions of dollars. The economy is, however, prosperous; American families enjoy success in business and unparalleled freedom.

However, America is at the end of a long reign as an indestructible power, and a self-proclaimed "World Police".

WASHINGTON DC 1967

Washington, D.C. is filled with neighborhoods distinguished by their political history, its varied culture, and its unusual architecture that showcases the International melting pot that so well represents the Nation.

Nighttime falls upon Washington DC; a **heavy fog lies silently over an old worn bridge** outside the city. Breaking through its thickness a black Town Car drives slowly to the middle of the old, wooden bridge that creaks with every movement of the car as it rolls forward.

The city lights can be seen from the bridge illuminating the sky like a big bonfire. A fifty-foot drop is exposed on the left side of the bridge while the vegetation on the right side hides whatever ground or lack thereof might be part of the side of the bridge.

The weather is unusually humid and cold; beads of dew can be seen on the vegetation. The Town car leaves its tracks on the ground as the wet and slightly muddy ground splashes out of the way of the car's tires.

The car stops. From inside the car the passengers can hear the busy flapping of birds as they make way for the Town Car that interrupts their night gathering. Crickets chirp, and then go silent; they too can sense the intrusion.

The vegetation is unkempt, overgrown, and it is hard to see past the worn out wooden railings of the bridge. Inside the Town Car, sitting in the driver seat is *Walter Crown,* mid 40's, 6' tall, African-American. Next to him is his wife, *Sandy.* She is a white woman, 5' 6", the same age as her husband, beautiful blond hair, good figure, in excellent physical shape. She lights a cigarette.

Sandy Crown is dressed in stylish clothing. A long black coat, her collar is flipped upwards and she nervously shivers from the tension. Walter crown is dressed in normal G-man business clothing. His coat is open in the front, his tie is loosened around his neck; he is tense, worried, and anxious.

Walter's hands shake, his face is tense and drained as if he hadn't slept for days. He speaks to his wife in a meek and apologetic tone.

Walter Crown: I thought you were quitting?

Sandy Crown: I told you not to speak to me.

Walter Crown: Sandy...

The inside of the Town Car is equipped with top of the line electronic equipment, a hardwired phone, and taping devices. The inside resembles a quaint office more so than the inside of a car. The driver is separated from his passengers by a thick opaque bulletproof glass. All the windows and windshield of the car are also tinted and bulletproof glass. A trap door is exposed on the bottom of the Town Car.

Sandy Crown: No, not a single word. How on earth could you put him in danger like this, he could be killed! Get our son back Walter, and that's the last I ever want to see of you.

Walter Crown: Sandy...

Sandy Crown breaks into tears, and tries desperately to regain composure.

Sandy Crown: Not another word. I want to hold him in my arms. I miss playing with him, rocking him to sleep.

Memories of the Crowns playing with their child, laughing, eating, and sleeping together flash through Sandy Crown's mind...

Walter Crown: Okay sweetheart, you know I'm sorry.

Sandy Crown: Sorry doesn't make anything right, it doesn't make me feel any better, Walter. What if they don't show?

Walter Crown: They'll show. I have what they want; I've done what they've asked.

We can see movement in the shadows. Government Agents awaiting orders to attack, set themselves in position taking advantage of the shrubbery and the side of the bridge to hide their presence. The bridge goes completely silent. Not a noise from a bird, a cricket, or a grasshopper can be heard. Nature knows that something very sinister is about to strike the bridge and everyone in it.

Sandy Crown: Yes, if they show and notice those Government Agents, then Xavier is as good as dead.

Walter: Those agents are part of the deal, they have to be there, or they'll haul me to Federal Prison for the rest of my life.

From the other end of the bridge a large black sedan approaches. It stops ten feet away from the Crowns' car. In the Town Car Walter reaches for his leather briefcase. He takes it with him as he exits the car alone and unarmed.

Walter walks nervously to the front of the Town Car; every step makes a creaking noise on the old bridge. Walter meets the three men responsible for kidnapping his four-year-old son face to face.

Mishka and Alex, two of the kidnappers are tall and husky; their faces show the weathering of many fights and a hard life. The third, Andrei, is just as tall, rather slender, dark hair, well-groomed, immaculately dressed, Brunello Cucinelli suit, Christian Louboutin shoes, Lorenzo Cana silk tie, David Yurman cufflinks.

Through the windshield of the kidnapper's car, Walter sees young Xavier, 4 years old, in the back seat of their car. The kidnappers, with stone cold faces, guns drawn, engage in a conversation with Walter.

PENTAGON - CONFERENCE ROOM - NIGHT [1967]

*The Pentagon is the headquarters of the United States Department of Defense. Approximately 23,000 **military** and* *civilian employees and about 3,000 non-defense support personnel work in the Pentagon. It has five sides, five floors above ground, two basement levels, and five ring corridors per floor with a total of 17.5 miles of corridors*

Deep inside the Pentagon, passing several intertwined hallways, a secret conference room comes into view, only accessible by activating a sliding wall to open. The wall marks a dead-end on that side of the building. There GENERAL BRAXTON, (50's, silver hair, 6'2") sits perched precariously in a leather chair at the head of a very long conference table. The American flag on his right and a photo wall filled with all the past and present presidents of the United States serves as a very impressive décor.

General Braxton discusses the ongoing events at THE COUNTRY BRIDGE, with MAJOR STANLEY (dark hair, balding, 5'8"). Sweat, anger, and frustration pours down his face; his breathing is heavy and labored.

General Braxton: They are meeting at the town bridge.

Major Stanley: Why there, sir? There is no escape route.

General Braxton snaps, with anger and defiance in his eyes that only the long lasting stress of "the cold war" can conjure, and that anger is aimed directly at his underling.

General Braxton: (In a loud voice...) They're not stupid, Major. Our surveillance reveals that they have a Trash Barge below the bridge, with a speedboat attached to it. They're planning to escape. I'm getting a bad feeling about this.

Major Stanley: We need to send in more men, sir.

The two defiant souls lock horns, but there can only be one winner.   Stanley realizes he has overstepped his boundaries.

General Braxton: I make the decisions, Major. We don't need any screw-ups. We've sent in SI-9.

Major Stanley: SI-9 sir?

General Braxton: Our new Deep Cover group; they're all assassins, true blue.

Major Stanley: Sir, we're the US Government. We can't use assassins.

General Braxton: (harshly) Major, we can... we just can't own up to it. Get it?

Major Stanley's face shows a mixture of fear and contempt.

General Braxton: There is work that needs to be done but we just can't be associated with it. There are jobs that the US government can't be linked to, but it's a must for National Security. *You can't send saints to do the devil's work anymore than you can send devils to do a saint's work.* Stanley, God help us... I've sent in the devil.

COUNTRY BRIDGE - NIGHT [1967]

Two of the kidnappers circle behind Walter Crown's car, the well-dressed one stands next to the back window of the Town Car. He speaks.

Andrei: Mr. Crown, good to see you.

Walter walks forward to take a closer look inside the kidnapper's car; he turns his back at the kidnappers, taking advantage of the fact that they are all circling his car.

Mishka, a tall 6'5" Russian, his face scarred, dark complexion, unclean, vicious, and rebellious smirks with defiance. Crown angles himself so he can see inside the kidnapper's car. His lips are parched, he wets his lower lip with his tongue, and beads of sweat begin to show on his forehead. He's at the lowest point of his life, scared, unsure of himself, ready to sell out the country he so much loves, endangering his only son's life, walking on the brink of possible death.

Walter Crown: Let's get down to business. I want my son.

Mishka: He Just few feet behind. You have papers?

His thick accent echoes, his empty icy eyes look through Crown and carefully scan the length of the bridge. His right hand in his trench-coat pocket clearly shows that he's manning a gun.

Walter walks back to the side of the Town Car and lays his briefcase on the hood of the car. He locks eyes with Mishka who has walked next to him. Walter opens the briefcase slowly so as not to get shot by the men and looks towards the black sedan.

Walter manages to get one last flash look of his son inside the kidnappers black sedan. Walter's son now sits quietly in the back seat of the car. That short snap look at his son seems to have given him strength. Walter smiles at him. Mishka takes a look at the documents, holding them up in the air.

Mishka: I vas exjpecting more.

Walter Crown: It's all I could get, (in a high strong tone) and it's more than enough...

Walter tries to muster enough strength to hide his fear, his palms start to sweat. He lets out a nervous cough and cowardly continues...

Walter Crown...but it's all there, the maps, all marked with exact target coordinates, codes, take-off and landing times, down to the second. All of it, Pentagon approved, not even sent to the Brass yet.

Mishka replies staring down at Crown...

Mishka: So ve have deyr orders before they do, da?

Walter Crown: Exactly.

From his peripheral view Walter notices *Federal Agents* climbing up from under the bridge. He wipes the sweat from his brow.

Mishka: Give him child.

Alex walks around Walter's car and approaches the black sedan. He opens the car door to grab the kid. Just as Xavier is brought out of the car, a loud shot comes from the bushes on the side of the bridge and a dozen Feds rush in shooting from all directions.

Mishka: I told you not cross me Mr. Crown. For dis you pay.

He motions to Andrei, who has been standing by the back door of Walter's car. Andrei opens the back door of the Town Car and shoots Sandy. Sandy lies dead inside the car. The bridge erupts in gunfire from all sides; amongst the Federal Agents, moving silently in the dark, the sinister figures of nine masked, clandestine SI-9 operatives close in on the battle. SI-9 Warriors fight the Kidnappers in the mist of the gunfire and confusion.

Other Federal Agents confused by the appearance of the SI-9 masked operatives, open fire on anything that moves. In the end, Walter lies dead in the street; one of the Kidnappers lies dead on the road. Alex jumps off the bridge and lands on the Trash Barge below. Mishka, a bruising 400 pounds, 6'5" gorilla grabs the child and attempts to take off with him as a hostage.

Shadow 6, head of the SI-9 unit, calls for a halt to the fire.

Shadow 6: We are here by orders of the Pentagon, everyone holster your weapons, and we will handle things from here.

The Federal Agents back down, but keep their hands on their weapons just in case things get out of hand. They are not sure what danger these mask men are bringing with them.

As Mishka runs towards the middle of bridge and as he reaches its half point, a masked black clad, SI-9 Warrior (Shadow 3) appears in front of him.

Mishka: You not take me alive.

Shadow 3: (in a calm soft voice) as you wish.

Mishka: Стоп! (Stop) Not come closer, or boy dead!

Alex grabs Xavier by the collar and hangs him over the edge of the bridge as he points the gun at Shadow 3. Xavier's feet dangle in the air fifty feet from the water. From behind him, a *Man* all in black (*Shadow 6*) places his hand over Mishka nose and mouth inserting a knife into the base of his spine. The kidnapper loses control of his legs and arms flail all over the place, dropping Xavier. His gun goes off as his arm jerks upwards, the bullet misses his target.

Shadow 3 locks eyes with Shadow 6, 6 nods slightly to his left.

Shadow 3 flings a long silk line off the bridge, from a pouch on his belt, in the direction of Xavier. Shadow 6 dives off the bridge grabbing the rope with his right hand as his left hand clasps on to Xavier's shirt preventing his deadly drop. Shadow 3 quickly wraps the silk rope several times on the handrail of the bridge to provide support for Shadow 6's dive. Shadow 6 holds steady on to the rope as Shadow 3 reels him back up the railing returning Xavier to solid ground.

A Government agent, bleeding to death on the ground, is shocked by the series of events of the mysterious *Warriors*. All in black outfits and Ninja-like masks, the Warriors maintain their silence.

The Government Agent forces his head upwards and asks...

Bleeding Government Agent: "Who the hell are you"?

Shadow 6 stares at him, knowing that the agent is beyond any help. No one responds. The agent takes his last breath.

Alex, below, is about to throw a grenade at the bridge. SI-9 Warrior 2, strides stealthily towards the bridge railing to get a clear view of Alex. With his right hand, he removes a weapon from the pouch on his upper left arm and with lightning speed and accuracy he throws!... from behind his back... making a complete circle and still in stride he glances slightly over his shoulder.

The Warrior's blinding speed and movements are in total contrast to Alex's view of his final moments as he seems to witness his upcoming death vividly in slow motion. His slow and clumsy movements cannot avoid the speed of the incoming weapon, *a Shuriken*, (throwing star). The shuriken impales Alex's throat. Alex, the kidnapper, drops dead on the floor of the barge. The grenade rolls out of his hands and into the water. It detonates. Solemnly and calmly the Warrior continues to walk forward without looking back.

In the foggy, dewy morning, the old worn bridge now holds the aftermath of an ambush gone wrong. Lying throughout the splintered floor of the old bridge, a succession of dead bodies; blood crawls slowly out of the bodies of two dead kidnappers, five Federal Agents and Walter Crown, mixing with the mud and dew and slipping quietly between the grooves of the old weather worn wood.

From the Town Car's back door blood drips slowly out of the bottom one drop at a time, hugging as hard as it can to the slick side of the car and inevitably dropping to the floor of the old bridge, mixing with the mud, dirt and wetness from the fog and dew. The rest of the Federal Agents left on the bridge watch in amazement of the Masked Warriors, realizing that their panic cost the lives of several of their team.

Shadow 6 holds the boy's hand, who gazes into space from the shock of what he just witnessed; his father dead and his mother nowhere in sight. The Warriors stand still, hands at their side, their piercing eyes staring into the horizon. A deafening quiet surrounds them. Shadow 3 speaks.

Shadow 3: Leave the boy?

Shadow 6: Negative 3, we are not leaving this kid on a bridge in the middle of nowhere next to his parents' dead bodies and Federal Agents with itchy trigger fingers.

Shadow 5: We'll take him back to H.Q., let them handle it.

The SI-9 Warriors leave, taking the briefcase and the boy. They all jump in two, aerodynamic, black, bulletproof, covert Military trucks with dark tinted windows that were parked nearby, hidden in the bushes.

Inside Shadow 6's vehicle, young Xavier sits with tears down his face, he looks up at Shadow 6.

Young Xavier: Where is my mommy, I want my mommy.

Shadow 6 removes his mask, Eric Stone, a white, male, 30's, chiseled face, piercing eyes. He stares out his windshield, his face reveals anger and frustration; he takes several deep breaths and looks at Xavier.

Shadow 6: Young man, your mother has gone to a better world. You won't be seeing her anymore, she wasn't able to say goodbye, but wanted me to tell you that she loved you more than life itself and that she is looking forward to meeting with you again in the afterlife.

Xavier puts his hands to his face and cries. Shadow 6 puts his arms around the little boy and moves him closer to him as he drives away.

Shadow 6: Don't worry young man; I will take care of you. Don't worry.

CHAPTER 2

HUNTING DOWN OF THE YOUNG WARRIOR

DEATH VALLEY DESSERT

As the night falls upon the Mojave Desert sand, two covert trucks speed through the tiny **Mojave Desert** community in Inyo County, California known as *"Death Valley Junction"*. The truck crosses the intersection of **SR 190** and **SR 127**, just east of **Death Valley National Park and heads straight to a seemly desolated area in an already desolated town that stands at** 2,041 ft. (622 m) elevation, population... fewer than 20... no gas stations, and only one restaurant.

The truck stops in the middle of a desolated area; SI-9 Warrior 3 jumps out of the truck, kneels down on the ground, and places a gadget on the sand holding it upright with his left hand. In his right hand he has what seems to be some form of reflective object.

He tries different angles around the gadget that cause a shadow effect on the sand. Warrior 3 nods as he looks at the trucks and signals to the right with his hand. He picks up his gadgets and jumps back in the truck.

The trucks speed ahead in the direction Warrior 3 pointed out. They travel several miles until in the middle of nowhere of the sandy desert they spot two figures standing as if guarding something behind them. However, there is nothing in front of them or behind them except... sand.

The covert army trucks pull up to two guards. The guards stand; legs spread shoulder width, their hands cupped in front of them, both guards looking forward. A set of thick steel gates, rise from the ground behind them.

Shadow 6 addresses the members of the Shadow team in his truck.

Shadow 6: They must be here for the meeting.

The truck approaches closer to the guards.

The two *Army Guards* signal to the tucks to halt; one of them shines a bright light against the driver's wristband. The wristband is shaped in the form of a Tiger that glistens when illuminated with their special light. A "safe to enter" green light goes on inside an underground complex. The gates retract underground, the ground lowers creating an underground ramp. The guards wave the trucks through. As the trucks clear the ramp, the ground lifts back up, the guards remain.

UNDERGROUND FACILITY IN DEATH VALLEY

Inside the *Underground Facility* the army trucks park. Shadow 6 unbuckles his seat belt and puts on his "Warrior Mask". Shadow 6 and the SI-9 Warriors step out from out of the trucks.

Shadow 6 carries the boy and the briefcase. The rest of the Warriors head to a designated rest area, while Shadow 6 walks through a long hallway to the CO's office. He enters, sits down across from General Moss, 50's, thick built, determined, self-assured, a true warrior that exudes an air of command and self-assurance. General Moss sits on a large black office chair behind a massive oak desk. He intensely studies several files marked "top secret". He doesn't look up.

The office is large and surrounded by glass walls with "one-way" tinted screens that automatically rise up and down. Two chairs sit in front of the General's desk. The American Flag stands proudly behind him, seven feet up from the floor on the ten-foot wall. Pictures of the General's wife and kids surround his desk amongst all the paperwork and two phones, one black and one red.

Shadow 6 places the child on a chair next to him.
The Masked Warrior just sits there for about a minute staring forward at General Moss. He slowly removes a Glock 19" from his holster and places it in front of himself on top of the desk, pointing in the direction of General Moss. General Moss's eyes look up and for several moments they stare at each other. The Warrior removes his mask.

General Moss: Eric, that's ok, if I call you Eric, or do you prefer Shadow 6?

Eric Stone: Eric will do.

General Moss: Ok then, we have two more top secret missions for your team. Same as always, no safety net; if compromised, you stand alone. This one needs special handling, here.

General Moss looks up as he stands and hands paperwork to Stone. Stone doesn't move.

General Moss: So listen....

General Moss's eyes shift right and he sees the child sitting on a chair next to Stone.

General Moss: (with clear distain) What the hell is this?

20

Eric Stone: (Stone ignores the question) They are all top secret... they're all dangerous... General, (with a smirk in his face) you have an uncanny eye for the obvious.

General Moss: The baby... Stone! (His face is now flushed his eyes wide, he pounds his fist on the desk.)

Eric Stone: (with humorous sarcasm) "The baby", it is sir. Wouldn't you know it? You send me out on a mission and I give birth.

General Moss: Eric, this is no joke. (With a look of disapproval) is this the one? What are you doing with him? He should be with his parents as planned. It's too early for us to have him.

Eric Stone: Before we get into this complicated matter, this briefcase was the matter of exchange between Walter Crown and the Russian spies at the bridge.

Stone puts the briefcase on the general's desk. They open it and go through the papers. Inside the briefcase contains microfiche documents, papers with specific satellite coordinates, and schematics.

General Moss: All this is gibberish to me Eric; this is way beyond my clearance level. I will pass this on and see where the leak was that released these documents to Walter Crown. How many people saw these?

General Moss closes the briefcase.

Eric Stone: Just you and I General, anyone else that saw them is dead now.

General Moss: On the other matter Stone, you went against all our plans by bringing this child here.

Eric Stone Well General, we couldn't just leave him on the desolated bridge as both his parents were terminated during the exchange. We couldn't wait for the local authorities because that would have compromised the top-secret nature of our....

General Moss interrupts Stone, a look of worry takes over General Moss' face, and his hands momentarily shake. He stares at Stone in frustration.

General Moss: Save it, Stone! This presents a problem bigger than us.

Eric Stone: Solution General?

The general reaches inside the desk's right hand drawer and pulls a wooden box of Cuban Cigars; he offers one to Stone who declines. The General removes a cigar from the box and puts it in his mouth rolling it right and left with his fingers.

He attempts to bite off the tip of the cigar but can't. He reaches into the right desk drawer once again and grabs a clipper. He clips the end of the cigar and lights the other end and takes a big puff. Lifting his head up, he slowly releases the smoke out of his mouth as if he had just accomplished some great un-accomplishable task. He continues to speak.

General Moss: I don't like this Stone. It goes against orders; I'll have no part of it.

Eric Stone: General, you don't have a choice. This is beyond our authority..."Protect him at all cost". Does that sound familiar General?

General Moss: Run him through medical, get the best four agents we got and have them take the child to our underground in Beijing, some of our best trainers are there. They'll know what to do.

Eric Stone: General, that's exactly where they'd look for him. Plans for SI-9 have been leaked to our enemies. They would expect us to institute the program in China, considering it's the birthplace.

General Moss: What? Lin Kuei? The training, the assassins, the mystery, all that crap?

Eric Stone: Exactly. Crap to you General, survival to him.

General Moss: Eric, you know I hate all this cloak and dagger shit.

Eric Stone: Chose another location.

General Moss: Are you questioning a direct order Stone?

Eric Stone: Nope. But then, I don't really answer to you, no one in SI-9 does.

General Moss: Stone I'm well aware of the fear that SI-9 instills in its enemies; hell, I know of some governments that would rather have an atomic bomb dropped on them than to be on SI-9's scope. But I'm still in charge of SI-9 missions Stone. This child was born for this purpose. We'll feed him, educate him and groom him to be a warrior; the ultimate purveyor of combat and war. He'll get more attention that any two parents could ever give.

Eric Stone: General...

General Moss: Stone, he's your responsibility. I'm giving you ten years to get him ready, after that I'm contacting every one of our enemies letting them know where the kid is.

Eric Stone: Fine. On one condition, I choose where he trains. It will be my secret.

General Moss: Tell me where, Stone.

Eric Stone: General, a secret remains a secret only when only one person knows it.

Silence overcomes the room, they both lock eyes in a silent test of wills. General Moss understands that it is not in Stone's DNA makeup to yield. Moss looks away and speaks.

General Moss: Your show, Stone. Succeed, and then the program succeeds.

Eric Stone: (matter-of-factly) I'll succeed, General, you can bet on that.

General Moss: No hard feelings Stone, but this is a matter of national security. When he's 18, we'll give him the choice, back to the States, stay with us doing the job he's already been trained to do at an instinctive level, or go out there in the world and make his own way. Either way, it's a lot better deal than most orphans get.

Eric Stone: I'll put him somewhere where he can get stability.

General Moss: Stone, he is "The Weapon" we'll spend years developing. Anyone near him runs the risk of ending up like his parents.

Eric Stone: You're right on that General.

General Moss: Hurry, take him. From now on it's your call. And Stone, I want him trained 'till he can kill without thinking. Then let him train the others.

Eric Stone: Yes General. Mathematics, Science, Geography, Language, Philosophy, Assassination, all in the same curriculum, got it.

General Moss: All in a day's work...

Stone exits the office with Xavier.

Eric Stone: (in a low thoughtful voice as he exits the office) Years of research point to Lin Kuei as the answer our government has been looking for. To create soldiers so loyal, so powerful, so intelligent, and so honest, that no money in the world would ever corrupt them. I will move forward, I will make it happen.

LIN KUEI

During the "cold war" period, the main dangers were Industrial Espionage, circumvention of Government documents, brainwashing, infiltration of the "American" way of life, underground assaults, and the creation of double agents seduced by large sums of money in a very short period of time. The ways of *"Lin Kuei"* were sought after by the US government as a means to take control of the "cold war' dangers.

The work of a *"Lin Kuei"* was usually on a one-to-one basis where the target needed to be eliminated without public awareness, or retrieving of crucial documentation or information while eliminating the enemy in the process.

Slowly, groups of 9 Lin Kuei were sent as a unit (SI-9) to overtake larger more obvious projects that needed immediate attention and extermination. Soon they were used to pave the way for an "invasion or interception" of foreign dictatorships. *The Lin Kuei, "The first ones in, the last ones out".*

In the seventies, small, inexperienced, subversive "assault" units were sent into countries around the "free" world to threaten the freedom and stability of the democratic world.

The 1972 Olympic Massacre.

"On the morning of September 5, with six days left in the Games, the worst tragedy in Olympic history hit. Eight Arab terrorists stormed into the Olympic village and raided the apartment building that housed the Israeli contingent. Two Israeli athletes were killed and nine more were seized as hostages. Eventually the horrible drama ended claiming the lives of all nine of the hostages, along with one policeman and two terrorists".

The 1974 Conspiracy Murder Of John F. Kennedy.

"On November 22, 1963, President John F. Kennedy arrived at Dallas' <u>Love Field</u> from Fort Worth at 11:37 in the morning. He was accompanied by Mrs. Kennedy, Vice President Lyndon Johnson, and Texas governor and Mrs. John Connally.

*At 12:30, as the open limousine carrying the Kennedys and the Connelly's moved west on Elm past **Dealey Plaza**, shots rang out.*

*Both the President and the Governor were wounded. The limousine picked up speed and raced to the **Parkland***

Hospital Emergency Room *where Kennedy was pronounced dead at 1:00"*

"On January 2, 1979, the House of Representative's Select Committee on Assassinations supported the Warren panel's conclusion that President Kennedy "was probably assassinated as a result of a conspiracy".

While attempting to infiltrate such subversive units with agents of their own, the US quickly found out that capitalism, moderated behavior, and self-survival rapidly overcame the loyalty to democracy and the "American Way". Numerous "secret agents" on both sides of the fence became "double agents' befriending each other and earning over twice the normal cash as well as staying alive to enjoy it.

The US needed "the true warrior" the "All American" spy that could not be compromised. One that could fight, kill, and not get personally involved or yearns for personal profits. A bright, dedicated, intellectual, socially calculating, politically endowed assassin. An incorruptible true blue all American super spy.

The only way the USA was to get such individuals was not by buying them, draft them, recruit them, but by simply growing their own. After years of searching, "before-and-after" WWII, special units were created using young orphans from the age of five. They were infused with the secret knowledge of "Lin Kuei", a successful ancient society of assassins in existence for over three thousand years.

The Lin Kuei clan, also known as "Forest Demons", was an ancient secretive cult that operated in northern China many hundreds of years ago. This individual clan's past and history is shrouded in mystery. However, it is believed that they resided in the deep parts of the forests, and captured unsuspecting travelers and forced them to breed with the clan in order to grow their numbers and members.

Children were usually chosen at birth and brainwashed to work as spies, assassins, and thieves for the benefit of the clan (similar to the Thugees in India). Their craft was so quick, so deadly, and so clandestine that they were feared throughout the nation.

The Lin Kuei were trained to kill an opponent in three seconds or less and became a living legend and anyone that needed to have someone terminated...quickly searched them out for hire.

When more and more people began moving into Lin Kuei territories, the Clan's numbers dwindled and they went their separate ways.

Probably during China's Tang Dynasty, some of the Lin Kuei members traveled to Japan to teach their secret arts and ways to the local villagers. Over the years, many of these methods were used and were incorporated into the art of Ninjutsu.

It is believed that some Lin Kuei stayed in Japan and made a living as mountain hermits or priests, known as the Yamabushi. They have since disappeared. Other Lin Kuei traveled to Korea and continued their teachings.

*It is believed that they were monks who practiced their ways and customs. They lived secretly in caves and in forests for centuries. After the clan's decline, the last **Shr-lin** (grandmaster of the Lin Kuei) moved to the United States to reform the clan.*

The last Shr-lin died during the 1970's, and since then, a clan member known as Li Hsing, who claims to have been a friend of the last Shr-lin wrote about its fighting secrets.

Today the government doesn't kidnap the prospect children to join the "Shadow Warriors", but instead they select children from various orphanages and test them from very young to see if they qualify to enter the program. Those that "make the cut" are adopted by the government and put into the "Shadow Warrior" program. After serving as a *"Warrior"* for twelve years they have the choice of staying with the group or to go out into the world and develop their own careers, all expenses paid by the Government.

ARGENTINA 1945

Argentina 1945, just days after the surrender of **Japan**, **German** influence still remains strong in **Argentina**, mainly due to the presence of a large number of **German immigrants**. Under Peron's leadership the government quietly allowed entry of a number of Nazi leaders fleeing Europe after Germany's collapse. The number of Nazi leader fugitives that fled to Argentina surpassed 300.

Argentina, at odds with **Great Britain,** furthered the belief that the Argentine government was sympathetic to the German cause. Argentina, due to their close ties to the Nazi Regime and insecurity of who would win the war, stayed **neutral** for most of **World War II.**

The United States kept heavy pressure on Argentina to join the allies, threatening to cut ties and impose governmental retaliation. The pressure and the turn of the war in favor of the allies finally forced Argentina to give in. On January 26,

1944 **Argentina broke** relations with the **Axis powers,** and declared war on Germany on March 27, 1945. Argentina delayed sending troops to back the allies and on September 2nd, 1945, World War II comes to an end with the victory in the hands of the allied forces.

Juan Peron is forced to resign from power; socialism spreads widely amongst the population. Amongst all the mayhem and intrigue, large numbers of tourists visit the city from Europe and Asia.

Peron is freed after major popular protest by those known as the *Descamisados (The Shirtless),* he is re-elected in 1951. Women's suffrage is approved. Argentina founds The National Atomic Energy Commission (*Comisión Nacional de Energía Atómica,* CNEA). Eva Peron dies; suspicion of foul play spreads throughout the country. Peron is ousted from office in 1955 by the *'Liberating Revolution'* military coup.

National unrest develops for the next seven years and in 1962 a military coup ends the presidency of civilian Arturo Frondizi. Four years of turmoil follow and in 1966 General Juan Carlos Onganía assumes power and represses political parties. The mixed feelings of love and hate for one of the country's most renowned guerrilla fighter comes to a halt in 1967, when the news of the death of Ernesto 'Che' Guevara reaches the Argentinean people.

ARGENTINA 1969

The average Argentinean finds himself out of work, or underpaid in his job. Families starve... tensions in the country run high. Sinister characters mix in with the large crowds of tourists that walk the streets in search for fun, food, drinking and dancing. *La Boca* becomes a center for various groups of assassins looking for a secret weapon to be delivered to the United States, hidden in the back streets of Argentina somewhere on *Caminito* Street.

On a cold rainy day, sightseers ignore the wetness and chill, swarming the back streets of *Boca*, Buenos Aires, enjoying the uniqueness and mesmerizing atmosphere of what develops in front of them. The colorful *Caminito* street in the otherwise run-down *barrio* of *La Boca* is unusually crowded with tourists rummaging through the commercial, touristy, *tiendas (stores)* while native men and woman engross the mass of tourists in a tacky, street tango waiting eagerly for *propinas* (tips) from the star-eyed travelers drunk by the colorful, ragtag *conventillo* housing that spreads throughout the *barrio*.

Caminito street is a reminder of where everyone had come from, not just in La Boca, but Buenos Aires, and Argentina, because this barrio and its port was - in its infancy - the gateway for around 6 million foreign immigrants that poured into Argentina between 1880 and 1930 who went on to make Buenos Aires and Argentina what they are today.

The streets are quaint and colorful, almost as if they arose from a fairy tale book. Behind all the mayhem, music, laughter, and dancing a young boy can be spotted engulfed in a cloud of mist and fog, arising from the shadows. His cold blank stare, his strong cat like walk, is totally uncommon of a child of about 5 to 6 years old. He walks slowly but attentively in the direction of the crowd. His body very close to the building walls, and in some instances blending with the structures; disappearing into the bricks and stones. He now comes slowly into full view and we can see him more clearly. His stare seems to spew fire, his walk firm, strong, determined, and fierce. As he comes closer we can see blood stains down his neck and shoulder. He advances... he disappears.

A FEW HOURS EARLIER

The "panther like" child effortlessly runs from HAGAR, a huge Mongolian man, 6'7", 480 pounds, husky, muscular, sweating profusely as he chases the boy. His clothes and his face are dirty, his filthy nails long and sharp, his beard unkempt, and his hair wild and unruly.

Hagar is one of the most dangerous paid for hire killers in the world. In his lifetime, he assassinated over 200 men for various mobsters, governments, and large conglomerates. He is amazingly fast for a man his size and he seems to rapidly gain on the young boy. As Hagar jumps on the boy hurling him backwards, the boy rotates his body and strikes him with a spinning round house kick right in the face. The boy now lies on his back, as Hagar unfazed by the kick just stands there and bursts into a loud maniacal laughter.

The boy's eyes are now wide and tense, but he shows no signs of fear. He concentrates on Hagar's eyes, paying strict attention to the movement of his arms, as Hagar draws a huge knife from his side holster and lunges towards the boy. The boy lies still and slowly reaches in his pocket pulling out a small object that resembles a box cutter.

As Hagar is about to land on the small boy, the boy waits for the perfect moment with the "cutter" knife in his right hand ready to strike. When Hagar is within the boy's reach, with the speed of light the young lad strikes a slashing blow on Hagar's right wrist.

With the small box cutter, he makes several turns and twists rendering Hagar's wrist useless. Blood gushes everywhere, as Hagar's knife is forced to drop from his hands. The boy, in one move, drops the box cutter and grabs Hagar's knife in midair – thrusting it across Hagar's throat. As the knife makes its swift and calculated dance, we can see Hagar's eyes widening to the size of saucers, for he knows there is nothing he can do to stop this fatal Tango. The knife strikes swiftly, with surgical proficiency bringing with its tune the final note to Hagar's life. Blood gushes out striking the young boy on the side of his face and shoulder.

The boy does a lightening flip off his back, landing on his feet to avoid Hagar's body to fall on top of him. Hagar's body thumps on the ground with extreme force. The body lays motionless as we see blood pouring on to the pebbled road. The boy slowly and quietly kneels over Hagar's body and with a cold calm stare, he whispers *"I let you catch up to me, but I couldn't let you kill me"*. The boy stands up and once again disappears.

MINUTES LATER

The young boy walks towards a house in the *La Boca* neighborhood. He reaches a faucet that is sticking out of the wall of a building. He removes his shirt and washes the blood off his face and shoulders. He throws the shirt in a garbage can nearby and enters his home shirtless.

The bright blue color on the outside of the house is bordered by a bright red line all around. The front door is painted with red paint to match the house's outline. The inside is modest, country, old fashion, with a wooden stove in the kitchen, tile counters, and floors.

A brown couch sits in the living room showing years of constant use by the indentations on each pillow and the discoloration of the backrest of the couch. Wooden chairs face the couch separated by a large tree stump used as a dining table. Pictures of gauchos and pretty flowers decorate the walls. An old brick fireplace rests on one of the walls and framed family pictures going back one hundred years decorate the fireplace wooden mantel.

The wooden floors in the living room creak through the large, thick rugs that lie on top of it, the stucco walls have not seen a coat of fresh paint for the last fifty years, and the thick blue curtains that separate the kitchen from the dining room release a thin layer of dust every time somebody moves them. The worn out paint of the three bedroom doors show marks of children prints, food stains, and years of weather damage.

Middle Age Lady: Xavier, huera is choir shirt mijo?

The Young Boy: Sorry, some boys stole it from me.

Middle Age Lady: Oh, Xavier, chu need to learn tu stand up for chourself, chu can't let those bullies abuse you like that, one day they keel you if you not careful.

The Young boy: Working on it... working on it.

Xavier walks to his room as he passes the kitchen; he feels the heat from the wood burning stove sitting in the corner. A *maté* with a gold tip *bombilla* sticking out of it, a half-eaten *flauta*, and a bag of *yerba* can be seen sitting on the kitchen counter.

Xavier enters his room and closes the door behind him. His room is a modest room with a wooden single bed and a wooden night table, a worn wooden floor that gives way with every step and creaks out loud as if asking for relief from the weight thrust upon it. A *trapo* covers the window, old and used up as if it was the remains of an old crusty t-shirt. A ceiling fan with a half an inch of dust on its blades is the only source of air circulating the room.

Young Xavier lies on the bed, his eyes fixed straight ahead, staring at the ceiling, stern, fierce, unblinking. Hours go by, the night darkness engulfs the room, silence becomes deafening... intense. In the mist of the obscure room we can barely see the shadows of a small boy masterfully gliding through the moves of an ancient martial arts system called Lin Kuei... the night rests.

The morning sun attacks the house with the much-needed brightness after a night of nonstop rain. A knock on the door is heard, a man stands at the door, Eric Stone - white, male, 30's, chiseled face, piercing eyes.

Eric Stone: Morning Elsa, is young Xavier ready?

Elsa: Chu no him, he always *como un gato*, climbing here, climbing there, then puff, gone. Señor Stone, chu need to make him more stronger. *Los matones de aqui...*

Eric Stone: In English Elsa, in English.

Elsa: Sorry señor Stone, the bad children steal jis shirt and he no say nothin' and come home with no shirt. They always pick on him, he no defend himself, I worry for him. Please make him more strong so he defend heself.

Eric Stone: (under his breath) If he gets any stronger he would be made of steel.

Elsa: What chu say seňor Stone, I no hear what chu say.

Eric Stone: Sorry Elsa I said that we will have to give him better meals; you know to make him stronger. I'll try to teach him how to box a little, but you know how the school frowns on violence.

Elsa: Ches, ches seňor Stone, chu a good man, Xavier very proud of you, he love you. You help him, no?

Eric Stone: I help him, yes, Elsa.

Stone smiles at Elsa, as young Xavier with the grace of a puma jumps from the roof of the house and lands behind him.

Elsa: Chu see, *un gato, siempre como un gato.*

Stone laughs out loud, Xavier patiently waits, staring forward.

Eric Stone: Let's go Xavier. We have a lot to go over today.

ARGENTINA 1970 - 1976

Chaos and instability continue once again in Argentina, as General Alejandro Lanusse emerges as President in 1970 after removing *Presidente* Onganía from power.

From 1970 to 1976 civil conflict and terrorist attacks rock the country, principally by left wing *Montoneros* and *Ejército Revolucionario del Pueblo* opposed by the *paramilitary Argentine Anticommunist Alliance.*

On September 13th, 1976, civil unrest comes to a head in Rosario, the largest city in the central **Argentinean province of Santa Fe,** with a population of over one million people.

On that September day, residents walk the streets window shopping and frequenting their favorite restaurants. Children play in the streets; policemen hang out in the corners talking to pedestrians, a group of policeman are enjoying a café (coffee) from their favorite corner restaurant, when a bomb goes off killing nine policemen, two civilians and injuring 30 people.

The bombings, shootings, and killings has the population in the mist of such turmoil and uncertainty that the public majority calls for the return of former president **Juan Perón, believing that he could restore order and prosperity to the country.** Answering the Argentinean outcry Peron returns from his 18 years of exile on June 20th 1973. Arriving in Ezeiza International Airport in Buenos Aires, Argentina, Peron is greeted by the Peronist masses, an estimated three and a half million, including many young people, that gathered there to acclaim Juan Perón's definitive return from an 18-year exile in Spain.

From Perón's platform, camouflaged snipers from the right-wing of Peronism faction opened fire on the crowd. The left-wing Peronist Youth and the Montoneros were targeted and trapped. At least 13 bodies were subsequently identified, and 365 were injured during the massacre.

Argentina had *"jumped from the fire into the frying pan"* in efforts to eliminate Marxism military and security forces entered the homes of anyone suspected of being a communist or anti-Peronist and incarcerated them and executed them.

Thousands of citizens, students, men, and women were murdered in the name of "freedom from communism". This was known as "The Dirty War" where neighbors turned on neighbors that they didn't like and accused them of being a communist. Students that gathered in Universities or on the streets to discuss any politics not favorable to the government were gunned down on the spot.

Democratic elections brought Peronist Héctor Cámpora to power; Perón was elected president in fresh elections later that year. During Cámpora's first month of governing, approximately 600 social conflicts erupted; strikes and factory occupations took place. Peron set himself to take over the government once again.

Traveling in safety through Argentina becomes difficult and dangerous. Eric Stone and his group of undercover military men decide to limit their movements in the country and stay put in Las Pampas until the "heat" dies down.

CHAPTER 3

THE CHILD ASSASSIN

LAS PAMPAS-ARGENTINEAN VILLAGE - (1973) – DAY

Seemingly unfazed by the political turmoil and the brutal deaths in Buenos Aires, campesinos, (farmers) in *Las Pampas,* a sparsely populated province of Argentina, located in the **Pampas**in, the center of the country, cheerfully continued their day-to-day routine.

Las Pampas, for many years has been the home of a secret training camp for a group of American stealth fighters known as "Shadow Warriors".

A number of South American Cowboys, *Gauchos,* and a mix of Indian and European cultures referred to as *Mestizos* sit by an open fire drinking *Mate* and sharing tall tales while the women work around the huts.

ARGENTINEAN VILLAGE - DUSK - PLAYGROUND

In the training camp where a number of children are being trained on the "Way of Lin Kuei", for months on end, young Xavier (10 years old) spends hour upon hour studying the moves and creating counter moves to the Boar, the Bull, the Leopard, the Tiger, the Cobra, the Viper, the Python, the Eagle, and … the Ghost of the Snowtiger.

All the animals were kept in captivity at the compound for the very purpose of Xavier to examine their behavior, understand their attacking moves and deception habits. Young Xavier's training was designed to understand and counteract every form of martial arts possible. This also included other fighting forms such as wrestling and boxing.

However the main and foremost fighting style that he was indoctrinated in and taught to master and control was the ancient deadly fighting style of Lin Kuei.

Lin Kuei is thought to be the forerunners of the Japanese Ninja, the Lin Kuei clan, also known as *forest demons*, who were an ancient secretive cult that operated in northern China about 3,500 years ago.

The history of the Lin Kuei is dark and mysterious as the warriors' very existence. They have historically been considered the most feared assassins, with much of nothing ever written about them, and looked at by the martial arts world as the 'holy grail' of the martial arts.

Not much is known about their beginnings other than which has been passed down orally one generation to the next. The Lin Kuei were masters of survival, they thrived in the woods and made their living there adapting to the ways of nature. The art is so secretive that no Chinese Martial Arts scholar or historian has ever spoken of their existence.

The "Lin Kuei" trained under the guise of a martial discipline known as "Snowtiger" and selected nine of the animal systems as the core base of training and combat. The animal systems practiced are the Boar, Bull, Leopard, Tiger, Cobra, Viper, Python, Eagle and the Ghost of the Snowtiger.

All ancient doctrines of the Lin Kuei became incorporated into the current training regimen, including that of weapons, stealth, camouflage, espionage, and sorcery. Known in the past as masters of disguise, they travelled in small groups, disguising themselves as magicians or circus performers, all the while with the intent of completing their task – assassination of a high-ranking politician or businessman. They went by a strict code of accepting assassination jobs of only those that were ethically or morally challenged.

The Lin Kuei were notoriously linked with the kidnapping of children, who were apparently taken back to their farms and homes within the forest and trained as assassins. Today, special government operatives, operating under extreme secrecy have special CIA clearance to extract children from orphanages to accomplish the same. Although once considered the most feared assassins of their time, Lin Kuei are now considered devout upholders of freedom and justice, fighting as soldiers, law enforcement and high level security personnel.

Today there are only a few, high-ranking practitioners of the Lin Kuei, expert in all nine animal systems. Their system of combat is considered extremely violent, with each engagement ending within three seconds. Master instructors of Lin Kuei are trained to 'become' the animal of the system they master and the result is a violent encounter of vicious proportions. The Tiger system specialist fights with the intensity, ferocity and speed of each animal they master, the Tiger; so too for the Boar system specialist and all other animal system practitioners of Lin Kuei - they adopt the physiological and psychological makeup of the animal.

It is now early in the morning, and young Xavier sits in front of a caged white tiger, watching every one of its moves, imitating him, staring right into his eyes. For every one of the tiger's moves young Xavier has a counter move. Li Ming, a young trainee, nine years old approaches Xavier.

Li Ming: Xavier, what are you doing? You have been playing with that tiger for four hours.

Young Xavier: Not playing with him, becoming him.

Young Xavier moves close to the cage, he now has his nose touching the cage, staring right into the caged tigers eyes.

Li Ming: Why are you staring at him so close? He is going to eat your nose Xavier! Why are you doing that?

Li Ming: (To herself in a low voice), *"My god Xavier you are totally crazy"*.

Young Xavier: Because If you stare a *tiger* straight in his eyes he is less likely to *kill* you.

Li Ming: Less likely? Xavier, does Mr. Stone know you are crazy?

Young Xavier: Shhhhhhhh...

Li Ming: Whatever Xavier, can you do that tomorrow? Come and teach me the way of the Snowtiger.

With a soft solemn stare, young Xavier replies...

Young Xavier: Tomorrow?... Tomorrow I'll be inside the cage with him...

Li Ming gives Xavier a weird look; Xavier leaves the stare-down with the tiger and shows Li Ming the way of The Snowtiger, The Viper, and The Boar.

Young Xavier: Not like that Li Ming. That is not the strike of a Viper that is the strike of a wet noodle.

They both laugh out loud. Xavier abruptly takes Li Ming down as she incorrectly finishes her move and has a knife on her throat.

Young Xavier: Your life may depend on this Li Ming, let's get serious.

Li Ming: Xavier, I like you better when you are funny, not when you are trying to get eaten by a tiger, or when you are so serious. My life will be OK as long as you are with me, right?.

Young Xavier: Li Ming, you are such, Drama...tic. Drama queen.

Li Ming: You promised my mom you'd keep me safe, that you'll always watch out for me, so promise me you will Xavier. Say it.

Young Xavier: I promise. No one will ever hurt you; I will always protect you....

Eric Stone approaches the children. He puts his arm around Xavier and Li Ming. He looks at Li Ming as he speaks.

Eric Stone: Li Ming, would you mind if I take Xavier away from you for a couple of hours? I need him to do something very important for me.

Li Ming: Ok, Eric, I mean Mr. Stone.

Eric Stone: That's right Li Ming, during training we must show respect, I am always Mr. Stone. When away from training its ok to call me Eric.

Li Ming: Yes sir, Mr. Stone, but don't take him by the tiger cage. The tiger almost ate his nose today.

Eric bursts into laughter.

Eric Stone: I am sorry for laughing Li Ming; I know how serious that is so you have my word on that. Xavier, come on I want to introduce you to some people.

Stone takes him to a large room in the facility. The floors are wooden resembling an old college gymnasium; several mats are set up in the middle of the floor, training weapons hang from the walls and in several wicker baskets on the floor.

Ten warriors stand in the middle of the gym staring at Stone and young Xavier.

Eric Stone: Xavier, I want to introduce you to martial arts masters from different disciplines: Master Cho, Taekwondo; Master Tennasy, Bartitsu; Tom Hess, Bare Knuckle Boxing; Master Garro, Manegra-Colombian martial arts; Master Perez, Brazilian Jiu-Jitsu; Master Stevens, Okichitaw; Master Kiwon, South African Musangue; Master Ping, Chinese Wing Chun; Master Wong, Chinese T'ai' Chi'uan; and Master Babu, Indian Vajira-musti.

Each of the Masters bows down as they are introduced. Xavier bows down to them at the end of the introductions. They all bow back to young Xavier. Stone directs his speech to Xavier.

Eric Stone: For the next ten days I will bring you ten new masters from different fighting styles for you to study.

Young Xavier: OK, but tomorrow I enter the cage with the tiger.

Eric Stone: Let's focus on this for now.

Young Xavier spends the next six hours studying the Masters as they fight one another. His eyes are focused, intense, his mind locked on the every move that each master executes. He mimics each one of their moves, then for each one of their moves, young Xavier mimics a counter move.

ARGENTINEAN VILLAGE - 5 YEARS LATER - [1978] DAY

A band of desperados searches the small, poor, and touristy town of La Boca for a kid named Xavier. An armed bandit catches a glimpse of a shadow between two buildings, hears a short whistle, and is lured into entering an alley. As he enters he shouts out loud.

Armed Bandit: Sali para afuera pendejo o te mato! (Come out of there kid or you're dead).

A few seconds go by, a loud thud is heard, a cracking sound, a quiet gasp... Then Xavier exits the alley, dragging the body of the dead bandit, neck broken, out of the alley and into the street. The young man steps calmly out of the shadows, he looks back, making sure that the other four dead bandits lying in the alley are all that is left of the group.

ERIC STONE'S VILLAGE HOUSE - DAY

Eric Stone's home is a modest one, full of artifacts and history from ancient Asian times. His furniture resembles those periods. The home is clean, almost a "model home".

Xavier, now fifteen years old, and Li Ming, fourteen, are snooping around in *Eric Stone's* private room. They open a strange looking *Chest* to find all sorts of unique looking *Weapons* and *Ancient Artifacts.* Xavier picks up a *Bracelet* and puts it around his wrist. Eric, now in his thirties enters the room. .

Eric Stone: What are you two doing?

Li Ming: Ah, nothing. We were just looking.

Eric Stone: You kids are just a bit too nosey, but that's OK, curiosity is good.

A somber trance overtakes young Xavier. Pain and anguish can be seen in his eyes.

Eric Stone: It happened again, Xavier?

Xavier: Yes, What do they want? Five more today. I had no quarrel, they attacked me.

Eric looks at Xavier and forces a smile, to hide his fears and guarded nature towards Xavier. He tries to keep up a positive attitude as he speaks.

Eric Stone: Xavier, they're evil. Stay strong, walk in the shadows; the darkness will always be your ally. Be alert and Xavier... "Remember you are the chosen one, and that comes with a price".

Li Ming: [Holding up the *Bracelet*] what is this?

Eric Stone: (Picking up the Bracelet) this is a very special *Bracelet*, Li. The day has come for this *Bracelet* to be worn by you, young Xavier. It is one of the true hidden meanings of the history of *Tatakai (Battle* in Japanese*)*. It carries a spiritual power and history that is over 900 years old. It holds all of the power and wisdom of the ancient warriors of *Lin Kuei*. When all nine wristbands have found their masters, miracles will be possible. Its powers will protect you.

Xavier: Ah...Lin Kuei?

Eric Stone: The art the inner strength of your spirit...well it's about time. Things are about to get turbulent. Come, sit. Let me tell you a story that will give you an idea where it all began. Knowing the roots of where your life will soon take you is important; the story goes as follows...

Eric's voice submerges young Xavier and Li Ming into his story and their minds travel to the ancient forests of China...

EXTERIOR - FARM AND FOREST - CHINA – DAY [3000 BC]

A farmer and his family work the land. In the distance the farmer's four year-old son plays at the forests edge, mesmerized by its mystique. He attempts to enter, only to be stopped abruptly by his father who grabs him and pulls him close to his face.

Farmer: (in Chinese; sternly) You are to never enter this forest. You understand me, there are many dangers; it is very dangerous. Never. Never. Ever. Enter.

The child shook up and crying runs back to the house.

The child stays indoors for the rest of the day but as nighttime falls upon the village and while the family eats supper by an outdoor bonfire, the farmer's son wanders away towards the forest. He chases a rabbit. Noticing that he is not being watched, he steps beyond the forbidden boundaries of the Forest in pursuit.

No one notices the disappearance of the young boy until after dinner. Inside the house the farmer discovers his son's empty bed. Panic strikes the farmer, he runs hysterically through the house screaming his son's name in vain. On the edge of the forest he spots his son's tracks

47

leading inside the forbidden territory. The farmer enters the forest in search for his son and finds him, his body still, bloodied, mauled by the wild beasts that inhabit the Forest.

Overcome with grief the farmer stands in the forest screaming and cursing, and vows never to leave the forest until his revenge is complete. For years the farmer secretly watches each forest animal, their habits, strengths, and weaknesses. He masters their ways.

When finally ready, he confronts and destroys each one of the animals with his bare hands: Lions, wolves, tigers, leopards, wild dogs, oxen, and jackals. The first of the Lin Kuei; the first of the "Forest Demons" was born...

INT - ERIC STONE'S VILLAGE HOUSE - DAY [1977]

Li Ming sits on the floor her mouth wide open, Xavier stares.

Xavier: That's why you have me spy on all those animals and study their ways.

Eric Stone: Yes Xavier, but it's not the four legged animals that you should fear, but the two legged ones that act and think like wild mad animals.

ARGENTINA - THE DIRTY WAR - DEATH SQUADS

The *"Dirty War"* (Spanish: *Guerra Sucia*) or *State Terrorism*, also known as the *Process of National Reorganization* (Spanish: *Proceso de Reorganización Nacional or El Proceso*) continues.

People fear for their lives in their own homes. Mothers' morn for their children unjustly slain, people stay clear of their neighbors for fear of being turned over to the police as Marxism sympathizers. Bullet holes can be seen in many parts of the city where police machine-gunned down groups of young men gathering to oppose the brutality of the police and the military.

The "disappeared" included those thought to be a political or ideological threat to the military junta, even vaguely, and they were killed in an attempt by the junta to silence the opposition and break the determination of the guerrillas.

The worst repression occurred after the guerillas were largely defeated in 1977, when the church, labor unions, artists, intellectuals and university students and professors were targeted.

BUENOS AIRES, ARGENTINA [1977] MONTHS LATER.

In the distance, *Gauchos* can be seen cooking *"Parrilladas"*, kids play with their *"Boleadoras"*. Old folks gather outside drinking *"Maté"* and telling tales to the children.

Death Squads approach the unsuspected, terrorizing villages, killing, raping, and pillaging for financial gain. Assassins from all over the world join specific death squads in search for "the chosen one," Xavier. The word was out and a heavy bounty was placed on Xavier's head, creating the ultimate test to see if Eric Stone's theory on the viability of creating a new, stealth, indestructible, underground team of Warriors loyal to the US government actually held water.

People on the crowded streets of *La Boca* run screaming as they scatter for cover trying to avoid the *Death Squads* slayings. As people get interrogated, beaten, and murdered by teams of "gun for hire" guerrilla types, the search for Xavier intensifies. The hired assassins compete for a large reward, in the millions, for the head of Xavier Crown.

Goon #1: (On horseback screaming at a crowd of people) Donde esta el muchacho que se llama Xavier. Diganos o vamos a matarlos como perros. (Where is the boy called Xavier? Talk or we'll kill you like dogs).

Goon #2: Estamos con ordenes de llevarlo, vivo o muerto. (We're under orders to take him dead or alive.)

Heavily armed men search through the village homes, a shadow lurks outside the buildings, waiting to strike.

Inside Xavier's home the assassins have Elsa, the middle-aged guardian of Xavier Crown in Argentina, kneeling on the floor; the 'Death Squad' Leader holds a shotgun to her head. Nine other armed GOONS stand by. One of them holds a knife to Li Ming, (14).

Death Squad Leader: Where is he? Talk now or die!

Elsa: (Shadow 6's foster mother) I don't know, and if I know, I no tell chu, chu, asesino (murdering) chancho (pig)!

Death Squad Leader: Maybe you don't care about going on living, but killing the little girl might persuade you. Where is he?

Elsa spits on the death squad leaders' face. Grabbing a knife from her boot, she attempts to stab her attacker. He steps on her hand grinding down on it.

Death Squad Leader: Easy, you might cut yourself.

He shoots her point blank on the head... Elsa lies dead on the floor. Li Ming runs to her, embracing her and sobbing. Another shot is fired and Li Ming collapses.

Goon #1: Damn it, I am out of here – that was his Mother! He will kill us! Don't you understand? The stories about this kid are real. He is a phantom, a ghost, he blends into the woodwork. How can we fight him if we can't see him? They call him "The Shadow of Death"...for a reason, you idiot!

Death Squad Leader: His mother died years ago, you imbecile.

Goon #1: Well, his foster mother, whatever, she took care of him, we are so fucked...

Goon #1 heads towards the door. The shadow of young Xavier moves through the house. At 14, Xavier is now immensely built beyond his years; he looks like a young man in his twenties. We see his face as he puts a mask on covering his identity from the assailants.

DEATH SQUAD LEADER: (to Goon #1) Stop! He's just a 15-year-old kid, you fool.

Goon #1 stops and turns as he speaks.

Goon #1: I'm out of here. Don't try to stop me. Dead is dead, no matter the age. Keep the reward if you live to collect it. We sent over 40 mercenaries to kill him and now they are *All Dead.* And they didn't even kill his mother!

As Goon #1 finishes his sentence he is struck by a giant shadow appearing from thin air. Goon #1 falls dead.

Death Squad Leader: What in God's...

Xavier: (In a soft, hollow whispering tone) God won't be able to help you now.

Goon #2 lowers his weapon to fire, Xavier overcomes him. The other eight goons join in to their demise. The first combat scene in a long line of battles as a "Shadow Warrior" ensues...

"Charge of the Bull"

> *The Bull stands still before charging, with a menacing posture, sizing up his opponent before he strikes. When the enemy foolishly accepts his challenge, he attacks with relentless aggression and blind rage, willing to sacrifice a direct hit just to strike and kill.*

One of the goons lowers his rifle aiming at Xavier's chest. With blinding speed Xavier grabs the barrel of the gun aiming it towards the direction of another of the villains. The rifle goes off and the bullet strikes the villain in the head and kills him instantly.

Xavier uses the barrel of the gun as leverage to catapult himself in the air as the goon holds on tight to the gun fearing losing it to Xavier. Xavier now air bound strikes another killer in the throat with a flying front kick.

Xavier lands with both knees on the back of the goon's knees bringing him to the ground. Xavier, still holding the barrel of the gun with one hand, now grabs the butt of the rifle with the other and pulls, striking the weapon against the throat of the goon, who lets go of the rifle as Xavier removes a knife from his belt and runs it across the goons neck. The goon drops dead to the ground.

A fifth attacker comes head on against Xavier. Xavier rolls forward head first, over the dead thug in front of him doing a perfect summersault landing on his feet in front of his attacker.

Xavier strikes the attacker in the heart with his knife. Without missing a beat, he grabs the attackers' rifle as the dead man's body attempts to fall to the ground but is held up by the rifle's strap, now tangled around his neck and arm. Using the hanging dead thug's body as a shield Xavier shoots three more goons dead.

Xavier turns to the Death Squad Leader, the last goon runs for his life. The Death Squad Leader shoots at Xavier, but Xavier is no longer in front of him.

Death Squad Leader: (Palms sweating, sweat dripping from his forehead) what are you? Where are you? Come out and fight like a man.

XAVIER: (in a soft whispering tone that seems to come out of the woodworks) A man? Like you? Killing a defenseless woman and a mere child? You...You are my number 50.

A cold air fills the room. The Death Squad Leader fires in every direction until bullets run out. Xavier charges the leader with the ferocity of the Bull — the Death Squad Leader lies dead on the floor.

Xavier removes his mask and kneels over Elsa and Li Ming, holding both of them in his arms; he hugs them tight as tears roll down his face.

Xavier: Oh, Li Ming, I am so sorry, I was supposed to always keep you safe, I am so sorry...

Placing a goodbye kiss on their foreheads, he disappears into the forest.

CHAPTER 4

CANDY WILL KILL YOU

MARFA, TEXAS - JOHNSON BANK - NIGHT

...Present Day...

The small town of Marfa is most well-known for the numerous sightings of mysterious lights reported in this small desert town of around 2,000 people, Marfa is also an off-the-beaten-path destination for Minimalist art attractions, and many artists have flocked the town to enjoy the art culture. With a charming town square, and various art exhibits, the town prides itself on the Marfa Lights Festival! In the middle of the quaint town stands the one and only Johnson Bank.

The inside of the bank has the air of the banks in the 30's when Bonnie and Clyde traveled the central United states with their gang robbing banks and killing people when cornered or confronted.

Inside the bank in a small computer room with large windows and a stale smell is a computer programmer working at night burning the midnight oil. The computer NERD (20'S), thin, curly hair, dressed in shirt and blue jeans, no tie, old worn cowboy boots, works on the final figures of the year-end audit. He fidgets with his hands over the keyboard.

Amongst the bank transactions on his screen, a "chat" box with the name "League of Superheroes" remains open.

Behind him stands the BANK MANAGER, (42), medium built, dark hair, thick mustache, nervous, distracted, and uptight. He is overweight and tends to look over his glasses when he speaks, he is dressed in a cheap Walmart suit, his shirt hangs over his belly, his tie is undone, and he wears a five o'clock shadow. His eyes cross slightly when he looks at the computer.

Paperwork lays all over the geek's desk, pencils, paperclips, small model planes, and comic books are mixed within all the work. Pictures of UFO's and sci-fi films crowd the grey painted walls. A waste paper basket full of crumbled paper spills all over the floor.

Bank Manager: How much longer? I'm exhausted.

Computer Nerd: Just a matter of giggle cycle partition spins sir.

The manager rolls his eyes.

Bank Manager: Freaks, geeks and audits. I hate them.

The computer finally stops and beeps.

Computer Nerd: Well this year's is done. Now we're all caught up with the audit.

Bank Manager: Excellent! Good work Mike. Just let me call the wife, and grovel, and we're out of here.

The manager walks down the hallway and steps into his office and calls his wife, as the nerd sits at the computer.

Suddenly, a *Pink Cartoon Pig* wearing a crown and a ballerinas' tutu appears on the screen. He dances and skips across the screen licking an oversized lollipop smiling and saying, "want some candy?"

The nerd's eyes widen to the size of large saucers, he can't even blink - he knows what that means. He nervously calls the bank manager.

Computer Nerd: Sir, ah, Mr. Bradley, you better come in here.

Bank Manager: (Shouting from his office) what's the matter?

Computer Nerd: I don't know sir, some kind of pig...I mean virus, or worm, has gotten into the main drive. Possibly a "code red' or an "I love You Virus", or a "Melissa Virus", oops, not that one, Melissa is pornographic, scratch that one, maybe a Nesser or a Sasser...

Bank Manager: Oh, Shut up! And talk...

Computer Nerd: Ok, which is it, shut up or talk?

Bank Manager: In English, damn it! Talk, in English! I am on a very important call here.

The nerd stretches out in his chair, throws his hands up in the air rolling his eyes backwards, for he knows the bank manager is speaking with his wife.

Computer Nerd: It looks like money is being pulled from our accounts. So let me ask you... is that call more important than having all the bank's money stolen?

Bank Manager: The hell you say! That's impossible....

The bank manager leaves his office and runs into the computer room and over to the nerd, his eyes twitching, holding tightly to a ruler with both hands.

Computer Nerd: Wait a second; it looks like... they're putting it back.

The Bank Manager smiles, scratching his back with the ruler.

Bank Manager: Why's it still adding?

Computer Nerd: If they put that money back, we aren't loosing anything, sir. Maybe they are just borrowing it...

The bank manager slams the ruler on the desk several times as he speaks.

Bank Manager: What? Nobody just borrows from my bank!

Computer Nerd: (intimidated) Sir, everybody borrows from banks. That is what banks do, lend...

Bank Manager: Oh, shut up!

Computer Nerd: Ash... sir, they just put a 72-hour hold on the entire bank's money. That is enough time I suppose...

Bank Manager: You suppose what??? What!!!

Computer Nerd: Just all conjecturing here, I don't know for sure, but it is enough time to take that money to a high interest account overseas and collect interest, and then put it back in your bank. I think this taking the money out and putting it back right away was a test to see if their virus worked or not. They are borrowing the principal to collect on the interest, how cool is that? I want in on that gig.

Bank Manager: Cool? That is crap! Thievery, fraud, money napping, or something!

Computer Nerd: It might not be a crime; it's just borrowing sir...

Bank Manager: Shut up, you mutt!   Not like this they don't. Not without paperwork! Not without my permission they don't! This is stealing. Get on the phone, call the FBI, then call the IRS, call Microsoft. I'm calling the sheriff; I have his card in my office.

Computer Nerd: Sir, I'm just here for technical support.

Bank Manager: Well, this is a technical problem! Handle it! Do as I say!

The Smiling Piggy dances across the screen and winks. Computer Nerd stares in admiration.

Computer Nerd: (under his breath) Nah, Mr. Bradley don't bother, this little piggy looks smarter than Gates.

CANDY FACTORY – LOS ANGELES CALIFORNIA

The inside of a candy factory warehouse in seedy Los Angeles, is attacked by the darkness of the night sky. The large stucco building is mostly warehouse with a half panel half glass office situated at the back end of it.

"The Candy Factory Warehouse" is the home of dozens of large plastic bags filled with white powder "Candy" the new state of the art designer drug.   A synthetic mixture combined with some of the most powerful drugs on the market.   "Candy", stronger and more dangerous than *"sleet", "rail", "woo-woo" and "snow seals"* put together is set up to be the drug of choice of millions of teens. The bags of "Candy" lay on an 8-foot folding table against the back wall of the office.

A pair of male hands type feverishly on a wireless laptop computer. Twenty pairs of legs surround him from behind.

The typing stops and both hands rise in the air forming two "V" signs.

Everyone behind the typist Cheer, jumping up and down.

Everyone: We did it...we did it.

The figure sitting behind the laptop spins in his chair and stands up, turns around facing the onlookers. It's "Jeffrey "The Geek" (25), 5'10" slim, glasses, oversize pants, shirt hanging out.

"JEFFREY, 'The Geek' is the mastermind developer of an electronic "worm" named "candy" that when activated compromises the world banking system making him the primary target of the FBI's Electronic Crimes Division. He is the 'Maestro Supreme' of "Hackers Inc." Jeffrey speaks to the crowd of thugs facing him with sarcasm and disdain.

Jeffrey: No. Gentlemen, I DID IT.

MARFA TEXAS – JOHNSON BANK

Back in Marfa Texas, in Johnson bank the bank manager and the computer nerd are both staring at the bank's computer.

Bank Manager: Is it over?

Computer Nerd: I think so. I hope so.

They watch *the Screen* in front of them; the pig standing there waving and laughing.

CANDY FACTORY- LOS ANGELES

Back at the candy factory in seedy Los Angeles, Jack Reed, (40's), dirty blond hair, unshaven, open shirt, jeans cowboy boots, the leader of the group of thugs confronts Jeffrey.

Jack: You little, lying, cheating weasel. The money is being pulled back from our account. What are you doing with our money? I'll break your pitiful neck. When we kidnapped you....

Jeffrey: I wasn't kidnapped; really, I work for Tex and Mr. Ven....

Jack moves in closer to Jeffrey, his face twisted with anger, his eyes exuding bad intent. Jeffrey starts backing up in fear.

Jack: (Lifting Jeffrey by the throat) We told you the deal; make it happen and we give you back your life and pay you 2 million dollars. You don't, you die..

Suddenly Jack seems to have digested what The Geek was trying to tell him.

Jack: What do you mean you weren't kidnapped? You sayin' you work for the Boss? You lying little...

Jeffrey gets a sign of relief, but is still choking. He smirks as he speaks, his right index finger waving in the air.

Jeffrey: You hurt me and they'll be mad.

Ten *Thugs* armed to the teeth with machine guns, automatic weapons, rifles and shotguns stand by. Jeffrey is dangling by his throat, his eyes bulging out of his head awaiting a response.

Jeffrey: (gasping for air) I swear I didn't do it, I am not cheating you. I am just doing what I was told.

Everyone backs up cocking their weapons, ready to shoot as Jack drops Jeffrey to the floor. Veins pop from Jack's forehead, his rage can be read through his warped face and bulging eyes. Jack stands to the side; Jeffrey is now in full view of the armed thugs.

Jack: Boys, I want to see nothing but bullet holes on this little lying weasel. If he doesn't look like Swiss cheese when you're done, you're all dead. Jack pulls a two headed silver dollar coin out of his pocket and flips it in the air.

Jack: (in a loud laugh) When the coin hits the ground and stops spinning, everyone fire.

The coin flips in slow motion. Terror can be seen on Jeffrey's face.

While the ordered execution of Jeffrey, "The geek" is being carried out inside the warehouse, outside the roar of the engine of the black Lamborghini can now be heard as it speeds inside the warehouse at 70 MPH as the front doors of the Candy Factory Warehouse, are slowly and automatically closing...

The black Lamborghini barely wedges through the doors.

Now we can finally see the Lamborghini as the light from the warehouse reveals the speeding black panther gobbling ground as if after an injured pray, its veracious nostrils flaring, its slick and shiny body, curvaceously cutting through the wind, its wings spread outwards as if it were about to take flight. It roars, menacing anything in its way.

Inside the warehouse the thugs are startled and stare in shock...as the coin strikes the floor spinning in slow motion. The thugs desperately back away in panic as the Lamborghini is on its way to crash right through the inside office doors. The car skids across the entire warehouse and spins sideways, stopping inches from the office door at the back of the warehouse.

The passenger's window rolls down. The coin can still be heard spinning on the warehouse floor. Tex, 6'3", well built, dark brown hair, light blue sparkling eyes, perfect white teeth, dressed all in black long black trench coat, turns towards to the passengers' seat, removes his night vision goggles and replaces them with a pair of dark sun glasses before facing the group of thugs.

As the dust clears, Tex pops the trunk of the car exposing a trunk full of bricks of "Candy", the drug. Jack cautiously approaches the Lamborghini.

Jack: Tex?

CHAPTER 5

YOU DON'T TUG ON SUPERMAN'S CAPE. YOU DON'T SPIT INTO THE WIND. YOU DON'T PULL THE MASK OFF THAT OLD LONE RANGER. AND YOU DON'T MESS AROUND WITH TEX!

CANDY FACTORY-LOS ANGELES

Inside the Lamborghini Tex can be heard talking on his cell.

Tex, an orphan as a young child after both parents were killed by thugs robbing their home, was born in Laredo, Texas. Tex, a man with a checkered past, and with a mystery that surrounds him leads to reveal a long tenure in law enforcement and military activities.

He now seems to have switched loyalty from defending the country to money and dark power.

Tex: (On The Cell Phone) Yes, BOSS, I'll make sure I get the Geek back before he gets whacked.

Tex: (continuing) No, not Johnny, sir, his name is Jeffrey. Yes sir, I know we need him. Call me back in five. I'll keep you posted.

Tex slowly steps out of the car. As his foot hits the ground, the coin makes its final spin. Tex carries a silver brief case in his left hand. His face is sculptured; his body radiates an air of total control.

Tex: (addressing Jack) I'm in a bit of a hurry old chap. My bulletproof Lamborghini and I have places to go. Where is the "Geek"? For your sake I hope he's still alive. I've got the money and the "Candy".

Candy: "The New Drug" A combination of chemically laced cocaine, heroin, ground mushrooms, choice chemicals, and morphine.

Jack: How do you have the drugs and the money, Tex?

With his right index finger Tex taps Jack's nose as he speaks.

Tex: Because I am the number-two banana in this outfit Jack. I am the boss's right hand, I make things happen. So you are asking all the wrong questions, Jack, are you a thug or are you a reporter for the New York Times?

Jack, Jack, Jack, is it fair for you to be so naïve and at the same time be on the wrong side of the law? You think maybe you should be applying for a job as one of the girls on "The View". Get with the program...

Tex pauses for a second.

Tex: Or get...dead. I can't believe that you complaining because I am bringing you both the money and the "Candy"? I can take them away if you want.

Confused Jack is not sure what to answer.

Jack: Uhm...Ye...ah? No, no, that's fine.

Tex: Yeah. Trust me, yeah. (A big smile radiates on Tex's face)

Jack: Well, this computer nerd you kidnapped for us is a total pain in the ass. To top it off after two weeks the disk doesn't work.

Tex: I didn't really kidnap him, he works for me. It's either the disk, my geek, or...

In Slow Motion, Tex drops his briefcase, flips his black trench coat back with both hands, revealing two high caliber pistols. He draws both pistols from the holsters. He presses the top of both slides of his weapons against his legs with a downward motion, racking a round into both chambers as the coat lingers in the air behind him. He points one gun at Jack and one at his posse.

Tex (continued)... you're all dead. So where is my boy?

The group of thugs burst out into laughter. Tex, poker-faced, stares down the thugs with the blank look of a heartless killer. His thumb flicks the laser sight on his weapon; he slowly moves the light from body to body. He smirks.

Tex: I'll take down seven of you before I take the first bullet, but I'll kill you all. Let's do it, my money is on my Glocks...any takers?

Jack's Thug #1: (Whispering to the thug next to him) Careful, I know him, this guy is insane. He's killed more people than all of us put together.

Jack's Thug #2: (To the group) He's got to be wearing a bullet proof vest, because I've seen him take a shot point blank before, get up and walk away. He ain't no superhuman.

The thugs quickly realize that they are no match for Tex, who seems to be itching to start a gunfight rather than finish his business. Something in his air of appearance, his look of invincibility, his readiness to invite danger begins to deter Jack's thugs. Their smiling faces change to obvious despair. With the thugs' attention on Tex, Jeffrey manages to quietly work his way to the back door. Tex holsters one of his weapons and picks up the briefcase.

Jack: OK, guys, it's OK, stand down. (starting to cower) Put those guns down now; the "Geek" is fine and he has the disk.

In the back of the warehouse, Jeffrey desperately yanks on a locked back door. All eyes turn to the Geek then back to Tex who's still staring down the thugs. Tex and Jack, guns drawn, slowly walk in unison towards "The Geek". The other thugs look on.

Tex: I think I am going to kill this little weasel; I don't care what the Boss wants.

Jack: He works for you and you want to kill him?

Tex: Jack... sometimes you just have to sacrifice somebody, just to feel good, don't you think? I am supposed to keep him alive, but let's see... Let me give it some heavy thought...

Tex looks up in the air as if he is debating his own question.

Tex: Yeah, what the hell – let's kill him.

Jack: (under his breath) You're a psycho.

Tex: Tomatoes, tomatos... Psycho, not Psycho...

Jack: Oh, I am sorry Tex, it just slipped out I didn't mean it...

Tex: I see everything, I hear everything.

Jack smirks at his comment. Tex and Jack take aim with their handguns and begin to squeeze their triggers. Jeffrey cowers and cries in desperation. Suddenly, a cell phone rings. Everyone reaches for their phone, looking at each other to see whose phone it is. Tex reaches in his coat pocket and answers his cell.

Tex: Excuse me for interrupting our execution; I have to take this. (into the phone)

Yes sir... It does...? Really, well he's right in my sight sir... Yes sir, I'll make sure to take good care of him.

Outside the warehouse we see nine Shadow Warriors putting on weapons, being briefed, looking at surveillance, photographs and charts off the back of their van. The Shadow Warriors then run in single file outside the warehouse, climbing up the warehouse walls.

Inside the candy factory warehouse Tex hands the phone over to Jack, a cold air overtakes the warehouse. Shadows of strange silhouettes blending into the background move swiftly in the loft above. They can be seen lowering themselves from the ceiling, head first, with their legs wrapped around their black rappelling ropes. Tex notices them; however no one else seems to.

Tex: It's for you.

Jack: Who is it?

Tex just stands there holding the phone, making a face at Jack with an expression that says "who cares, just take the phone". Tex just stands there waiting without saying a word, staring at Jack. Jack takes the phone from Tex.

Jack: Hello, who is this? Hello? (to Tex) There is no one there.

Jack looks at Tex with a puzzled look.

Jack: (continued) Hey, what the hell is going on?

Tex: Oh, yeah, it was Mr. Venezie he wanted me to give you a message.

Meanwhile *Black Shadows* continue to climb down from the loft behind the thugs. Their bodies blend into the background colors. Tex sees that they are getting close and reacts quickly. The slight sound of helicopters can be heard outside. Tex raises his gun and shoots Jack point blank.

Tex: Message delivered.

Tex keeps the thugs at bay by moving in a circle pointing his weapon at them and talking. Jack's thugs lift and cock their weapons.

Tex: I am under orders from *Unity*. I am the new under-boss; the disk works. That means more money for all of us, any objections?

Tex scans the room with a "you better not challenge me" look. He flicks a button that unlatches the briefcase full of money and tosses it in the air towards the thugs. Two million dollars suddenly fills the air. Tex makes his way over to Jeffrey in the confusion, as the thugs scramble for the money.

The masked shadowy figures all dressed in black land on the ground without making a sound, ignoring the money and drugs while neutralizing the goons in an attempt to break through them and get to Tex and Jeffrey.

Tex reaches Jeffrey by the back door

Tex: (to Jeffrey) the disk, where is it? Do you have it? Answer, I don't want to have to kill you.

Tex holds a gun to Jeffrey's head.

Jeffrey: Tex, what's wrong with you? (pushing Tex's gun hand away) Take that gun away from my head, you lunatic. You almost let those psychos kill me. Here, I got the disk in my pocket, you can have it.

Tex: This is the disk with the virus and also the anti-virus code in it?

Jeffrey: Yes, you jerk!

Tex: Little man, your words are cutting deep into my heart and hurting my feelings now.

Tex looks at Jeffrey with a grin on his face as Jeffrey "The Geek" hands the disk over to him. We can see big bold letters printed on the label "CANDY".

Tex: My little Geek partner, I wasn't going to kill you, we are a team. But I made you sweat didn't I?

Jeffrey: (under his breath) Psycho.

Tex: (Putting his arm around Jeffrey and hurrying him towards the back door in a mocking voice) Ok, little man I am now really hurt by your comments.

As the fight ensues the Warriors try to get to Tex and Jeffrey with the "Candy" disk.

Shadow 1: Shadow 2, let's get through the mess and get that disk back.

Shadow 2: I'm all over it Shadow 1.

The thugs, believing that the Shadow warriors are after them, fight the shadowy figures obstructing them from their true goal. A second combat ensues for the Shadow warriors...

"Way of the Snowtiger"

The Combat is fierce and savage as all the animals of the Snowtiger attack the enemy quickly and mercilessly crippling and killing with dispassionate intent.

The Shadow Warriors athletic and acrobatic disposition elude the thug's gunfire as they strike with the force of A Boar, the slick movements of The Leopard, the vicious stinging of The Python, the elusiveness of The Tiger, the savage charge of The Bull, the choking grip of The Cobra, the vicious flight of The Eagle, the quick and silent attack of The Viper and the stealth and blood chilling movements of The Ghost.

Tex grabs Jeffrey as they swiftly and calmly escape the mayhem and walk towards Lamborghini, with Tex dragging Jeffrey along the way. The front door of the warehouse opens as the majestic figure of Shadow 6 walks through it. Shadow 6 stands still in front of the Lamborghini.

Jeffrey: (pointing at Shadow 6 and screaming) who's that giant lunatic, who is that lunatic?

Tex: Uh...Oh.

Tex opens the passenger door and throws Jeffrey in the passenger seat of the black Lamborghini. He closes the trunk keeping his eyes fixed on Shadow 6 all along, as the thugs fight off the shadowy intruders and compete to scoop up the most cash. Tex gets in the driver's seat. The car locks automatically and starts immediately.

Jeffrey: (screaming) Run him over, run him over!

Tex: (calm, cool and collected) No way. That's what he wants. He won't lure me into a fight, not now...the time is wrong.

Jeffrey: You know this psycho? I should have known; one psycho knows the other psycho! He wants us to run him over? Any bets on who'll end up on a gurney? Ever seen one of these cars in a hospital bed?

Tex: (slapping Jeffrey) Shut up! You don't know who we're dealing with. I would never be able to touch him with this car. Lay back, we've got work to do.

All attempts to stop Tex fail as he does a 360 on the spot burning rubber. Two thugs get hit by the spinning car and are catapulted into the air. One lands onto the mix of thugs and shadowy figures and the another crashes through the office glass, landing directly on top of the plastic bags full of powder, causing them to burst and quickly filling the room and warehouse with white powder. Two of the Shadow Warriors run stealthily and swiftly after the car as it starts to speed away.

The warriors throw *shuriken* at the car tires, and unload several bursts of rounds from their fully automatic pistols as they run. The Lamborghini barely gets away, the two Warriors stand in the wake of its dust. Tex floors it and heads straight for the side wall of the warehouse.

The Lamborghini runs over huge bags of powdered "candy", the drug. As the bags explode and powder continues to fill the warehouse, the Lamborghini crashes through the warehouse walls. The thugs try to warn Tex, but he has no intentions of avoiding the piles of drugs.

Jack's Thug #1: Watch out! The "CANDY", that's worth milli...

Before he finishes his sentence he gets knocked unconscious by the side of the Lamborghini that tosses him in the air several feet away on top of the *Candy.*

As quickly and swiftly as the shadowy figures appeared, they vanish.   *Police* with weapons drawn enter the warehouse to find the group of gangsters unconscious and money flying everywhere.

A cold draft fills the warehouse. Everyone's heads turn in the direction from where it came from, in time to see a tall, well built, imposing figure of a masked man dressed completely in black. His long black coat flaps as a gust of wind blows through the warehouse, causing money and powder to mix and scatter throughout the warehouse from the powerful draft.

Shadow 6 exits the warehouse.

As Tex' car smashes through the side wall of the warehouse, the Lamborghini spins and the car slides, stopping twenty feet from the warehouse. The car is instantly bathed in spotlights. Tex speeds off. Confusion falls upon the scene, some of the thugs that weren't badly injured or dead run outside.

The policemen look at each other asking one another "who was that?" No one seemed to have the answer.

As Tex speeds off, he speaks into a hidden microphone in his coat sleeve.

Tex: Now. Move now.

A group of several matt black Lamborghinis now appear on the scene.

Lamborghini driver #1: (yelling to the group) Whatever you do, make sure TEX gets away, set the decoys at the designated spots, protect him, the cops can't get them. Protect him. Protect whatever "CANDY" is left.

Ten of the Lamborghinis' outside rush away from the scene and take to the streets in efforts to confuse their followers. Three additional black Lamborghini's come out of the shadows and speed away following Tex as he heads towards the freeway. The other ten Lamborghini's draw as many police towards them as they can so Tex has a better chance at his getaway.

As Tex continues his escape, two black, unmarked police helicopters follow Tex' car. Shadow 6 and the Warriors follow the Lamborghinis in their black, supercharged Humvee. Two thug cars follow the Warriors. Numerous police cars follow the ten Lamborghinis but have difficulty keeping up with the high speed and the skilled driving of the criminals on the run.

The three cars identical to Tex's Lamborghini follow behind Tex's car and all four begin to play the "shell game" between them to confuse the police helicopters above.

The four *Lamborghini's* speed down the freeway changing lead positions frequently, their Speedometers' reading climb, 110 MPH... 180 MPH... 210 MPH... 220 MPH, and have to slow down due to *Heavy Traffic*. One of the Lamborghini's makes a sudden exit and leaves the freeway as four of the other Lamborghini's that had taken to the street now join in. Shadow 6 follows them.

The LA freeway is packed, it's rush hour at 2 AM.

Tex: Rush hour at 2 am? Welcome to LA!

Tex enters the carpool lane intimidating other cars to get out of the way. He pulls a police flashing light from under the dashboard and sticks it on the roof of the car. All the other Lamborghini drivers do the same. Meanwhile the other three Lamborghini's speed through adjacent lanes going in and out of the lanes attempting to get the other cars to clear the way for Tex.

Tex Lamborghini's speedometer reads 90 MPH, 100 MPH, and back down to 20 MPH, slowing down due to heavy traffic, he is in and out of the shoulder on the road. As Tex again speeds down the road, he passes a CHP. The CHP goes in pursuit of the speeding car.

Jeffrey: Where did you get that police light? That's against the law.

Tex: News flash... we are criminals...Do you think I should turn on a siren too. Since the light is against the law already...

Tex breaks into laughter.

Tex sees that there is no traffic on the other side of the freeway and crosses over now driving against traffic. Jeffrey panics and holds on for dear life.

Jeffrey: You madman, you are going to get us killed!

Tex: There you go again little man, showing no confidence for your friend and savior. I am traveling in the diamond lane.

Jeffrey: Yes, but against traffic!

With a smirk on his face Tex replies.

Tex: Do you think I'll get a ticket?

Jeffrey: Oh my God, there is a car coming at us at full speed on this lane. Get out of this lane! Get out of the lane!

Tex: I can't do that, I was here first, he needs to move.

Jeffrey is now rolled up in a ball, hanging on to anything he can and peeking from under his arm.

Jeffrey: You crazy nut, you are driving against traffic. We are going to die.

Tex: Maybe I should send him a message, you think?

Jeffrey: What message, get out of the lane! You have the whole freeway empty...

Tex: As you ask my little buddy, let's send him a message.

Tex moves to the empty lane next to the diamond lane. Jeffrey has a sign of relief in his face as he releases some of his grip from the car door. Tex presses a button on the dashboard that releases some kind of oily liquid from the bottom of the car. The road under the Lamborghini becomes wet and sleek.

Suddenly with expert precision Tex slams on the breaks and floors the accelerator at the same time as he turns the wheel to the left making the car spin in circles and landing back in the diamond lane.

Tex floors the car at full speed challenging the car heading in his direction. The driver of the other car pulls out of the lane on the nick of time. The cars miss each other by less than an inch. The other vehicle hits the sleek road, loses control of his car, and crosses over to the oncoming traffic, crashing into a truck.

Tex: Little man, little body, he got the message, just like you said he would. But you know he wasn't a good driver, crossing over the medium like that and crashing into a truck. Hmm, hmmm.

Jeffrey: Help! Help! I am being kidnapped by a suicidal madman! Help!

Tex: Little man, you are so funny! That's why we get along so well.

Tex bursts into a loud laughter as he speeds down the freeway, traveling on the wrong side of the road and chased by police cars and helicopters.

CHP car #1 - Speaks into his radio.

CHP: Car 20 to dispatch, we have a huge problem here.

VENEZIE'S MANSION

In the middle of beautiful *Beverly Hills* California, the home of the rich and famous stands 34 acres of land with a lavish mansion in the middle of it. The driveway twists and curves for what seems "forever". Suddenly a well-guarded structure at the end of the long and laborious driveway is finally disclosed. Standing before them, like the great Coliseum of Rome, a colossal mansion makes claim to the grounds. It is the headquarters of *Gabriel Venezie*, the head *Capo* of the most dangerous and criminally wanted organization on earth – *Unity*.

The interior of the mansion is beyond lavish. Ceilings over twenty feet tall, with large floor-to-ceiling glass windows and doors. Statues from ancient Rome and Greece decorate the rooms.

Slightly past the mansion's front lobby, left of the double stairs and elevator, is a den where the "Boss" spends most of his time these days.

Gabriel Venezie, The Boss mid-60's, dark hair, slight built, slicked hairdo, clean shaven, very well dressed in a pants suit a silk shirt and a silk vest, sits in his wheelchair, sipping on a glass of Brandy in front of the TV, channel surfing and stops the remote at a news channel.

The TV screen is showing the helicopter chase, reporters are discussing the earlier developments of the chase with the three black Lamborghini's, at two o'clock in the morning.

The Boss tries to sit up in his wheelchair, to no avail; he is startled by the news.

Gabriel Venezie: Oh shit! God damn it Tex! Not good, this is not good! Gina! Make preparations for traveling to our home in the Italian Alps. This is going to have repercussions.

L.A. FREEWAY

The Lamborghini chase in the middle of the Los Angeles freeway at 2:00 Am continues.

CHP: Car 20 to dispatch. I've got several black Lamborghini's, no license plates, lights off, and exceeding 100 to 150 MPH, heading east. They're getting way too close to other vehicles at high speed, and then they turn on police lights to move them out of the way. One of them is traveling east on the westbound freeway exceeding 150 MPH. They're going to kill someone. Officer requires assistance.

Dispatch: Police lights? They are cops?

CHP: Negative on that. Just crooks with police gear.

The Southern California freeways are a network of interconnected freeways in the mega region of Southern California, serving a population of 22 million people. Dozens of freeways blend, mix, inter-mesh, cross, twist and turn with the finesse of a seasoned ballerina giving her best performance at the Bolshoi Theater in Moscow, Russia and the sudden exchanges of an unsuspected cliff in the middle of the German Autobahn.

Tex gains some distance. He's now going 155 MPH. Three additional CHP cars join the pursuit. All three Lamborghini's are now traveling in the carpool lane on the eastbound freeway.

CHP Car #2: (on the radio) these guys are going too fast, we're going to lose them.

VENEZIE'S MANSION

Now back to the Bosses mansion in Beverly Hills the TV still reporting on the freeway chase. The police helicopters bathe the cars with their spotlights, but it's no deterrent to Tex and his gang.

TV Reporter: I'll tell ya guys, I've reported on and seen a hell of a lot of car chases but never one like this. Four black sports cars...they look like Lamborghini's and cops all over the place. One of the cars is traveling like a bat out of hell on the wrong side of the freeway.

They even have police lights to clear the freeway. These guys are certainly prepared for everything. Whoever's driving those cars are really driving like the devil, they might just get away. I've never seen cars go so fast and so skillfully on the freeway. They're even faster than our helicopters. We're going to try to stay on this.

Back on the road, Jeffrey holds on, terrified, white-knuckling and praying for his life as he watches Tex. Tex, with the expert skill of a racecar driver, swiftly maneuvers the Lamborghini at the top speeds of 150 MPH, 170 MPH and beyond.

Jeffrey: The lights, they are still behind us. They're going to catch us, or worse, we are going to crash, get shot, or blown up. We are going to die.

Jeffrey turns around intermittently to check out the flashing lights in pursuit of the Lamborghini.

Tex: Relax, calm down, and sit still. I would hate to have to use the ejector seat; the landing can be hell.

Jeffrey: I'm down. I'm calm, as calm as one can be under the circumstances. Please don't kill us.

Tex smirks as they easily speed away from the CHP cars. He now crosses over to the right side of the freeway, but travelling too fast for the police that chase him. The CHP cars give up the chase as they call dispatch for back up.

CHP Car #1: Dispatch, they are getting away, we need air support – they're topping 200 MPH!

The Lamborghinis race head to head, down the road now being chased by only the two unmarked police helicopters.

Helicopter Pilot- Alpha One: (on his radio) Headquarters, we are chasing something moving over 200 MPH on our radar. We cannot get low enough to see what it is. It appears to be two objects...no make that three. Well...four.

The Lamborghinis reach a freeway crossing, where multiple LA freeways meet and split off. The Lamborghinis take hard lefts and right turns without slowing down. Suddenly, the four speed demons split from one another; three going straight and the other turning right onto another intersecting freeway.

Helicopter Pilot-Alpha Two: (on his radio) They have split up ALPHA-ONE, we will cut right and stay on the one heading south. You follow the three heading east.

Helicopter-Alpha One: Roger, ALPHA two, we are on it.

The helicopters split to follow.

BACK AT THE MANSION

A reporter comments on the Bosses' TV station. In his mansion sitting in front of the TV the Boss stares in a transfix state. Once again the television reports on the car chase from the news helicopter. The Boss' fingers tap nervously on the arm of his wheelchair as he hears the developments reported on Channel 4 News.

Reporter: Sweet Jesus! Did you guys just see that? What speed!!!

With every news report, the tapping on the wheelchair armrest gets louder and harder.

Tex turns onto a dark deserted road in efforts to lose the helicopter following them. Tex keeps speeding away, and Jeffrey now more at ease, hasn't blinked for two hours. Tex drives silent. Jeffrey keeps on looking up through the glass roof at the helicopter.

Jeffrey: I think they're on to us.

Tex: Hmmm, really? What's gave it away? That flood light above our heads? Hmmm, don't panic my little idiot, watch this...

Jeffrey: We going to outrun a helicopter? And I'm not an idiot.

Tex: In this thing? Ah, we could, but no we are not. Not today. We are going to have some fun first. And I'll be the judge of your psychological condition; you're an idiot. Right now a live idiot...wanna change that?

Jeffrey: Oh, no, no, that's what I meant, not an idiot, a live idiot!

Tex flips a switch and deploys the Lamborghini's Targa roof, which flies off into the road together with the police light on it. He pulls a flare pistol from the center console. The flare has a large spike sticking out of the barrel.

Tex: Close your eyes.

Tex fires the gun straight up at the under belly of the chopper. The Co-Pilot looks at the FLIR night vision monitor, and sees a glowing ball traveling up towards them.

Co-Pilot: Oh shit Jimbo, incoming!

Helicopter Alpha One-Pilot One: What?

Alpha One - Co-Pilot: It's a rocket! Roll out, roll out!

NEWS STATION

TV Reporter: Yeow! These guys are firing something at the police helicopters. Looks like a missile!

At the news station, the news desk anchors react with shock as they look at the video coverage of the chase from their news desk.

L.A. ROAD

The flare smashes into the bottom of the chopper making a loud bang, with the spike attaching firmly to the bottom. Their *FLIR* monitor goes all white, and there is a bright glow around the bird from the still-burning flare.

Co-Pilot: (on the radio) We've been hit, we've been hit! Tango Niner to base – we've been hit by what looks like a small SAM.

Helicopter Pilot One: (to radio) Negative base, Negative.

Radio Voice from H.Q.: Tango Niner, what in Sam's Hill is going on up there, over!

Helicopter Pilot One: If it was a SAM, we'd already be dead. It was a flare.

NEWS CENTER

News Reporter: Looks like it was only a flare. Wow. Talk about gutsy. These guys are not fooling around; I wonder what they have in store next.

LA ROAD

We see the flare continue to burn as the Lamborghini below takes off; 175 mph and out of sight.

Radio Voice from H.Q.: Do you still have visual on the vehicle?

Pilot Two: That's a negative base; we lost him.

Radio Voice from H.Q.: Well, where did he go? The car didn't just disappear, did it?

Pilot Two: You could say that.

Helicopter Pilot One: We need to refuel. Tango Niner, heading for home.

Tex and Jeffrey are now in the clear from the police and head down the road. A second Lamborghini paces Tex on and off.

Jeffrey: Wow that got rid of them!

Tex opens a small flap in the console of the car sitting next to him. A detonator light flashes red and the digital read out window labeled "#1" quickly counts down from ten to zero. Nothing happens.

Jeffrey: We fooled Jack and his punks, Tex. They thought we would keep the money in their accounts. Like I always say most criminals are imbeciles... (Shaking and moving his head towards the window) No offense Tex, um, you're not an imbe....

Tex: You're about to get slapped, boy.

Jeffrey: What I mean is that they thought all the money was going to them.

Tex: Whatever, dork. The patsies... the designated idiots got what they deserved. Keep your eyes open, we don't want any surprises.

Pushing down on the switch with no results Tex gets annoyed.

Tex: What's wrong with this piece of crap?

Jeffrey: Hey, there's still another Lamborghini next to us. Isn't he supposed to divert the cops for us?

Tex keeps pressing on a switch on the box sitting inside the arm divider. He calmly answers Jeffrey.

Tex: No, His job is done. Now he probably wants to kill us both. He was supposed to disappear by now, but my magic box is not working.

Tex removes a grenade from the center console. It's covered with a sticky, see-through, gooey substance. He hands the grenade over to Jeffrey.

Tex: Hold this.

Jeffrey: This is a grenade! It will go off; we'll be killed!

Tex: You're so dramatic my little genius. When something doesn't go according to plan, one must what... little man?

Jeffrey: Use another plan? Run? Hold a grenade?

Tex: Two of those three answers were correct. See this pin? We would have to remove it to activate the grenade...like this.

Tex calmly removes the pin from the grenade. Jeffrey freaks out yelling in panic.

Tex: Don't worry little Jeffrey, we have 7 seconds...6...5...I think you are missing the point little man, you are supposed to throw the grenade into the other car before he kills us.

As Tex counts down, the second Lamborghini rides beside them. Jeffrey tries to toss out the grenade, but hits the window with his fist, the grenade's still stuck to his hands. Jeffrey panics again.

Tex: You think it would work better if I roll down the window for you?

Jeffrey: Hurry you madman, it'll go off...

Tex rolls Jeffrey's window down.

Tex: You better toss that really hard or it will go off in your lap. Then I'll really be pissed.

Jeffrey gives the grenade a real hard toss as Tex accelerates away from the other Lamborghini. The grenade leaves Jeffrey's hand.

The grenade lands on the windshield of the other Lamborghini. The driver of the car swerves all over the road trying to disengage the grenade from the windshield to no avail. As the *Driver* looks on in horror at the grenade stuck on his windshield, he extends his hand out the window as he drives to grab and remove it. Just as his hand closes on it, the grenade goes off and the Lamborghini blows to pieces.

NEWS CENTER

TV Reporter: Looks like this chase has come to an explosive end. Well folks, a new height in the never-ending LA freeway chases. Back to you at the studio.

Anchor 1: Good work Jim, crazy but exciting stuff.

GABRIEL VENEZIE'S MANSION

Back at the Bosses' Mansion, the Boss switches off the TV. He smiles and shakes his head.

Gabriel Venezie: (in a low voice to himself) I should probably stop doubting Tex's skills or he is going to give me a heart attack. (He smiles again). Italy, here I come anyway.

CALIFORNIA ROAD

On the long and lonely California road Tex turns off his headlights, puts on night vision goggles and turns on a radar scrambling device.

Helicopter Alpha 2 Pilot: We spotted them after the explosion, but it's getting too dark now. We are losing them – he is moving too fast. Send ground support 20 miles east of the old Miller road heading south.

Tex and Jeffrey in the black Lamborghini tear down the road at a demonic speed.

Tex opens the small flap in the console of the car next to him once again. The detonator flashes red and the digital read out window labeled #2 quickly counts down from ten to zero. A second explosion is heard.

Far behind Tex's car, pieces of the third *Lamborghini* can be seen flying all over the road. The HELICOPTER turns around.

Helicopter Pilot: Headquarters, we lost the bogey. It looks like he crashed. Send ground back up two klicks east of the old Miller farm. We are heading back.

CHAPTER 6

GUN FIGHT AT THE "OK CORRAL"

Tex answers a video call on the car's dashboard screen. It's Gina Venezie, mid 30's, 5'9", long black hair, smooth silk skin, big brown eyes, beautiful, evil, sophisticated.

Gina Venezie FBI Code Name "Panther" is a spoiled girl from a wealthy criminal family. Gina is her fathers' (The Boss) right hand person. Tex' sweetheart, considered one of the most dangerous criminals in history, Gina is not without merit in the "underworld". Gina has been involved in every major international financial crime for the past eight years. Lack of proof keeps her out of jail, but in the vigilant eye of the FBI.

Tex: What's shaking baby?

Gina: Do you have the nerd?

Tex: Yes ma'am.

Gina: Is he acting as geeky as always?

Jeffrey: You know I can hear you, right?

Gina: Good boy my dear Tex. You know we were just watching you on TV, that chase interrupted every other program.

Jeffrey: You also know that I have a name, right? I may be a nerd, but I'm not the idiot that threw two million dollars away...

Tex smacks Jeffrey in the face while bursting into a cynic laugh.

Tex: Counterfeit my boy, counterfeit. Show me some respect, you'll live longer.

Jeffrey grabs his face in pain.

Jeffrey: Ouch! That hurt!

Tex: My mother would have washed out your mouth with soap for a comment like that. You know... the one about me being an idiot, not the "ouch" one. (Tex laughs).

Gina: Get that rude boy back here so I can thank him personally.

Jeffrey: Thanks... For what? You don't have to do that. I am already hurting from Tex's thanks.

Tex: Nah. I think I'll just toss him out of the car at high speed. I'm sorry Gina, you know the code. I have to do it. He hurt my feelings, he called me names.

Jeffrey sits there horrified, Tex and Gina laugh.

Back at the chase site for Tex's Lamborghini by Shadow 6 and his warriors, they notice a black Lamborghini parked at the "OK CORRAL" Gas Station and Mini Mart. They pull into the gas station with their black "Humvees" right behind the black Lamborghini.

Close behind them, *two sedans* loaded with Tex's *henchmen* follow Shadow 6 and his Warriors.

The driver of one of the sedans following Shadow 6 gets on his walkie-talkie and reports the location of Shadow 6 and the Warriors.

Driver of the Sedan #1: They are stopping at the Mart. We'll trap them there. Kill them all. Make it look like a robbery.

All the thugs in the other sedan acknowledge the order.

Seven Warriors exit their vehicles and visually scout the area. Shadow 6 warns them to be extra careful, for if it is really Tex in that gas station Mart, he will come out shooting.

Shadow 6: Shadow 4, Shadow 5, let's check out the Lamborghini.

Shadow 6 and his two team members check out the Lamborghini at the gas pump up close. It's empty. Shadow 6 feels the hood of the car with the back of the hand...it's cold.

Shadow 6: (to the Warriors) Is this a coincidence? This car was not in the chase. Yet there are no coincidences in life. Proceed with caution, I smell a trap.

Shadow 5: We'll be careful. I'm going inside for some snacks. Shadow 4 heads for the Hummer.

Four of the *masked Warriors* walk casually inside the Mini-Mart.

Shadow 6 speaks to the Warriors inside the Hummer.

 Shadow 6: (Tapping on the Hummer) It doesn't look like the right car, but be careful.

The three warriors inside the vehicle nod.

The four warriors walking into the gas station mart ask if anyone wants any drinks.

Warriors in the Hum v: We'll take bottled water. We'll come out and stretch our legs.

Shadow 6: (as he joins the other Warriors walking in the Mart) that will be 5 waters coming up.

Shadow 6 enters the MINI-MART and sees the attendant standing frozen behind the counter with his hands up in the air. The four masked Warriors just stand there without saying a word, looking at the attendant.

Shadow 6: Are we robbing him or are we shopping?

The Warriors look at each other. They shrug their shoulders.

Shadow 4: Nah, let's just shop.

The all laugh.

Shadow 6 speaks to the Mart clerk, trying to keep him calm.

Shadow 6: You can put your hands down sir, we are the good guys. Ignore the masks; we'll be out of your hair in five minutes.

Outside, the two *cars* filled with *henchmen* screech into the station's lot blocking the Hummers and the Lamborghini from front and back. Five *men* in black ski masks step out of the cars.

Shotguns are drawn. They start shooting into the mini-mart. Bullets fly everywhere. Inside the mart Shadow 6, and the four Warriors take cover by diving over the mini-marts' counter and landing behind it. The Mini-Mart attendant, *Rajeev* - East Indian (30), covers his head while diving to the floor.

Rajeev: Oh, sweet mother of Shiva, no! Theese are not guud guys, for sure!

Another 5 *Thugs* enter the mini-mart through the back door. The Warriors are surrounded. Rajeev mumbles prayers as he cowers behind the counter.

Rajeev: I worship thee, O sweet lord of transcendental vision...

The four Warriors left outside take cover by jumping in one of the Hummer's, the bullet proof closed doors protect them from the incoming fire, as the Warriors quickly retrieve their weapons from inside. They return the thugs fire. Inside the mart the Warriors motion to each other with their fingers, showing three fingers up and nodding in acknowledgement.

Outside the Hummer doors open.

Four "Shadow Warriors" jump out and engage in battle:

The ruby-eyed "*Viper*" extends her long, hinged fangs as she leaps out of the Hummer, ready for her speedy and venomous strike.

The "*Python*" uncoils from the Hummer as he jumps lands and rolls on the ground delivering a myriad of venom filled daggers and stars.

The "*Tiger*" pounces off the Hummer at a speed of light, landing and spinning, avoiding incoming bullets, and pouncing again until he reaches one of the thugs who falls under his fierce attack.

The "*Cobra*" with a show of elegance thrusts her body off the Hummer, landing and rolling and back on her feet acquiring a prideful stance while throwing a series of venomous stars with uncanny accuracy while masterfully unleashing poisoned darts on the enemy.

As the Warriors in the outside carry through their vicious and stealth attach, The "*Boar*" crashes through the glass pane window of the Mini Mart in flying fashion ignoring the incoming firepower and landing on the enemy with ferocious and deadly strikes.

The Warriors successfully ambush the rest of the men from one of the sedans outside, skillfully disarming them as a ferocious battle ensues.

"Rush of the Boar"

> *With complete contempt for its opponent the Boar keeps rushing and hitting its attackers with relentless fury and wanton disregard. The enemy is struck with a multiplicity of violence, brutality, and speed that only a Boar can execute.*

The thugs from the second sedan start opening fire to give aid to the other henchmen under attack by the Warriors. Inside the Mart Shadow 6 gives the order to move forward and attack.

Shadow 6: Shadow Warriors, ready?

Shadow Warriors: We're on.

Shadow 6: Take the fight to them Warriors!

All Warriors: Ninpǒ Ikkan!

Ninpǒ Ikkan: *'The Law of the Ninja is our Primary Inspiration'.*

As in a slow motion capture of an action film, Shadow 6 and the four "*Shadow Warriors*" emerge from behind the counter with lightning speed and athleticism, fully automatic pistols drawn, blasting away. Shadow 6's team defeats the intruders. Battle scene three comes to a close.

Shaking his fist in the air at the injured gangsters and screaming in his Indian accent Rajeev voices insults.

Rajeev: What jave you done to my shoop? "May the *fleas* of a thousand camels infest your armpits!"

As Rajeev turns away, he pauses, turns around and speaks once again in anger.

Rajeev: And your crotches too!

Shadow 6 assembles the Warriors outside by the Hummers. As the last two Warriors are finished tying up the rest of the defeated thugs, Shadow 6 lifts his left arm half way in the air and calls out.

Shadow 6: Warriors *Yame Yoi!*

Yame Yoi: A command to stop and be ready, attention.

Warriors: Rei!!

Rei: 礼 A command in Japanese Martial arts meaning "Bow with Respect"

All Warriors drop on their right knee with their heads down and their left arms up in the air, fists clenched tightly. They stand up; legs spread shoulder width, in a circle formation. (Standing up with their hands clasped in front of their chest) each emulating a Kuji-In Symbol of the Kuji-Kiri, "nine-hands-cutting" five horizontal and four vertical, alternating. This is a preparatory ritual of protection, to cut off demonic influences. They sound out.

Annie stands with her hands together, fingers interlocked. Her index fingers are raised and pressed together. *"The Seal of the **thunderbolt**." She* sounds out!

Annie (The Viper): Rin – Strength of mind and body.

Bobby has his Hands together, pinkies and ring fingers interlocked. His Index finger and thumb raised and pressed together, his middle fingers cross over index fingers and the tips curl back to touch the thumbs' tips, the middle-fingers' nails touching. *"The Seal of the **Thunderbolt**." He* sounds out!

Bobby *(The Bull)*: Pyǒ – Direction of energy.

Carmela sounds out with her hands together, index fingers cross each other to touch the opposite ring fingers, the middle fingers crossed over them. Her ring and pinky fingers are straight. The tips of her ring fingers pressed together, the tips of her pinkies pressed together, but both sets of ring and pinky fingers are separated to form a "V" shape or bird beak *"The Seal of the Great **Thunderbolt**."*

Carmela *(The Ghost)*: Tǒ – Harmony with the Universe.

Chao Fang has his hands together, his ring fingers cross each other to touch his opposite index fingers, his middle fingers crossed over them. His index finger, pinky and thumb straight, like the American Sign Language "I love you". *"Seal of the Inner Lion." He sounds out!*

Chao Fang *(The Eagle)*: Sha! – Healing self and others.

Ed stands with Hands together, fingers interlocked. *"Homage to all-pervading diamond thunderbolts. Utterly crush and devour!"* He sounds out!

Ed *(The Cobra)*: Kai! – Premonition of danger.

Fernando with his hands together, fingers interlocked, with the fingertips inside. "Seal of the Inner Bonds." Sounds out!

Fernando (The Boar): Jin! – Knowing the thoughts of others.

Max sounds out with his left hand in an upward-pointing fist, index finger raised. His right hand grips his index finger, and his thumb is pressed onto left index's nail. "Seal of the Interpenetration of the Two Realms."

Max (The Python): Retsu – Mastery of time and space

With her hands spread out in front, with thumbs and index fingers touching. "Seal of the Ring of the Sun." She sounds out!

Ding Su (The Leopard): Zai – Controlling the elements of nature.

Shinobi forms a circle with his hands, his thumbs on top and his fingers on the bottom, his right hand overlapping his left up to the knuckles. *"All hail!"*

Shinobi (The Tiger): Zen – Enlightenment.

CHAPTER 7

HOME SWEET HOME

THE SALT FLATS OF DEATH VALLEY

The sun rises on the low desert, and nothing can be seen for miles in any direction, with the exception of two black Hummers driving fast across the salt. The Hummers turn a white dusty trail in their wake.

Suddenly, Shadow 6 slams on the brakes, the Humvee slides to a halt. The dusty cloud catches up to it, enveloping the vehicle. The second Hummer stops.

The front door opens and Shadow 6 steps out. He walks a few feet, removing the dusty sand from the ground with his boots. A single gloved hand clears away some of the sandy salt exposing a key pad and tracks of a gate that normally rises when triggered by the weight of a vehicle several feet away.

Shadow 6: They disconnected the gate.

Shadow 3: I guess they weren't expecting company.

The Warriors break into laughter inside the Hummers.

Shadow 6 types in a code in the exposed keypad and suddenly the ground begins to lower around them. An elevator lowers them into the facility.

Shadow 2: Now that's what I call service!

The black Humvees and the Shadow Warriors are lowered down to the main deck of the compound as one by one they take off their masks. Salt and sand pour down the sides of the platform as it lowers the Warriors down.

It's now for the first time we see the faces of all nine warriors - six men, three women - accompanied by Shadow 6, who removes his mask revealing him to be Xavier Crown, an African American (43), light skin, well built, chiseled face, piercing eyes, leader of The Shadow Warriors.

The warriors are met at the dock by Eric Stone, now in his sixties, still in excellent shape and the head of the agency.

Eric Stone: Well... made it home for breakfast.

Shadow 6: Yep, morning' sir.

The Warriors step off the platform and Shadow 6 tosses the truck keys to a mechanic waiting to service it. Eric follows Shadow 6 into the locker room, talking as they walk. Shadow 1 speaks to shadow 3.

Shadow 1: Hey I'm counting on you to be at the party at my house this weekend.

Shadow 1 stresses the word "the" motioning, the "quote" sign with both hands in front of him, as if his party was the happening of the century.

Shadow 3: Yeah, got it. The wife will be there too.

Shadow 1: (Shouting to the rest of the team) Hey, guys don't forget about the party at my house this weekend.

Shadow 3: You guys are all coming, right?

Shadow 5: I'm there, I'm bringing the beer.

Shadow 2: Count me in.

Shadow 1: Great, that accounts for everyone. I'm going to catch some Z's now.

All the Warriors head to their bunks.

In the locker room of the underground facility, Eric Stone continues his conversation with Xavier.

Eric Stone: So I hear from H.Q., that you didn't get me that hacker. Of course, I had to tell them how impossible that was. All the years of training under your belt, all the money we spend on this program to keep it functioning at the highest level. So tell me they're lying to me, so I can go back to my coffee and morning paper.

Shadow 6: I never failed you before, Eric; I'm not going to start now.

Eric looks at Xavier with a smirk on his face.

Eric Stone: What about the time you peed on my couch, when I asked you specifically if you had to use the bathroom before you went to sleep?

Shadow 6 bursts into a short laugh.

Shadow 6: I was five, and it was your fault. Bad parenting, Eric, bad parenting...

Eric Stone: Bad Parenting? That's the thanks I get for raising you?

Shadow 6: Raising me? You abandoned me in South America; it took you years to come back for me.

Eric Stone: I was following orders, Xavier. I sure miss the parrilladas, the maté, the gauchos, the good company.

Shadow 6: You think it doesn't bother me they got away? It's like they knew we were coming.

Eric Stone: Listen kid, if I can tell you one thing, is that nobody, I mean nobody, ever knows what you're going to do next; heck probably not even you. You'll catch that Tex guy, no problem.

Shadow 6: There is a mole on the inside Eric. Have it checked out.

Eric Stone: I doubt it, but I'll have it checked out. Hey at least the trucks are in one piece. First time that's ever happened. You keep that up and I can fire the mechanic, cut back on spending, maybe get you another helicopter.

Shadow 6: I see you forgot what happened to the last one.

Eric Stone: No, no, it's now a heap of trash and we are still paying for that one. How about breakfast? A power bar?

Shadow 6: No, I'm going to hit the sack for a few, catch up on some Z's.

Eric Stone: No dice pal.

Eric pats Shadow 6 on the back and laughs.

Eric Stone: You got a class in 20 minutes.

Shadow 6: (under his breath) you've got to be kidding.

Eric Stone: Perk up sport, you're molding the minds of the future. (Patting Shadow 6 on the back) Now there's a scary thought.

Shadow 6 looks at Eric rolling his eyes. Eric Stone continues dialogue in a sarcastic tone.

Eric Stone: Then of course. If you don't teach them, who will?

Eric takes off, as Shadow 6 stays sitting on the locker room bench. Eric yells back to him, his voice resonates through the locker room as he exits.

Eric Stone: By the way I've got a walk through with the Pentagon today, so, wear a tie or something. And I don't want any complaints. Somebody's got to sign our pay checks, you know.

We hear the door shut, Eric is gone, and Shadow 6 sits alone.

Shadow 6: I don't kiss up and I don't do ties...

The door opens back up, Eric sticks his head in. He speaks and then makes a puckering face.

Eric Stone: Fine, then just look presentable...and start practicing kissing up.

Shadow 6 smiles and reflects on previous training days with the Young Warriors.

CHAPTER 8

TIGERS, AND COBRAS, AND LEOPARDS AND PYTHONS, OH, MY!

FLASHBACK TO A MONTH AGO

The young Warrior's training is extensive. It consists of nine consecutive days of one-on-one individual training, followed by one day of rest and reflection, then three days of combined animal system compact training, followed by a second day of rest and reflection. Then the whole cycle starts again on a nine - one - three - one day basis.

The nine one-on-one individual training days with Shadow 6 consists of one day for each animal system with each prospective master of that animal. While the single system training takes place, the rest of the Warriors observe and take notes.

The lessons take place in an isolated training room for which Shadow 6 holds the only key.

In the private closed training room a daily chart hangs on the wall:

Day	Animal System	Warrior	1	2	3	4	5	6	7	8	9	10
1	**[The Eagle]**	Max Long										
2	**[The Viper]**	Sarah Long										
3	**[The Cobra]**	Carmen Ramirez										

4	[The Tiger]	Ethan Perez										
5	[The Bull]	Jimmy Traves										
6	[The Leopard]	Mike Nelson										
7	[The Boar]	Tom Ellis										
8	[The Python]	William Spencer										
9	[The Ghost]	Alexa Evans										

On day one, Shadow 6 meets with ALL the Young Warriors in the training room. The large room is comprised of wooden floors; weapons hang in each of the walls. Training dummies line up one of the walls, boards and bricks for training purposes stack up in one of the corners. A huge gong is centered in one of the walls. Shields, throwing stars, spears, and swords decorate the rest of the room.

The Young Warriors enter the room and proceed to sit down, legs crossed, making a large circle with each of them facing outwards from the circle, while Shadow 6 walks inside the circle to choose the first Warrior for lesson one, day one. Shadow six calls out a warrior.

Shadow Six: Max, (The Eagle Warrior).

DAY 1

The lesson starts. Max stands up, turns around, and walks into the circle to face his master. The Eagle Warrior bows down to Shadow 6 in respect. The rest of the Warriors, keeping the same sitting position, spin in place and turn around to witness the lesson.

Shadow 6: Tell me about the weapons of the eagle.

Max: The beak, the wings, the claws.

Shadow 6: Think Max, what else.

Max: His vision.

Shadow 6: What about his vision?

Max: It can spot it's pray from way up in the sky.

Shadow 6: Good Max, what else?

Max: It can break the prey's neck with one strike.

Shadow 6: Yes Max. His grip is strong enough to break bones, his flight makes him elusive and unattainable, his wings, his feet, and his beak can strike simultaneously. His attack is fast, furious and incredibly accurate. He is fearless, protects his young, and lives a long life. In some cases, where the eagle stood in perfect conditions, it has lived to seventy years.

The talons and beak are two of the three best defining features of what makes *The Eagle* "raptors". Without the sharp talons for catching prey and the strong, sharp beak for tearing food, *The Eagle* would certainly die of starvation. So protect your weapons.

Max: Yes sir.

Shadow 6: What is his third defining feature?

Max: His wings.

Shadow 6: Correct, why?

Max: It allows him to strike, surprise, avoid, elude, and escape danger.

Shadow 6: Correct, Max. What are his weaknesses?

Max: It can only cripple and kill large pray where they stand. He cannot carry or lift them, but he can sure cripple them. Speed rather than force, speed is power.

The eagle is a dangerous adversary, because the Eagle has the ability to strike with several weapons at once.

Shadow 6 yells out two consecutive strikes at once.

Shadow 6: Kakushi-zuki, (隠し突), Hidden Fist Punch. Wari-uke-zuki, (割受突), Split-block Punch

Max strikes, Shadow 6 defends. Shadow 6 strikes, Max defends.

Shadow 6: Max, there is hundreds of attributes to the power of the Eagle, each day we will disclose a few. Shadow 6 yells out several more commands.

Shadow 6: Kamae! Kyobu-morote-shuto-uchi, Shi-zuki Toride-zuki! (Fighting Posture), Take a Stance, Double Chicken Beak Thrust, Bird Hand Strike, Knife-hand Strike (to the chest area).

Max and Shadow 6 engage again in a hand-to-hand combat war for hours on end, with Shadow 6 yelling out strike after strike commands.

DAY 2

Shadow 6 chooses Sarah, (The Viper Warrior) out of the circle. Sarah stands up, turns around and enters the circle. The ritual for the rest of the Young Warriors is the same as day one. The Young Warriors witness the lesson. The Viper warrior bows down to Shadow 6 in respect. The lesson starts.

Shadow 6: Tell me about the weapons of the Viper.

Sarah: Their hidden fangs, their venom, they are just as at home in the desert as in the forest, they only strike in self-defense, their coiling before attacking gives them speed and unusual mobility.

Shadow 6: Their thermoreceptors?

Sarah: On their head below and in front of their eyes.

Shadow 6: They are their body heat sensors.

Sarah: Their stealth like movements. Their ability to blend in with their territory.

Shadow 6: Their element of surprise. Their ability to strike and disappear.

Shadow 6: What are the Viper's weaknesses?

Sarah: Their enemy must be within touching distance. The viper cannot move or lift an enemy. While the Viper is quick in close quarters, it cannot chase, catch, or kill an enemy that is twenty feet or further away from its grasp.

Shadow 6: Solution?

Sara throws a succession of *Shuriken* at Shadow 6 who is always prepared for an attack in and out of training. She throws the Shuriken overhead, underarm, sideways, and rearwards, in each case the blade slides out of her hand through the fingers in a smooth, controlled flight. Shadow 6 blocks some of the stars with a shield from the training room. He steps aside avoiding others.

Sarah grabs four *Bo-Shuriken* (throwing weapons consisting of a straight iron or four-sided steel spike) and tosses them at Shadow 6, who is again ready for that attack and easily avoids getting hit. At blinding speed, she grabs a *Kunai* (a Japanese dagger,) and throws it at Shadow 6. Shadow 6 catches it in midair.

Sarah: The solution is to use distance weapons that can reach the enemy.

Shadow 6: Very good Sarah.

Shadow 6 yells out a command.

Shadow 6: *Kumite-dachi* (Fighting Stand) *Haito-uchi!* (Reverse knife-hand Strike).

Sarah does a summersault landing on the edge of a shield. On the other end of the shield a *Kunai* is tossed in the air, Sarah jumps to meet the *Kunai* in midair and spins attempting to stab Shadow six. Shadow 6 is not there, he now stands behind her. Sarah follows with a Reverse knife hand-strike which is blocked by Shadow 6.

Shadow 6: Speed, deceit, strike. Very good Sarah!

An all-out fight ensues, Shadow 6 yelling commands for Sarah to attack as he blocks her attempts. The Shadow 6 yells defensive blocking moves as he attacks the Viper bringing her into submission.

Sarah gets to her feet bows to Shadow 6 as a sign of respect, lets out a yell and continues to attack. Hours pass by with the two fighting back and forth.

DAY 3

Shadow 6 chooses Carmen, (The Cobra Warrior) from the circle of Young warriors. Carmen stands up and walks inside the circle as the Young Warriors holding the "Eastern Sitting positions" turn towards the inside of the circle to witness the lesson. The Cobra Warrior bows down to Shadow 6 in respect. The lesson starts.

Shadow 6: Tell me about the weapons of the Cobra.

Carmen: Intimidation, threatening posture, sense of smell, its venom, its hiding abilities. Its spitting venom abilities. Its ability to strike numerous times at rapid speed. It is feared and respected by foe and friend alike.

Shadow 6: What are the Cobra's weaknesses?

Carmen: The Cobra must be able to strike the flesh. The Cobra cannot move or lift an enemy. While the Cobra is quick in close quarters, it cannot chase an enemy at a fair distance away.

Shadow 6 yells a command.

Shadow 6: Gedan-barai (Lower Sweeping Block).

Shadow 6 attacks Carmen. Carmen's defense is solid and she counter-attacks at any chance she gets. Carmen is cornered against a wall. She retaliates enough to get some elbowroom. The Cobra Warrior then turns and runs up the wall and with a skillful summersault she lands behind Shadow 6.

Shadow 6 anticipated her move and grabbing a sword from the adjacent wall spins and slashes Carmen across the chest. Carmen bends backwards, almost like a scene out of "The Matrix" and is able to avoid the fatal attack.

109

They continue fighting with back and forth attacks and defenses for hours. The sparring training finally comes to an end. They bow to each other.

Shadow 6 steps out of the circle, walks into another room and comes back in rolling in a large glass cage holding a large Cobra into the room.

Shadow 6: Mirroring time.

Shadow 6 wheels the cage inside the Warrior's circle.

He has Carmen stand in front of the glass cage and mirrors every move that the caged Cobra makes. Carmen mimics the Cobra's facial expressions, the movement of the tongue, the twisting of the body, the posturing.

The Cobra slowly rises up the glass cage, staring at Carmen as if she was her dancing partner. The cobra crawls over the top of the glass and is now face-to-face with Carmen. As the Cobra attacks, Carmen counters.

As Carmen counters the Cobra's strikes, she is able to run her hand and caress her opponent's long sleek body, causing a soothing effect on it. The snake and mouse game continues for a couple of hours and slowly the Cobra gives up her attack and moves with Carmen as if performing the La Sylphide Ballet, choreographed by Fillipo Taglioni at the Paris Opera House. The Cobra slowly and smoothly wraps around Carmen as Carmen pets her former foe and lulls it to sleep.

Shadow 6: Good work Carmen. You don't always have to kill your enemy.

DAY 4

Shadow 6 walks the inner circle several times before picking Ethan, (The Tiger Warrior). The rest of the Young Warriors follow the same daily procedure by turning into the circle and watching the training. Ethan stands up, turns around, and enters the circle. The Tiger Warrior bows down to Shadow 6 in respect. The lesson starts.

Shadow 6: Tell me about the weapons of the Tiger.

Ethan: His claws, his speed, his patience, his physical power. He does not panic, he does not hesitate, he does not regret. He is direct and fearless. He can take his enemy down with one swift strike.

He does not know from yielding ground, he is strictly an aggressor. He is righteous, he is definite. He knows every inch of his skeletal structure and how to use it to his advantage. He thrashes and pounces, slashes and thrusts with power, certainty and finality. He can take down an opponent twice his size without hesitance.

He loves the darkness. He is a master at camouflage. He is graceful in his actions.

Shadow 6: What are the Tiger's weaknesses?

Ethan: His unwillingness to go on the defense; to back down. His short life span. The Tiger has few if any weaknesses.

Shadow 6: A heavy burden to bear, big shoes to fill, don't you think? Invincibility.

Ethan: I will keep at it until I live up to the high standards of a "Tiger Warrior" sir.

Shadow 6: Ethan, when I was a mere child, I spent countless hours studying tigers. Even then I appreciated the benefit of completely understanding the power and seduction of such animal.

I would stand face to face with a caged tiger, staring sternly into his eyes and I noticed several things. When he sensed my fear, he became aggressive. When I looked away from him, he would strike. When I ran away from him, he tried to chase me. When I stared at him without fear he would calm down and walk away.

By the age of ten, I had learned all his moves, all his moods, the way he thought, his strengths, his weaknesses.

By the time I was 11, I entered the tiger's cage, unprotected, without weapons.

Ethan: What happened?

Shadow 6: We became best friends and I learned all his secrets. At this stage of your training, your goal is to do the same.

Shadow 6 picks up a mallet and strikes the gong in the training room twice. Two men rolling in a cage entered into the room. Inside the cage was a Bengal tiger. The cage is wheeled into the inner circle.

Shadow 6: Shadow him, charge him, run from him, stare him down, look away, back him down, and make him your friend.

Ethan: Now sir?

Shadow 6: No Ethan, first we square off.

The "Tiger Warrior" attacks, his hands swiping from side to side, leaping in the air to get the advantage angle over Shadow 6. Shadow leaps up to meet the "Tiger" clashing into a four-hour war.

The Bengal tiger inside the cage demonstrates his fearful growls and roars and his sleek movements as he leaped and jumped exhibiting his powerful and mesmerizing attack with every one of Ethan's moves. The circle of Warriors watched in fascination, committing to memory "The Way of the Tiger".

Shadow 6 and Ethan square off for hours and at the end of the lesson, the Bengal tiger is wheeled to the side of the training room, where Ethan is directed to shadow the tiger, copy his moves, counter his actions and learn to make this powerful foe into a friend.

DAY 5

Shadow 6 paces back and forth behind the *"Circle of Young Warriors"* once again and calls out Jimmy, (The Bull Warrior). The rest of the Young Warriors once again pivot on their spot and now face the center of the circle sitting down in an "Eastern Sitting Position". Jimmy stands up, turns around, and enters the Young Warrior's circle. The Bull Warrior bows down to Shadow 6 in respect. The lesson starts.

Shadow 6: Tell me about the weapons of the Bull.

Jimmy: His horns, his body strength, muscular body, aggressiveness, his strong neck, his bony head, his low gravity.

Shadow 6: What are the weaknesses of the Bull?

Jimmy: His limited lateral movement.   Poor depth perception, poor stamina, and weak legs in comparison to his body.

Shadow 6: What is the Bull's main action in an altercation?

Jimmy: The Charge.

Shadow 6 shouts a command to Jimmy.

Shadow 6: 電荷、攻撃 Denka, kōgeki (Charge, attack). 戦い始めましょう Tatakai hajimemashou (let the fight begin).

The "Bull" attacks with the strength and violence of a runaway train.   Shadow 6 blocks the Bull's initial strikes. The Bull rears and commences a second intense and furious attack, but Shadow 6 allows gravity to take over the Bull's raging speed and with one swift move, he tosses the Bull off his feet and forward.   The Bull rolls out of the Young Warrior's Circle, as they open to allow for Jimmy to pass. Jimmy crashes into the gong, postures back up and delivers a third attack.   The fighting goes on for hours.

DAY 6

Shadow 6 crouches down in the middle of the circle of Young Warriors, his right hand on his jaw, his elbow resting on his knee. He stands up and calls out Mike, (The Leopard Warrior).   Mike stands up, turns around, and enters the training circle. The Leopard Warrior bows down to Shadow 6 in respect.   The lesson starts.   The rest of the Young Warriors once again pivot on their spot and now face the center of the circle sitting down in an "Eastern Sitting Position".

Shadow 6: Tell me about the weapons of the Leopard.

Mike: His strength, his agility, his power, his gracefulness. His climbing ability is unique; he is so strong and comfortable in trees where it often hauls its kills into the branches. By dragging the bodies of large animals aloft it hopes to keep them safe from scavengers such as hyenas. The **leopard can carry three times his weight up a tree.**

Leopards can also hunt from trees, where their spotted coats allow them to blend with the leaves until they spring with a deadly pounce. They are nocturnal predators; they stalk antelope, deer, and pigs by stealthy movements in the tall grass.

The Leopard will attack when hungry and when threatened. When human settlements are present, leopards often attack dogs and, occasionally, people. Leopards are strong swimmers and very much at home in the water. The Leopard is stealthy and cunning.

Shadow 6: True, Mike. Well done on the study of your craft.

Mike: ありがとうございます Arigatōu gozaimasu (thank you sir).

Shadow 6 acknowledges with a nod.

Shadow 6: What are the weaknesses of the Leopard?

Mike: The "Panthera Pardus" is a loner and has a short life span. If he misses his target he will abandon pursuit.

Shadow 6 yells out commands.

Shadow 6: Genkaku-dachi, (Rigid Crane Stance), Tsuri-ashi-dachi (Crane Leg Stance), Sagi-ashi-dachi (Heron Leg Stance).

Mike quickly jumps to each stance that Shadow 6 commands.

Shadow 6: While you will master the way of the Leopard, you must also learn every other form of fighting there is. That will assure you that in combat you will never be a stranger to any action of attack against you.

Mike: Yes sir.

Shadow 6 retrieves two swords from the training room wall and hands one to Mike.

Shadow 6: Yoi, Kah-wah-tay (Ready, on guard).

The leopard pounces forward, its long claws swipe downwards on his prey. But his opponent is not a weak and defenseless prey, and has claws of his own. The Leopard's attack is easily blocked by his opponent. Shadow 6 attacks the Leopard with a barrage of slices and direct hits from every direction making him back into a defensive posture.

The Warriors stand face to face, the Leopard initiates a second attack with his own series of slashes and with the swift and slick moves that only a Leopard can have, he takes flight above his opponent and with a summersault he attempts a final strike.

With years of experience and the ability to read the moves of thousands of his attackers before the encounter with the Leopard, Shadow 6 summersaults back behind the Leopard, disarms him, and stops short of a fatal blow.

Both Warriors stand up and bow to each other.

The circle of warriors watch, taking mental notes for future use.

Mike: Arigato Gozaimasu Hanshi ありがとうございます 範士 (thank you very much Master Teacher).

Shadow 6: Do Itashimas'te Senshi どういたしまして 戦士 (You are welcome Warrior).

Shadow 6 walks over a stack of wooden boards on the training room floor and commands.

Shadow 6: Yoi, Kawate, Hajime! (Ready, on guard, begin).

Shadow 6 starts throwing the boards at Mike, "The Leopard Warrior" in "Frisbee" fashion. As the flying boards get within the Leopards reach, he strikes each and every one – breaking them to smithereens. Shadow 6 increases the speed of each throw, but the Leopard is ready and successfully destroys the flying boards.

For hours, Mike is trained by Shadow 6. Fighting, attacking, blocking, breaking boards, sword fighting, stealth moves, etc, etc. The training continues into the night.

DAY 7

Shadow 6 is down to three more choices to complete the nine-day training period. He walks behind Tom, (The Boar Warrior) and taps him in the back. Tom gets up turns around, bows down to Shadow 6 as a show of respect and enters the *circle* as the rest of the Warriors pivot in place to witness day seven's lesson. The lesson starts.

Shadow 6: Tell me about the weapons of the Boar.

Each day of training, the Young Warriors must find a new weapon that their animal system possesses. Each day their performances are rated from 1 to 10, ten being the highest scoring rank. To graduate a Warrior must get a score of 10 every training session for a period of six months.

The warriors are graded for fighting knowledge, alertness, cunning, stealth, creativity, respect, quickness to the kill, knowledge of all fighting styles of Lin Kuei, and fairness.

Shadow 6: What are the strengths of the Boar?

Tom: Constant movement, incredible sense of smell, sharp tusks, powerful, thick hide, their speed when attacking, and dense bones. A Boar can attack at the speed of 11 miles per hour and is extremely dangerous when injured.

Shadow 6: What are the weaknesses of the Boar?

Tom: Poor eyesight. Only attacks in small quarters.

Shadow 6: What is the average successful attack of a Boar?

Tom: Under a minute.

Shadow 6: What is the best fighting scenario for the Boar?

Tom: Quick striking counter attack then taking the opponent to the ground.

Shadow 6: What is the preferred weapon of the "Boar Warrior"?

Tom: Twin daggers, swords, and nunchacku's for close in fighting.

Shadow 6: Yoi, (用意), Rei (礼), Hajime (始め). (Ready, bow with respect, begin.)

The Boar attacks with relentless speed using every weapon available to him. He strikes, head-butts, and attempts overwhelming moves against Shadow 6, who is readily prepared to overcome every obstacle. They fight for hours.

DAY 8

Shadow 6 enters the Young Warrior's circle and from the center he calls out William, (The Python Warrior). The Python warrior bows down to Shadow 6 in respect and steps inside the circle. All other warriors pivot facing the center of the circle. The lesson for day eight starts.

Shadow 6: Tell me about the weapons of the Python.

William: Their ability to crush the enemy, their ability to camouflage while stalking an enemy, their size, they can grow to 30 feet, their heat sensing abilities. They are excellent swimmers.

Shadow 6: What are the weaknesses of the Python?

William: They are slow; their rectilinear progression while moving restricts their lateral movements. It takes them too long to eliminate a prey.

Shadow 6: What is the best assault of the "Python Warrior"?

William: A quick and overwhelming attack. Wrapping the enemy to restrict their movement and then strike the fatal blow.

Shadow 6 gives a command.

Shadow 6: Kōgeki! (Attack!)

The Python engages Shadow 6, attempting to take him to the ground. Shadow 6 defends by sprawling. The Python throws a lead hook; Shadow 6 blocks and grabs the Python's wrist and inside elbow, bringing him to the ground. The Python rolls forward escaping the throw. A battle ensues that lasts for hours.

DAY 9

Shadow 6 walks outside the circle looking at each and every one of the Young Warriors. Shadow 6 speaks.

Shadow 6: All nine of you represent one body, one mind, one soul. In battle you will feel the pain of the other. You will respond to the safety of the team and will succeed as a team to accomplish the goal for the good of all. Today ends the nine days of training. Tomorrow you will reflect on what you witnessed and what you experienced for the past nine days.

Then a three-day training period with three warriors, each day fighting in the art form of the other, will follow. You will dig deep and rely on what you have learned today and from the last nine days to be able to fight in an animal form not familiar to you. You will learn to draw strength from each other and become one in thought and action.

After another day of reflection, the circle begins once again, mounting knowledge to your current understanding and therefore making you a true Lin Kuei "Shadow warrior". These last couples of weeks are crucial training for you to complete your graduation. So listen, watch, and perform to the very best of your ability.

Shadow 6 enters the circle and calls out Alexa, (The Ghost Warrior). Alexa stands up, turns around, and bows down to Shadow 6 in respect. The Ghost warrior enters the circle. The rest of the Warriors spin in place and face the inner circle. The lesson starts.

Shadow 6: Tell me about the weapons of the Ghost.

Without hesitation Alexa leaps in the air attacking Shadow 6 with a series of leg and fist strikes. She promptly disappears and appears in front of "The Python Warrior" attacking at full speed with punches and slicing blows. The Ghost once again disappears only to attack the "Boar warrior" with a combination of spin kicks and back spin elbows. Now everyone in the circle stands up and takes a fighting stance, waiting for the apparition of the "Ghost" once again.

Shadow 6: She is wearing the new invisibility suit. Listen and watch or you will become her next victim.

The "Ghost" reappears striking, sliding, moving and disappearing at will. Each one of the Warriors is attacked and then left without a target for retaliation. The fighting goes on for hours with all of the Young Shadow warriors participating.

Shadow 6 oversees the ongoing combat.

CHAPTER 9

THE BIRTH OF THE SUPER SOLDIERS

THE INNER SANCTUM ROOM

The Inner sanctum room is like an armory of sorts with several antique swords, knives, and other miscellaneous weaponry where the Warriors' train in deception, stealth, and intelligence skills. Shadow 6, is accompanied by the Assistant Director of base Operations and Master Trainer, Elisa, (30's), 5'9, brown hair, sexy built.

Elisa Frank is a tutor and intelligence advisor to the "Shadow Warriors". Elisa is highly skilled in the art of deception [she practiced and was schooled in the art of magic from the age of 9]. She is wise and witty, and because of her ability to "blend-in" in almost any situation, she goes unnoticed in most situations. She is a martial arts master and a seasoned strategist.

She was recruited by SI-9 out of the CIA's intelligence transfer program. The NSA took her and then she migrated into SI-9 as part of the new Pentagon Global Initiative on terrorism.

The nine Warriors are gathered around a circular glass case in the middle of the room.

Each Warrior takes a special *Bracelet* from their wrists and returns them to the case. Each of the gold *Bracelets* have the likeness carved and intricately engraved of the animal system that they master in. They all bow for a second in silence, then leave the room.

Outside at ground zero, a helicopter lands on the desert floor, a procession of limousines, with government insignias and American flags on them can be seen approaching the helicopter.

The ground next to the helicopter and the limousines opens up. A large structure resembling an enclosed conference or meeting room rises from the underground. There are chairs set up all around the perimeter of the room. A communications counsel sits in the middle.

The group of Generals and Senators from the limousines and helicopters enter the structure that lowers them to the underground facility. As they exit the structure, they are all escorted into a conference room where they sit surrounded by one-way glass walls on all sides. Eric activates the one-way mirrors, one at a time.

TRAINING AREA - DAY

The training area can be seen from the conference room one-way mirrors. A video of a series of various animals engaged in ferocious combat plays on one of the four walls. Meanwhile in the training room, visible through the one-way glass, several *Masked Warriors* in all out combat drills take on the disposition, veracity, viciousness, and aggression of each one of the animals on the screen. Their style and acrobatic skills are mesmerizing. The scene is a paralyzing vision of the metamorphosis of each warrior.

Senator Marshal, a man in his 50's, grey hair, dignified looking speaks in astonishment.

Senator Marshall: My God, those soldiers are the most incredible fighting acrobats I've ever seen.

Eric Stone: Senator Marshall, it's a pleasure to meet you. By the way, soldiers is an understatement.

They shake hands.

Senator Marshall: Sorry, I can see that. The boys at the Pentagon have a lot of great things to say about you, and from what I have seen so far, I can see why.

Eric Stone: Just old war stories, I'm sure. But what you have not seen yet will be the most fascinating.

Senator Marshal proceeds with introductions of his group.

Senator Marshall: This is Annie Crothers, just hired to head my office here in California and her assistant Anusha. Senator Perez, Senator Jackson, and Senator Rice. They each are accompanied by their assistants.

Annie Crothers is a tall 5'9", long brown haired young woman in her 20's. She is attractive in spite of her faulty complexion and the nose that only a Greek God would love. Anusha wears a *Burka (a full body cloak);* she seems timid, almost nervous.

Eric Stone: Miss Crothers; Anusha. A pleasure.

Eric Stone shakes hands with all the senators and their aids.

Anusha bows her head, her beautiful green eyes rise staring intently at Mr. Stone. She smiles meekly and stays silent, clutching tightly to the handle of her briefcase.

Annie Crothers: General, a pleasure.

Eric Stone (speaking to the group): Now, let's begin. The program was created in 1956. The effects of the Second World War were just wearing off and our government was desperate to create a force that could battle any enemy.

We took all the information we acquired from the Chinese and the Japanese at the end of WWII, and thus created the first Shadow Unit, of which I was a member. The Project was so secretive, so clandestine, that neither the Secret Service nor the office of the President of the United States knew about it.

A second senator speaks, William Perez, 6', 35, clean shaven.

Senator Perez: Tell me, General Stone, what exactly separates this program from say, the Green Berets or the Navy Seals?

Eric Stone: Just watch.

Stone points towards the training studio that can be seen through the one-way glass; they all watch. A *Masked Warrior* standing in the center of the training room, motions a group of trainee assistants to move forward.

The trainee Warriors form two lines and proceed to attack him. The Warriors move into an all-out response drill; unprepared, unrehearsed, they systematically attack. One by one The Warrior in the center of the room disposes of each attacker. It is quick, abrupt, and brutal. The fighting is still captivating, as the mock combat crescendos with volatility, a loud yell comes from the Warrior in center of the room.

Warrior: REEII!

The Masked Warrior now unmasks. It's Shadow 6. The rest of the Warriors stop fighting immediately and bow down humbly. They take off their masks and gather to begin class. They are all students around the age of 17. Entering the classroom formation, they take their designated places.

Max Long [the Eagle], the nerdy-type with glasses and curly hair, sits scratching out a math problem on his laptop, while Sarah [The Viper], the nerdy shy girl, stares at Ethan.

Max and Sarah, at ages 4 and 3 respectively, were kidnapped by a group of International Terrorists while their parents attended a business seminar somewhere in Asia.

Upon their return from the business seminar their parents surprised the kidnappers in the act and were murdered in the process. The kidnappers belonged to a ruthless group that kidnapped children and trained them to become assassins for their cause.

Max and Sarah were trained in several forms of martial arts as well as the art of deception and conning. They were also trained on the making of explosives, and in the creation and use of various lethal, undetectable poisons that could be used to eliminate their designated target.

Max and Sarah were the only children that were successful at escaping the terrorist camp after six years of rigorous training and brainwashing. After their escape, they were able to lead the authorities back to the camp where the terrorist group was eliminated and many of the surviving children rescued. Max and Sarah are the only two members of the Young Warrior team that were indoctrinated at such late age after rigorous months of retraining. Max was a high school letterman in Gymnastics and soccer from his sophomore year on. Sarah was a lettered gymnast, an A+ student and a varsity athlete in high school.

Carmen Ramirez, [The Cobra] the girly cheerleader type, touches up her lip-gloss.

Carmen is a straight "A" high school student, trilingual, athletic and very beautiful. Carmen's parents were machine gunned down as the bank that Carmen's father worked in was the target of terrorists. Carmen's father was a computer programmer [hacker]. She saw her parents die at the tender age of 4.

Ethan Perez [The Tiger], the jock frat boy type, sits starring at Carmen.

High school athlete, president of the "Lettermen Club". He became an orphan after his father that was "jumped" into a Hispanic gang at age seventeen, and his sixteen-year-old mother had apparently overdosed on heroin. He fought hard to break away from his apparent current destiny. He was sold to overseas Human Traffickers at the age of 2.

Ethan with the help of a couple of concerned religious travelers, escaped the traffickers in route to Europe and made his way to the Amazons, where he lived in the Jungle where his only friends and playmates were the wild animals of the jungle.

Captured by poachers, he was brought into the USA and sold illegally at the age of 4. He was then recruited by "Shadow 6" as a warrior, after Shadow 6 conducting an in depth investigation into another murder case, found that both his parents were gunned down in a drug deal "gone bad" and their death "staged and covered up" by the police as a drug overdose.

Jimmy Traves [The Bull], the bad boy, sits with a file reviewing mug shots of the "FBI most wanted".

High school wrestler and football jock. He spent his childhood in a foster home after both his parents were murdered while shopping at a local convenience store by a group of drug addicts and dealers.

Jimmy witnessing the gruesome murders at age 3 never forgot the face of the assailants and vowed to spend his life trying to find them.

After reviewing mug shots and motion clips of almost every criminal alive for the past 14 years, Jimmy developed a photographic mind where faces and body language is concerned. He has the uncanny ability to identify almost any criminal by quickly studying their faces and referring back to the database in his mind.

He has a photographic memory in regards to numbers, faces, places, and occurrences. He has the ability to see through disguises and is a language "accent" expert.

Mike Nelson [The Leopard] reads from his textbooks.

High School long distance runner. Mike lived in a foster home, both foster parents were alcoholics that were brought up on child molestation charges and mistreated him every chance they got.

He was extracted by SI-9 out of the orphanage that took care of him from age 3 to 5. Mike is in constant research to find his real parents. His hobby of rock climbing combined with his athletic ability, have made him one of the best competition climbers in the US.

Tom Ellis [The Boar] whispers to Alexa.

Tom, a 17 year old was recruited by Shadow 6 as a Shadow Warrior when Shadow 6 while checking out records of foster children found out that Tom was adopted by a small town policeman.

After being kidnapped from his real family as an infant and held captive 3 years. One day the authorities found him walking alone on the streets of New Mexico at the age of 4.

Tom's parents had moved out of the country and were unable to be located by the police. Tom was placed in a foster home. To this day Tom has no knowledge of his real heritage.

Tom is a high school athlete, a gymnast and a lettered first-string varsity quarterback for his team. He studied yoga and Tai Chi on his off time since age 10. He is a Mensa International Member.

William Spencer [The Python], sits wrapping his hands with athletic tape.

Son of an international trader, William at the age of 4 was never picked up from daycare on a Friday afternoon. Their disappearance got the curiosity of Shadow 6, who 30 days into foster care brought William into his care. William's parents have never been found to date. William still believes his parents are alive and continues to look for them. A student of martial arts since childhood, trained in the art of Brazilian grappling and a lettered varsity wrestler, he was a State and National wrestling champion in high school.

Alexa Evans [The Ghost], the blind intellectual sits in a lotus position listening intently to her surroundings, with a smile on her face as she listens to Tom's whisper. She then continues reading a book in Braille. Elisa, their Master Trainer sits there taking it all in.

Alexa became an orphan when her parents were killed in an automobile crash. Their car was struck by a drunk driver driving an 18-wheeler. The truck landed on her parents' car and killed them both instantly.

Alexa, age 2, was the only survivor, sitting in the back of the car strapped in her car seat. She was blinded by the violent impact of the accident. She sustained injuries to her head that were diagnosed as fatal. 'Till today she is known as the "miracle child". Firefighters had to use "The Jaws Of Life" to get to her freed from the wreck and the automobile exploded within seconds of her release.

She was recruited by SI-9 at age 4 after the orphanage in which she was cared for was closed due to lack of funding.

In high school, attending the University of New Mexico, Alexa was always the mischievous one. Trained in several disciplines of martial arts, such as Aikido and Savate, "the Ghost" was trained and recruited by "Shadow 6" and his ancient martial arts teachers since childhood.

Senator Perez: They're all kids!

Shadow 6 replies from the training room, ignoring the comment.

Shadow 6: Great observation senator. Let's move on.

Shadow 6 motions with his hands to the screen. Eric Stone narrates as the group witnesses on the screen a montage of Warriors sparring with each other.

Eric Stone addresses the group through a loudspeaker as everyone pays attention to the screen in front of them.

Eric Stone: Gentleman, when these Warriors entered our program, they engaged in the most extreme and intense training ever given to a law enforcement agent or military operative.

The Senators look at each other, some in amazement others with skepticism.

Eric Stone (continued): The CIA Special Operations Group is faced with one success out of one hundred applicants selected. When our training program was incorporated by them, only one out of one thousand passed it.

Inside the training room Shadow 6 turns towards the Warriors.

Shadow 6: Warriors, stand ready.

The group listens intensely.

Shadow 6 nods, the screen shows visual renditions of Lin Kuei Combat. The young Warriors sit in a circle listening to Shadow 6.

Shadow 6: Warriors, the end of this stage of your Snowtiger training is near complete after 12 years. Your skills as a well-rounded individual will soon be tested for graduation.

We continue see renditions of Lin Kuei in combat. The montage ends, Shadow 6 exits the training room and joins Eric Stone and the group of Pentagon officials.

For the benefit of the senators in the audience, the trainees ask questions. Shadow 6 asks questions to the Senators as the young Warriors give their take on the questions asked.

Carmen: Sir one question, please, why do we recite the Hannya-shin-kyo?

The Hannya-shin-kyo is called the Heart Sutra because it represents the heart of great wisdom and was written between the first and the sixth century A.D. Common to all the different forms of Buddhism, it is certainly the most well-known of the sutras.

Shadow 6: *Good question, for the benefit of our guests, recite it, Cobra Warrior.*

Carmen: *There's no eye, ear, tongue, body and mind. In darkness there is sin, in darkness there is death. Sin negates spirit and the killing of beings without spirit shall only be looked on as an act of charity.*

Shadow 6: So question #1, what does this mean to you?

Carmen: Anyone without spirit or a conscience is evil, so it's a forgiven act to kill them?

Shadow 6: Kill them randomly?

Carmen: No, killing shall only be allowed in self-defense and in the act of protecting the United States of America and the safety and liberty of all its citizens.

Shadow 6 contemplates Carmen's answer and replies.

Shadow 6: Very well, a question for you Warriors. Has God created everything?

Carmen: Yes he has.

Shadow 6: He?

Carmen: Ahhh...

Shadow 6: Everything?

Carmen: Yes.

The battle of wits and the *"verbal cloak and dagger"* continues.

Shadow 6: *Next qu*estion then. If that's the case then, since God created evil and you are what you create... therefore, is God evil?   Everyone sits in silent contemplation, shocked at the implication of the question.

Shadow 6 (continued): Stumped? Well then how about this. Does darkness exist?

Max: How about you Senators, what do you think? Does darkness exist?

Senator Jackson, a white male, 5'7" slightly overweight, dark hair brown eyes replies.

Senator Jackson: Childs play, so I'll play along. Of course it does, we experience it at nighttime daily.

Max: Wrong, senator, darkness does not exist; darkness is merely the absence of light.

They all sit again silent. Shadow 6 looks around the room at the expressionless faces of the senators.

Senator Jackson: So very well, you tricked me; so what? It's all a matter of interpretation.

Sarah: So senator, then...cold exists?

Senator Jackson: I know you probably are going to tell me that it doesn't, but it does. I am cold in this room right now.

Sarah: Wrong again senator, cold is the absence of heat, if you take away heat slowly; you are left with coldness to the point where life ceases to exist.

Once again, the Senators sit silent. Shadow 6 watches as none of the other senators wants to get mixed up in this psychological word game.

Max: So one final question for you senator... does Evil exist?

Senator Jackson: Of course, look at all the atrocities that men commit against each other. Pick up any newspaper, listen to any radio or TV station and you will get your answer.

Senator Jackson is now frustrated and angry, fearing that he is being made a fool of. His face turns beet red.

Max: Wrong once again Senator, Evil is merely the absence of God in your heart; therefore all that is God is good and all that is good... is God. Do you understand Senator?

Senator Jackson: This is the most foolish conversation I have ever been part of. Children, only an idiot would have come up with those questions and worse with your answers.

Shadow 6: You are right Senator Jackson, that idiot was Albert Einstein, you might have heard of that name before. Gentlemen, these "children" as Senator Jackson refers to are not only some of the best offensive and defensive lethal fighters in the world, but also extremely educated in every field possible, Mathematics, Geography, Philosophy, Psychology, Technology, English, Chinese, Japanese, Russian, History, and other disciplines. Our government's best spent money in counter intelligence.

The group of Senators smiles at Shadow 6's explanation. There's something reassuring and clever in his psychology.

He exudes confidence and makes those around him feel protected and at ease. The Senators are then guided into the training hall. Shadow 6 is introduced to a group of Pentagon Officials.

Senator Peters, in his 40's, 6'5", blond hair, well built, addresses Shadow 6. Pointing to Alexa, the Senator asks.

Senator Peters: Nice speech. Is that the blind girl?

Shadow 6: She would probably be the best to answer the question Senator.

Senator Peters: Well, what would you say?

Shadow 6: Only in sight Senator. Why not have a couple of your boys rush her and you'll see what I mean.

Senator Peters: Not sure, I wouldn't want my boys to hurt her...

Alexa: I might be blind, but I can hear Senator...

The senator chuckles.

Alexa walks closely to him as if she was not affected by her blindness.

Alexa: ...and I can smell your fear...

Senator Peters: [reacting nervously] What?... Why should I fear?

Alexa: Because people are afraid of the unknown, and to you I am an unknown.

Alexa continues to approach closer to the Senator. Two bodyguards step in front of the Senator.

Senator Peters: Well, you are taking an aggressive stand, and they are doing their job.

Alexa: Then you feel comfortable with their protection?

Senator Peters: I do

Alexa: You know Senator, these bodyguards are trying to protect you from a blind, harmless girl. Senator, are you sure you need protection from a blind girl?

Senator Peters: Blind, probably, harmless, I doubt it.

The Senator and his group begin to feel uncomfortable. One of the bodyguards tries to grab Alexa, and that spins her into action.

She grabs his open hand and holds tightly to his right thumb, pulling it outwards with her left hand. With her other hand she reaches under the bodyguard's elbow, pushing it up towards his face while pulling outwards on his thumb.

This move takes the bodyguard off his feet. Alexa places a roundhouse kick to his head, and without setting her foot down, she places a side kick into his solar plexus. The bodyguard is knocked out cold on the ground.

The second bodyguard moves to grab Alexa. Without ever putting her foot down from the sidekick, Alexa extends her leg backwards and with a heel kick, connects to the second bodyguard's jaw. He is knocked unconscious. Now both bodyguards lay unconscious on the floor. The group of senators gasps in shock. Alexa calmly walks away. She stops, turns and addresses the group.

Alexa: Gentlemen, being afraid of the unknown is something that one needs to overcome to be able to successfully destroy evil. Underestimating the enemy and not knowing when to take aggressive action against them is a fatal mistake. We train to understand and act at the proper moment with the proper force to protect you, your family, your friends, your children, and the constitution of the United States of America.

Alexa sits back in the circle.

Senator Jackson: How in the world did she do that? She can't see. I really like that girl.

Senator Jackson smirks.

Shadow 6: Never underestimate a 'Warrior'... blind or not. You wanted a demonstration of our group, so what is more real to life than experiencing contact with our children, sorry I meant Warriors. We're pressed for time so we must move on. This way please...

The group hesitantly, but full of adrenaline, moves on. Senator Rice, 5'9", African American, 200 lbs., speaks.

Senator Rice: I'm afraid to ask questions, I don't want to end up like the senator's bodyguards, but is that boy going over confidential CIA files.

The group laughs. Tension is relieved.

Shadow 6: That's Jimmy, "The Bull" he's case studying Senator. He has a photographic memory, he can recite names, physical descriptions, and the crime committed from over 5,000 FBI and CIA files.

Senator Rice: What a wonderful hobby.

Shadow 6: No senator, he's looking for the people that murder his parents in cold blood.

Senator Three: I'm so sorry for his loss.

Shadow 6: Senators, understand a very valid point here, and I know I am somewhat repeating myself, but these Warriors are trained in every scholastic facet possible as well as every aspect of assassination for one reason and one reason only...to seek and destroy the enemies of the State. Those that murdered his parents just picked the wrong family to victimize. We're on a tight schedule, so we must hurry. Follow me.

They all head to the Training Area.

Some of the young warriors go over some new and creative martial arts moves, some study the balance and correct movement of weapon fighting, some young warriors discuss the development of science for the past 40 years. Some are deeply involved in history and the success of major wars around the world: World War II; The American Civil war; The Mongol Conquests; The Taiping Rebellion; The Three Kingdoms War; and so forth.

They move through several combat scenarios. Some study films of several animals in action. Sarah and Max mix lethal poisons as well as explosives. Ethan studies videos of tigers fighting. Will puts a lethal choke on one of the male wrestlers. Mike climbs an almost flat wall.

Shadow 6 raises three fingers slowly, (one at a time, index, middle, ring). Reminding them of the "three-second rule".

Senator Marshall: What is that signal you just made?

Shadow 6: That is a reminder of the three-second rule senator.

Senator Marshal: What is the three-second rule?

Shadow 6: Jimmy, "Bull" Warrior, what is the three-second rule?

Jimmy, who is studying the movements of several animals from a film, responds.

Jimmy: *The Three-second rule: A successful Warrior must kill his attacker within three seconds, or less, in every encounter if he expects to become part of the elite group of Shadow Warriors.*

Shadow 6: Jimmy, the Senator would like to know why there is such rule.

Senator Marshal: Yes sir, that was my next question. I wasn't briefed on your mind reading capabilities.

Shadow 6: Like Sherlock Holmes would say *"Elementary Senator Marshall"*. Elementary.

Jimmy: It saves time, injury, and maintains focus. The longer a fight continues the more likely that all participants will sustain injury. It shows focus, commitment, and sends a message to your enemies that this is not a game, but a final exchange no matter the cost. No one should ever raise their weapons unless they are prepared to use them, quickly, swiftly, aggressively, and finally.

Senator Marshal: Impressive indeed.

Shadow 6: Good answer "Bull warrior". Gentleman, and ladies of course, I must leave you now. I have urgent matters to attend to. General Stone will finish the tour.

Everyone turns to say good-by to Shadow 6, but he's gone as fast as he said his goodbyes.

CHAPTER 10

THE WARRIORS' FIRST WEEK OF SCHOOL

The group of Senators chat as they move through the complex examining the premises.

Senator Perez: Oh, Lord, I just can't get over the fact that they're just kids. Dangerous kids no doubt, but still...kids.

Eric Stone: Senator, The average age of the soldiers in The American Civil war was 25.8 years old. Twenty percent of the soldiers in the United States Civil War were soldiers younger than 18 years of age. The average age of an infantryman that fought in Vietnam was 22 years old. Over 250,000 boys under the age of 18 served in the British Army during World War I. Should I go on?

Senator Perez: No, no Stone, you have made your point.

Eric Stone: The seemingly innocent faces of children trained from very early in life to become the defenders of our freedom...quick...stealthy...deadly. Not unlike the Gladiators who fought to greatness in ancient Rome, those who gave their lives for freedom in World War II, and the great soldiers of today keeping peace and freedom for America – The "Shadow Warriors" or "kids" as you put it, battle the enemies and wars that the Government cannot and will not attempt to fight.

The Senators all look on as Eric Stone speaks. There is an air of uncomfortable truth in the minds of the Senators.

Eric Stone: These warriors are not just deadly fighting machines; they are smart, intelligent, calculating, resourceful, and clever on the spot thinkers and above all "true blue" loyal to the United States of America. There is no amount of money that can buy them, there is no threat that they fear. Given what you witness here so far, do you care to challenge them again Senator? You can go ahead, bring in your best; choose your weapons.

Senator Marshal: No, ahem, not necessary, but certainly mesmerizing, unique, surprising and once again, educational. I certainly learned a lot. Things I never thought existed. All is good Stone, all is good.

Eric Stone: Gentlemen, for one, members of the Shadow unit are raised from very young as a family, in groups. Each group remains ready in case of a needed replacement. Each member of the group becomes a perfect and unique weapon. The "kids" once again, as you refer to them, which you had the chance to meet, have not become an active team yet. They'll be graduating next Tuesday.

Senator Rice: Have they always been raised into the program from infancy?

Eric Stone: The original unit was made up of career military types like myself, and we were good, believe me we were damn good; however it was just another tour of duty – but not today. Since the late sixties, all the units were raised into adulthood together.

Senator Rice: Where do they come from?

Eric Stone: Orphanages, mostly. Either abandoned by their parents or their parents were brutally terminated. They are all thoroughly tested physiologically and psychologically, as well as their resiliency and their moral fiber strength, to see if they qualify to be part of the Warriors at the age of 5. Here we give them a chance, a life, and a trade. Every member on our staff has a doctorate in history, education, or science, as well as field experience, the kind you can't get from a book.

Senator Rice: At the age of five, moral fiber, resiliency?

Eric Stone: Yes Senator, even at an earlier age such signs can already be detected on all individuals.

Senator Rice: Is it...? Well, is it right that we force these kids into a lifetime of servitude?

Eric Stone: On the contrary. Until they are 18, this facility isn't much more than the nicest foster home in the country. When they are of age, they choose whether to stay or go.

Senator Rice: And how many have left?

Eric Stone: None. To date, everyone that reached 18 has continued into the program. We've had some leave the program later on in life and some we have retired.

Senator Marshall: I find that hard to believe.

Eric Stone: Think about it, a chance to serve your country, fight the bad guys, armed to the teeth with the best Intel, weaponry, and technological advances our Government has to offer. We all dream of being a superhero; what child or adult wouldn't want that opportunity?

The group convenes back at the Conference Room.

Eric Stone: Here is the icing on the cake.

Eric Stone lowers a video screen in the conference room and a slide show begins. Eric Stone points to the screen with his laser pen.

Eric Stone: (as he points the laser light, a series of pictures flash through the screen) Thomas Weesly; Attorney at law, Robert Genre; plastic surgeon, Tim Knewly; Real estate tycoon, Betty Sharp; Scientist, Shirley Beets; actress....

Stone turns to the group and continues.

Eric Stone: Ladies and Gentleman, all these are former Lin Kuei operatives that served their country and retired. These are the emergency task force. And there are HUNDREDS of them. They walk amongst us as professionals in every field.

Senator Perez: All this Martial Arts stuff is great and all, but you still have to get close enough to use it. People have guns now General.

Eric Stone: You underestimate the right tools in the right hands senator.

Senator Perez: How so?

Suddenly Shadow 6 becomes visible before their eyes. He has been following them all along, wearing a special suit that makes the wearer invisible to the naked eye. Senator Perez jumps back, shocked by Shadow 6's sudden entry.

Senator Marshall: Oh Jeez... How did he do that?

Eric Stone: Senator Marshall, I hope you and your entourage are getting a small understanding of the skills and strength of the group.

Senator Perez: What the He--?

Shadow 6 unmasks.

Eric Stone: Like I said, we're state of the art here, this suit was developed ten years ago; it bends the light just enough to become invisible. It was recently upgraded to model TX7 and now it even works with low light activity as well as with the exclusion of light. Remember, the Ninja were renowned for their skills in 'invisibility' and stealth. We've just taken it to a higher level with our current technology.

Senator Perez: So he's been following us this whole time?

Eric Stone: And you had no idea?

Senator Perez: That's amazing.

Eric Stone: Yes it is, thank you.

Shadow 6: And by the way Senator, we also carry guns, big ass guns.

Shadow 6 pulls a fully automatic handgun from his holster.

Senator Perez: Oh... very well, I see.

Shadow 6: The statement that you made, with concerns that the enemy uses guns, tells me that you are not aware of exactly what we do here Senator. We are the team that goes in way before things get heated up with the enemy. We are the ones that work in the shadows to remove, cripple, or confiscate the enemy's arsenal before they can use it against our troops. We are the ones that put our lives in danger to strike at the head of any conspiracy regardless of their power, or strength in numbers.

When we are forced to fight in the open we use stealth state of the art technology combined with thousands of years of experience from ancient and effective fighting techniques foreign to most of the evil that threatens the United States of America today.

Senator Marshall: Most of the evil?

Shadow 6: That's correct Senator Marshall, while most of the *"evil"* that threatens us is unaware of the ancients techniques that we use, *"evil"* also works very hard at overthrowing *"good"* and through research they have come close to matching some of our current techniques. Thus more funding is essential to our success in protecting the American way of life.

Senator Marshall: Very well Shadow 6.

Eric Stone: As I was explaining, upon entering full service into the unit, each team member is given their number and only responds to that number for the duration of their career. As a team member I was Shadow 1, The Boar. The leader is always called "Shadow 6". I eventually became the units' leader and thus Shadow 6.

Eric Stone activates another one-way glass exposing the bulletproof glass case holding the Warrior's bracelets.

Senator Marshall: What's in there, jewelry?

They all stare through the glass at the sanctum, getting a good view at the glass case holding the nine bracelets.

Eric Stone: That is the core of the program.

Senator Marshall: Looks like a pretty fancy jewelry case to me.

Eric Stone: Much more than that. There are *"Nine Bracelets"*, one for each member of the team. This is another one of the stolen spoils of war by the Japanese, like the book of the Sun Tzu. Each *Bracelet* represents one of the animals used in the fighting style of *Lin Kuei.*

Senator Marshall: What do they do, make you fly?

The rest of the group laughs.

Eric Stone: Better. Number one: they are embedded with a special chip, which contains the complete history of Lin Kuei and all the Shadow 6 leaders.

Number two: they're used as a communication device between the Warriors.

Number three: they are a physical representation of the unity of the team. When the unit is active, it's a spiritual connection between the bearers. They are all controlled by the main *Bracelet* unit that Shadow 6 wears.

Number four: once the bracelet is on, it conforms to every bone, ligament, nerve, and joint of the arm. Only the master of that fighting style can wear the bracelet, anyone else attempting to put it on will suffer pain and injury.

Senator Perez: Okay, that sounds like hocus pocus to me. You're losing me now.

Eric Stone: We've studied them for half a century, and still can't explain it.

Senator Perez: Explain what?

Eric Stone: Ancient mysticism. It's a link, call it spiritual or psychic, it connects the unit in a manner in which they can function as one, each of them aware of the others presence, actions and thoughts. With it, 9 men can share one mind.

Senator Perez: (turning to Shadow 6, sarcastically) Right. I have to try one of these out, I'll be "mind number 10". Bring them to us please?

Shadow 6 stares at him silently and shakes his head.

Shadow 6: Sorry.

Eric Stone: I wish I could show you exactly what I mean, but you'll just have to take my word for it on this one. Come let me show you the cafeteria, they have an exquisite brunch awaiting us.

As Stone ends the sentence Alexa approaches the glass case and removes her bracelet. Putting it on, she approaches Senator Perez.

Alexa: Senator Perez, it seems that you carry a shadow of doubt about our culture and our efforts to keep you safe from harm.

Alexa extends her arm out.

Alexa: Here is my bracelet Senator, its power fuses with my knowledge, my mental, and physical being. It senses the teachings of Lin Kuei and understands an evil heart from a good heart as well as the balance of negativity and positive thoughts. If you choose to remove this bracelet from my arm, after I mentally accept it, then you will bear full responsibility for any damage to your being senator. Are we in agreement?

Shadow 6: Alexa, stand down.

Alexa ignores the command.

Mocking Alexa, the Senator speaks.

Senator Perez: Oh, all mighty one, I accept, let me remove this mystical bracelet from your wrist.

Senator Perez attempts to remove it, but it won't come off, he tries with both hands as hard as he can, but it won't come off.

Senator Perez: What is the trick here, I can't remove it.

Alexa speaks as the Senator has both his hands on the bracelet.

Alexa: I now mentally and physically release the Bracelet of "The Ghost" to you Senator Perez, should you be worthy of its power it will cause you no harm. Should it be otherwise, may the powers of the Ancient Lin Kuei protect you from harm.

The senator pulls on the bracelet one more time and it easily comes off.

Senator Perez: What in the world?

Senator Perez proceeds putting the bracelet on and screams in agony. He tries to remove it but the bracelet burns into his wrist.

Senator Perez: Help! Help me; this thing is eating my wrist!

Alexa blocks anyone from helping Senator Perez, and if as she was not hindered by blindness; she looks at him straight in his eyes.

Senator Perez: You...you are looking straight in my eyes... ca... can you really see?

Alexa: Not with my eyes Senator, but the Bracelet you are wearing guides me to everywhere my mind desires. My spirit and my soul can see your eyes very clearly.

Senator Perez: Help me...

Alexa: I do feel the fear and pain in your eyes Senator, do you willingly and rightfully so relinquish the control of the

Bracelet of "The Ghost" to its rightful owner, me, Alexa, *"The Ghost Warrior"*.

Screaming Senator Perez responds, now falling on his knees from pain.

Senator Perez: What control; it's controlling me! Yes, yes! I relinquish, please take it off, I can't stand the pain!

Alexa puts her hands on the bracelet and removes it, placing it back on her wrist. The bracelet of the "Ghost" burned a mark of a perfect silhouette of the bracelet all around his wrist.

Senator Perez's wrist begins to blister.

Shadow 6: Max, get some ice for the Senator.

Max runs to get some ice from the fridge.

Alexa gets next to the Senator and whispers in his ear.

Alexa: *Do you understand now Senator?*

Senator Perez: Yes, I do, I think I do. I have no idea what I do.

Shadow 6, not very happy with the events that just developed shouts out.

Shadow 6: Alexa! (Motions her to follow Him). (To Stone) Sir?

Eric Stone: That'll be all for the demonstration Shadow 6, you may go now. Senator Perez, I am so sorry for your injury.

Senator Perez holds a pack of ice on his wrist.

Senator Perez: No need to apologize, it was my fault. I was warned and disregarded the warnings for my safety, and if I may add, I apologize for my disrespect.

Shadow 6: Thank you sir, apology accepted. Gentlemen. Ladies.

Eric leads the Senators off down the hall, as Shadow 6 once again disappears. The Shadow Warriors leave the area. Stone and the Senators chat.

Senator Perez: How does the bracelet do that? If I had not seen it, I wouldn't have believed it

Eric Stone: As I told you Senator, we don't have all the answers.

SHADOW 6 LIVING QUARTERS

Jimmy and Carmen walking through the compound decide to sneak into Shadow 6's room. It's decorated in a Japanese style, very basic, paper with Japanese writing and silhouettes hanging from the walls, a few plants, and an aquarium.

Jimmy looks around the room for a secret passageway as Carmen admires the fish.

Carmen: This is a bad idea.

Jimmy: Quit being such a girl Carmen.

Carmen: Jimmy, I am a girl.

Jimmy: Aren't you just a little curious? I thought women were like cats, meowww, always curious.

They both laugh.

Carmen: Well, I wouldn't be here if I wasn't, you jerk.

Jimmy: I saw it before, there's some kind of switch around here somewhere.

Suddenly, Jimmy finds a button on the wall; he presses it. One of the walls rises up, exposing a hidden armory. The wall is lined with every variety of Asian weapons of war and the latest in high tech weaponry available to the armed forces.

Jimmy admires a Ninja "To" (sword) and runs his fingers softly over it.

Carmen sees a folder with her parents name on it amongst a number of files lying on Shadow 6's desk. She opens it, revealing pictures of her parents and their crime scene. Carmen breaks down in tears as she seats on the bed reading the file. Her mind goes back in time.

FLASH BACK

INTERNATIONAL BANK IN SWEDEN

In The International Bank's computer room, Carmen's parents *Tim* and *Becky* work furiously to meet a deadline.

Tim: Good thing they let us bring little Carmen to work with us.

Becky: That's because we are working 22 hours in a row and my Mom can't watch her, and your Mom won't. It's a wonderful day out today; we should be outside, running through the grass playing with her. Swimming, lying in the sun; oh, please let a magical wish take us there.

Tim: Oh, cheers to the wonderful life of marriage and working together. This is not our fault; we are getting overtime and saving for her college education.

Suddenly, a crash is heard and several bullets from an automatic weapon sound off as a group of *Terrorists* take the bank hostage, gunning down everyone and making their way for the computer room.

Becky and Tim are now in full panic as they witness the slaughter through their close circuit monitor system. Carmen (4) hears the commotion, and leaves the back room and joins her parents. Unnoticed, from behind her parents Carmen looks at the monitor in astonishment. Filled with fear and fright, and unnoticed by her parents, she hides under a desk behind a false sliding compartment in the computer room.

Becky: (with terror in her voice) Oh my God, Tim! Where is Carmen?

Tim: She is in the back room playing video games on the old computer. Get her and run!

Before Becky can move, the gang of terrorist's breaks into the computer room.

Becky: Please don't shoot, take what you want but don't hurt us.

Becky and Tim put their hands up and get gun down as Carmen peeks out from the slightly open false compartment under one of the desks.

Aden Workoff, 6'2", bearded, unclean, wearing a heavy jacket and carrying a *"Leader Dynamics Series T2 MK5"* assault rifle speaks.

Aden: Get the disk; check all the drives.

The group of terrorists finds the disk they want, remove it from the drive, and leave after machine-gunning the whole room. Carmen crouches there, under the desk, paralyzed with fear, her eyes closed, her tiny hands covering her eyes.

END FLASH BACK

Back at Shadow 6 Living Quarters Jimmy tries to console Carmen.

Jimmy: Carmen, Oh, no I'm sorry. Your parents… how awful.

Carmen snaps out of it. Jimmy holds her tight in his arms and rocks her back and forth.

Jimmy: Sorry, really Carmen.

In efforts to divert Carmen from her anguish Jimmy tries to change the subject.

Jimmy: Hey do you remember when Shadow 6 enrolled us into our first of three public schools?

Carmen with a broken laugh wiping off her tears looks at Jimmy.

Carmen: Ha, ha, ha, that didn't last long.

Jimmy: Yeah, one week in one public high school and out to the next one.

Carmen: Yeah, that whole thing with Max was so funny!

They both laugh.

FLASHBACK - JEFFERSON HIGH SCHOOL THREE YEARS AGO

Max Long, "The Eagle Warrior" was gathering books from his locker after class. Roger, a high school senior, a jock, 6'2", red hair, muscular 230 pounds, letterman's jacket, approaches Max. He is followed by two other high school jocks, football players with letterman's jackets and bad attitudes.

Roger: Hey, nerd, are you stealing all those books from the school?

Max now holding seven books in his arms doesn't respond.

Roger: Hey moron, I am talking to you. Are you stealing those books fart face?

Max calmly looks up and then goes about his business as he replies.

Max: Nope.

Putting one hand on top of the locker and blocking Max' exit to his right Roger keeps taunting Max.

Roger: Are they all yours?

Max: Yeap.

Roger: Can I have a couple?

Max: Nope.

Max attempts to leave, but the three boys block his way. Max smiles.

Max: Hmmm.

Roger: Well for a guy with so many books, you certainly don't talk much. Do you think that if I kick your ass right here you would be more talkative?

Max: Well, why would I let you "lick" my ass? That's...

Roger pounds his fist at the locker in threatening fashion. Max looks at Roger's fist then back at Roger.

Roger: I said kick, not lick!

Max: (In a sarcastic tone) Well, no. I specifically heard "lick".

Roger: I did not say...

Max: I am sorry, but I am not into boys. However if you and your boyfriends here decide to lick each other, I would suggest that you don't do it in the school hallway. I am sure there is some sort of school rule you would be violating... and the undressing and all, a sad sight...

The two other boys attack Max. Peter, 200 pounds, 5'9", Samuel, 5'11", buff. Peter throws a punch at Max's face. Max lifts his books up to his own face and angles them against his locker, so Peter's strike hits the edge of the hard cover books, injuring his hand.

Peter screams in pain. Samuel quickly comes to the aid of his buddy and throws a roundhouse punch at Max. Max holds tight onto the bottom and top of his books with both hands and strikes Samuel's forearm redirecting the fist to the edge of the locker. Samuel screams in anguish. Now both boys are doubling over holding their damaged fists in pain.

Max: Your friends here are the aggressive type; I assume they are the ones that will force you to do the licking in your Ménage á trios?

Roger lifts his fist as if to strike Max.

Roger: I am going to kill you, you mother fucker!

Max calmly replies.

Max: I don't think I ever had the pleasure, or the disgusting act of ever having sexual relations with your mom. Maybe someone that looked like me... Think for a moment, I am sure there are so many faces that you have to go through in your mind... I can wait...

Roger losses his cool and with his fist raised tries to blast Max. Unexpectedly, Alexa jumps in between Max and Roger, striking Roger's arm to deflect the punch and with open hands, she slaps Roger three times, hard and fast. Fingerprints can be seen imprinted on Roger's face.

The three football players stare in shock, Roger is paralyzed, not knowing what to say or do.

Alexa: Boys, this matter needs to be resolved outside school grounds.

Roger: Bitch, you slapped me!

Alexa: Yes, three times, and I think you liked it.

Roger: I am going to kill...

Roger now stares at her, his eyes widening some more...

Roger: You... you are blind...

From behind the group Jimmy speaks. All the rest of the young Shadow Warriors stand against the lockers on the other side of the hallway listening to the five quarreling. They lean on the lockers behind them observing the developments with a smile on their face. Twenty to thirty students are now standing watching the altercation.

From behind them, Jimmy shouts.

Jimmy: (The Bull Warrior) she slapped you fair and square. Too fast for you to stop her. She embarrassed the captain of the football team. You are now HER BITCH!

The crowd cheers. Roger is now enraged.

At this point the three football players are starting to think that they might have gotten too far over their heads with this provocation.

Ethan: (The Tiger Warrior) It's all set, we meet in 30 minutes by the alley behind the liquor store. It will be you, what's your name?

Roger with a puzzled look and hesitant answers.

Roger: Hmm, Roger

Ethan: Ok, Roger against Alexa…

Roger: I am not fighting a girl, besides she is bli…

Before he can finish the sentence Alexa slaps him twice, harder than before and turns around with the speed of a *Ghost* and slaps the other two jocks just as hard.

Roger: Fuck you, fuck you, I am going to kill you!

Peter: We are going to kill her.

Samuel: Yes we are! (holding his cheek) Damn, that hurt!

Ethan: Then it's settled, in 30 minutes, Alexa against Roger and his two boyfriends.

Carmen The *Cobra Warrior* yells to the crowd.

Carmen: Tell everyone to be there; don't let the teachers find out, get front row seats!

The crowd cheers and yells and scatters to spread the word.

Half an hour later a multitude of teenagers can be seen walking towards the local rundown liquor store, windows covered with advertising, red flashing signs saying "Lotto Here". A homeless man lies asleep in front of the store, a bell rings every time someone enters or leaves the liquor store.

Across from the liquor store's alley there is a huge parking lot, where 75 to 100 kids gather to see the fight.

Mike, The Leopard Warrior walks to the designated arranged spot carrying 8 boards, one and a half feet square, about two inches thick. As the Warriors arrive each grab a board, stand next to each other and spread out forming a circle. Inside the circle stand Alexa and the three jocks facing each other. The crowd surrounds the Young Warriors.

The three jocks feel confused as they witness the strange happenings. From behind the jocks, Jimmy speaks in a loud and commanding voice.

Jimmy: Gentlemen, before this battle begins a small test of what you, Roger and your boys, will be facing. The test will be demonstrated by "The Ghost", Alexa, standing in front of you. Boys, I advise you NOT to move or you will incur severe injuries.

The three jocks stand there, legs spread apart, shoulder width, ready to fight, not knowing what to expect.

Everyone watches in curious fashion.

Jimmy yells the commands.

Jimmy: Ushiro-hiji-ate! (Backward elbow smash).

Alexa jumps and spins twice in the air and throws a backward elbow at Roger's head. Just as the blow is ready to strike Ethan puts his board about one foot away from Roger's head. Alexa's elbow strikes breaking the board to pieces and avoiding Roger's head. Alexa spins away from the strike and stands facing the jocks.

The three jocks are now frozen in place. Jimmy yells the second command. Mike hands his board to Ethan, as the Warriors move their board forward clockwise from one warrior to the next as to always have one ready for Ethan to block Alexa's blows.

Jimmy: Sayu-zuki! (Double Side Punch).

Again Alexa leaps towards Samuel, who is standing last one in line to her right. As she gets within a foot of Samuel, his eyes open as wide as saucers; he is frozen, he can't move. Alexa then turns punches twice at Peter who stands in the middle between Roger and Samuel.

Before her punches connect Ethan positions his board a foot away from Peter's head. Alexa punches twice and the board splatters. She spins to the other side of Peter and delivers two blows to his head as Mike intercepts with a board that explodes upon contact.

As Alexa breaks the last board Jimmy yells another command.

Jimmy: Kyobu-geri! (Chest Area Kick)

Without missing a beat Alexa throws a chest kick at Samuel, which is blocked by another board that Ethan puts in front of Samuel's chest. The board breaks in pieces.

Alexa spins backwards and lands on her feet facing the jocks that are now paralyzed with fear.

Out of the crowd an attacker runs towards Alexa, the Warriors open the circle to let him in. The attacker is carrying a switch blade and as he jumps to strike down at Alexa's head, she swiftly steps sideways grabbing his knife carrying hand with her left hand, around his pinky finger and palm and twisting it upwards as her right hand presses against the thumb in the opposite direction, pulling his whole arm towards her. She ducks under the attacker and yanks back on his arm dislocating it.

The attacker stumbles back and Alexa turns away, exposing her back to him. The attacker stands now holding his right arm and with an uncontrolled fury attacks forward. Alexa turns with the speed of a pouncing tiger and places a front punch in the attacker's cheek. A cracking noise can be heard. Without pause Alexa throws a front kick to the attacker's solar plexus knocking him out before he hits the ground.

Alexa turns to the three jocks and asks.

Alexa: Ok, then, let's start our quarrel, show's over. Come at me, let's go – fight me!

The three jocks stand there frozen, without being to make a coherent sentence.

The Three Jocks: Hmm, ah, oh, no need…

Peter: Are you blind or not? I am just saying (shaking with fear).

Alexa: I am blind of sight, not mind and spirit. My soul can see things most people can't even notice.

Roger trying to save face and a little shaky, speaks.

Roger: Well, ahem… if you apologize.

Alexa walks slowly towards Roger as he backs up. Alexa lets out a yell.

Alexa: Gedan-zuki! (Lower Level Punch)

The Warriors acknowledge.

Alexa lunges towards Roger as she drops on one knee with extreme forward force and delivers a punch one inch from Roger's crotch as she strikes another board held by Ethan between Roger's legs. The board breaks to pieces. Roger's eyes widen and he grabs his crotch as he speaks.

Roger: Ok, ok, I apologize to you; it was all entirely fault, please, please. I started the fight with your buddy Max, I insulted you, I deserved the slaps; I am good. I am so sorry I started all this.

Alexa: Fair enough.

Alexa walks away and joins the circle as Max takes her place. Max is carrying a coconut in his hands.

Max: Girls, I am glad you enjoyed Alexa's exhibition. Just for the record, I taught her everything she knows.

He pauses, staring down at the three jocks waiting for one of them to speak.

Roger: Really?

Max: Oh, really!

Roger: Oh, ok, I believe you.

Max: Thank you, but I don't do exhibitions; I just come out fighting...

Roger: No, that's not...

Max: Do you know what this is? (Showing Roger the coconut from several feet away).

Max holds it in one hand in front of him, shaking it and turning it.

Roger: Hmmm, ah, a coconut.

Max: Correct Roger, do your girlfriends here know what this is?

He points to Peter and Samuel with the same hand that he holds the coconut as he smirks. Peter and Samuel give him dirty looks.

Max: Well girls, this is the "Coconut of Truth". This coconut will tell me if you want to fight me or apologize to me.

Max puts the coconut to his ear as if the coconut was a telephone and he was listening for an answer from the other side.

Max: Oh, really? Well I will tell them.

Max shakes his head

Max: Do you know what the "Coconut of Truth" just told me?

The jocks look at Max with a weird look on their faces. The crowd laughs, enjoying Max's antics.

Max: The Coconut of Truth said that you will not fight me, that you will apologize...on your knees. Don't take my word for it, you listen.

He throws the coconut to Roger, who looks at it, and turns it in his hand.

Max: Well put it to your ear, so it can talk to you.

Roger hesitantly puts it against his ear.

Roger: I don't think I hear anything...

Max: Pass it to your girlfriend there (Pointing at Peter).

Roger passes it to Peter who slowly and hesitantly puts it to his ear. Peter shakes his head as to say that he can't hear the coconut.

Max: Well maybe your other girlfriend can hear it.

Peter passes it to Samuel. Samuel grabs the coconut, and puts the coconut to his ear all the while staring at Max. He shakes his head.

Samuel: I don't hear anything...

Max: Well, maybe it's cracked, check it out. Is it cracked?

Each one of them examines the coconut to make sure is not cracked. As each one of them examines it, they conclude that the coconut is not cracked. The coconut is now back in Roger's hands.

Max: (Motioning to Roger) well, gently toss it over to me. And I mean gently, your life depends on it.

Roger tosses the coconut to Max. Max holds it in between his hands, fingers laced under the coconut, legs shoulder apart, his eyes piercing into the eyes of the three jocks in front of him. He yells out loud.

Max: Karate Ni Sente Nashi! (The Martial Artist does not attack first) A phrase to denote that, only in self-defense will a Warrior inflict pain or death to his enemy.

As he screams with his fingers laced under the coconut, Max squeezes his hands and bursts the coconut.

The three jocks drop to the floor on their knees and ask for forgiveness trembling from witnessing Max's exhibition. The crowd of teens screams clap and cheer in amazement.

Max walks towards the jocks, gets on one knee and speaks to them in a low voice.

Max: Don't ever, ever again bother me or anyone else in this school because if you do, I will inflict serious pain unto you girls. (The three shake as they listen.)

Max: Your actions are those of evil men, those without spirit, do you not agree?

All three nod their heads as they look down at the ground in fear. Max speaks to them in a soft, slow, but strong tone.

Max: *There's no eye, ear, tongue, body and mind. In darkness there's sin, in darkness there's death, sin negates spirit and the killing of beings without spirit shall only be looked on as an act of charity.*

CHAPTER 11

THE KILLING OF NINE ANGELS

THE NEXT DAY AT JEFFERSON'S HIGH PRINCIPAL'S OFFICE

The principal of Jefferson high has a large office situated in the first floor of the High school. Sitting on the right side of the principal's desk are Samuel, Peter, Roger, and Billy, Roger's brother, 6' tall, dark hair, 220 lbs., also a jock wearing a letterman's jacket draped over his shoulders. His right arm in a cast, his left cheek swollen, and his left eye black and blue.

Standing behind them are Roger's parents. Louise Williams, 45, short red hair, overweight 5'3" and Daniel Williams, 5'5" light brown hair 220 lbs., both of them are dressed business casual.

On the other side of the principal's desk sits Alexa, Max, and Jimmy. Behind them stands Shadow 6. He is dressed in a tight fit designer t-shirt, his muscles bulging out of it, dress pants, and dark sunglasses, emotionless, intimidating.

The door to the office remains open and a big glass window covering from floor to ceiling has its shades drawn up exposing the view of the school's office front desk. On the other side of the door stand the rest of the *Young Warriors* listening to the conversation.

The principal enters his office, Mr. Stuart, 5'7" dark hair, mustache, 165 lbs., dressed in a suit.

Mr. Stuart: I asked all of you here today because of the circumstances that took place yesterday after school, on private property. Jefferson High School carries the liability of the behavior of the entire student body it enrolls and that being the case I will not tolerate such animal behavior as it was displayed yesterday. At this point I have conflicting stories and some statements by young Roger and his brother which are very difficult to believe.

You, Roger stated to me that this young lady, Alexa, who is blind, no offense my dear.

Alexa: None taken Mr. Stuart.

Mr. Stuart: Well, Roger, you stated that Alexa threatened your life, slapped all of you, and attacked you so violently that you and your brother as well as Samuel and Peter feared for your lives. That in the process she broke Billy's arm, his jaw and gave him a horrendous black eye.

Roger: Well sir... and Max...

Mr. Stuart: Do not interrupt me young man! In this short time that we had the pleasure of having Alexa in our school, we know her as a sweet, kind, very studious young lady, which often needs help even finding her own desk in class, no offense Alexa.

Alexa: None taken Mr. Stuart.

Mr. Stuart continues with his speech.

Mr. Stuart: And this sweet "BLIND" girl that could probably have difficulty finding you in plain daylight, not only found you, but chased you slapped you attacked you and intimidated ALL four of you, not to add the damage to Billy's face? I have difficulty believing that!

Roger's and Billy's parents stare in shock realizing that Alexa is actually blind and not a ruthless assassin as described by their boys.

Mrs. Williams: Roger, Billy, boys, this young beautiful girl is blind, how could you make up such terrible story about her?

Roger: but she doesn't act blind...

Mr. Williams: Roger, you are a disgrace; you are making me ashamed that you are my son. What really happened out there?

Max: If I may interrupt, what really happened out there is very embarrassing to your sons and his friends; maybe that's why they created such story.

Everyone stops talking and directs their attention to Max.

Max: It is not like we are some stealth clandestine group of assassins that feel like the killing of beings without spirit is looked on as an act of charity and on one of these very dark and dreary nights Alexa and I would seek them out and break every bone in their bodies. How ridiculous does that sound?

Roger's eyes widen with fear, Roger and his friends get Max's message and are now sweating bullets looking at each other and Roger's parents for help. Shadow 6 just looks on desperately holding back a laugh, but keeping a serious face.

Alexa interrupts in a sad soft voice.

Alexa: Max is right, Mr. Stuart, allow me to explain. Mr. and Mrs. Williams, I want your promise that after I explain the correct circumstances, you will not be ashamed or judgmental over your sons and his friends.

Mr. Williams: You have my word sweetheart.

Mrs. Williams: Of course we would never pass judgment over our boys and their friends, go on young girl.

Max, not knowing where Alexa is going with this, but following her lead adds.

Max: And I am sure you boys won't make any lame excuses when Alexa is done.

Roger and his group shake their heads in fear.

Alexa: Very well. Your sons, Roger and Billy, have an affinity with tights, please don't laugh. You know ballet tights, and often they secretly dress in tights with their friends here. They help each other dress, because as you know tights can really be difficult to put on, especially for guys.

In any case, they love to dress and touch each other as they dress in tights, not any boys, primarily their friends here. I am not suggesting that your boys would just touch any boy, if you know my meaning here. They are very much into each other.

Roger and his friends are now infuriated, but can't say a word in their defense.

Alexa: Well as luck would have it for them, Max here is an outstanding ballet dancer; *I know this because he has taught me everything I know.*

Mrs. Williams: You do ballet?

Alexa: Well, not very well because of my condition, but Max is so patient with me, he is a great teacher and has done so much for my self-esteem. He just makes me forget my blindness.

Mr. Williams's eyes just keep getting bigger and bigger, his eyes failed to blink from the moment Alexa started explaining her side of the story.

Alexa: So when he saw your boys strip naked and put on tights in the locker room, he asked them if they would like to learn some ballet, for that would add some very much-needed sexiness to their relationship. You can see how fast your boys and their friends took on Max's offer.

Mr. Stuart: (Now somewhat interested and excited) Ahem, continue young lady.

Alexa: Yes, Mr. Stuart. After several private lessons with Max, they decided to take their first audition outside of school grounds. Max suggested the parking lot behind the liquor store, because it is seldom if ever traveled and they could have some privacy. Max, being the kind soul that he is, asked me to joined them.

Alexa, still angry over Max's comment on her "Ghost" training continues.

Alexa: You know, join them so it could boost my morale and make me feel worthwhile, *because Max has taught me everything that I know.*

Mr. Stuart and Roger's parents listen attentively, mesmerized by Alexa's power.

Alexa: I must add that Max doesn't like other boys in tights as you sons and his friends do; he is just studying to be a professional dancer in his off time and loves to help other boys in tights.

Max is now giving her this look like saying ok, you better shut up, the rest of the Young warriors are texting everyone in school Alexa's speech. All the students are now laughing and texting the others. The news spreads throughout the whole school. Shadow 6 now turns around to secretly smile and shakes his head. He turns back around, not knowing what to expect next.

Alexa: In any case, your boys excited over the possibilities of what they had learn and wanting to show off their newly acquired skills in the art of ballet, told a number of their friends about the ballet exhibition, and of course the word spread throughout the school.

A very large group of students circled around the boys and Max to watch. Maybe 100 kids or more showed up at the parking lot.

Mr. and Mrs. Williams and Mr. Stuart listen in shock and disbelief that they never knew this about their sons.

In the course of the lesson, Max had me do one of the spins he taught me during early trainings. I was a little disoriented because of not being familiar with my surroundings so as I spun, my hands were up in the air and I accidentally slapped Roger in the face. Roger yelled out that he loved it and directed my hand to his, hmmm, Gluteus Maximus and yelled "Slap it! Slap it hard!" Well, I did. Then his friends wanted me to do the same and guided my hands to their faces and other areas several times so I could slap them.

Mind you this was not part of the lesson that I know of. It was just that your boys felt so happy and free to show their true self in front of hundreds of the students here at Jefferson High that they just wanted to be slapped. Go figure, who can ever understand that, but I certainly respect it. Yes, Mr. and Mrs. Williams, Principal Stuart, I'll be darn if I understand it, but it was the way they expressed themselves.

Roger, Billy, Samuel, and Peter just stood there in embarrassment without being able to talk, with their mouth open.

Alexa (continues): During this whole event, your son Billy, overexcited by his friends dancing in tights, in front of hundreds of their peers in front of him missed a step and fell on the floor. Just before Billy hit the floor Roger and Samuel while performing an Allegro Pas de Deux, from the steps Max taught them, inadvertently struck Billy in the face with their foot, damaging his jaw.

Billy to his credit showed no pain and insisted on continuing the lesson and while taking an Arabesque position, he slipped and fell again this time dislocating his shoulder.

Who would have thought that ballet would be so dangerous? In all the time that Max has been *teaching me everything I know*, and with my condition, I have never experienced any injury, you know...being blind and all.

Mr. Stuart: (Shaking his head in amazement). Wow, what an amazing story.

Alexa: Mr. Stuart, Mr. and Mrs. Williams, can you see now why your sons had to make such horrible story about me? Can you see how ashamed they felt about their sexual preferences? They were scared of your reactions, if you found out their true feelings. Do you see why you must support them with what they were born to be?

171

Mrs. Williams hugs Roger and Billy – and cries.

Mrs. Williams: I do, I support you both, I love you no matter what your sexual preference is, you are my sons and I stand behind you 100%.

Mr. Stuart: What about the knife inference?

Max: Oh, sir that wasn't a knife, it was a nail file and some silver nail polish.

Mr. Stuart: Oh... Well, what about the coconut?

Alexa: Ah, the celebration coconut!

Max: That is correct sir, Roger wanted a coconut celebration. He asked me to break a coconut so they could....

Alexa: So they could rub the juice all over each other while they dance, sir...

Mr. Stuart: Very well, very well then, I don't think I need to hear any more. Case closed!

Max: Sir, let me expla...

Mr. Stuart: Enough said! I don't need to know any more. You are dismissed, all of you!

Shadow 6: Now that we have everything straighten out here, I will be taking the kids home with me for the rest of the day.

Mr. Stuart: Oh, yes as you wish, go on. Mr. and Mrs. Williams, I need a word in private with you. You kids can go back to class, please.

Mrs. Williams is still hugging her boys; Mr. Williams is just standing there in a daze.

Roger: Mom, please stop, we have to get to class.

Mrs. Williams: Go on my little Roger and Billy, go on, I support you one hundred percent, just remember that. You don't have to play football.

Mr. and Mrs. Williams stay to talk to the principal, the texting by the Young Warriors has passed on to the whole school. As Roger, Billy and Samuel and Peter walk out of the school's office, boys whistle at them. A boy asks them what lipstick they recommend for their mother. Another boy asks if they get really excited when they are in the huddle and the quarterback keeps the ball between his legs. Everyone laughs. Roger and his boys are infuriated.

PARKING LOT OUTSIDE JEFFERSON HIGH

Shadow 6 and the young warriors walk towards their vehicles.

William: Alexa, you are a lunatic, what stories...

All the young Warriors break into uncontrollable laughter. Alexa speaks as if nothing unusual had gone down.

Alexa: Sir, it is a school day, we have to go to class.

Shadow 6, making believe that he is angry with the Young warriors, but hardly being able to burst into a laugh, scolds them.

Shadow 6: No you don't. The only class you are getting from now on is with me fifteen hours a day, no more free time.

William (The Python Warrior): Max you should have known better than to say that crap... that you taught Alexa all she knows? Ha, ha, ha.

Max: You guys, I was creating drama and an atmosphere of suspense. You are so not with it, William.

Tom (The Boar warrior): Yes, suspense in tights and a tutu, ha, ha, ha.

Mike (The Leopard warrior): Well I hope you teach us that Grande Jeté position, so we can dance against Evil man. Ha, ha, ha.

Jimmy (The Bull Warrior): I am personally glad that Alexa told the truth on what happened.

Ethan (The Tiger warrior): Yes that poor blind girl that can't even find her school desk.

Carmen (The Cobra Warrior): that is so heart breaking.

Sarah (The Viper Warrior): My brother in a tutu and tights, that's hilarious. I love Alexa, what a mind!

Max: Alexa, I can't believe you made up that crap. Me in tights, ballet, what load of crap.

Alexa: Oh, like the crap that you told everyone on how "you taught me everything I know in the art of "The Ghost"?

Alex: Alexa my love, I was bringing suspense and credibility to my abilities as a tough "hombre'. You saw them shake when I said that, right?

They all laugh.

Shadow 6: Alexa was always very clever and creative from a very small child till adulthood. The head trauma that made her blind also gave her special powers.

Jimmy: A bullet?

Shadow 6: No, not a bullet Jimmy. Can I tell them Alexa?

Alexa: Yes sir, we are all family, they deserve to know.

Shadow 6: Alexa became an orphan when her parents were killed in an automobile crash. Their car was struck by a drunk driver driving an 18-wheeler. The truck landed on her parents' car and killed them both instantly.

Alex: How old was she?

Shadow 6: Two years old. She was the only survivor, sitting in the back of the car trapped in her car seat. She was blinded by the violent impact of the accident. She sustained injuries to her head that were diagnosed as fatal. 'Till today, we know her as the "miracle child". Firefighters had to use "The Jaws of Life" to get to her freed from the wreck and the automobile exploded within seconds of her release.

Carmen: The program adopted her then?

Shadow 6: No, I met her at age 5. I knew she was one of us the minute I met her.

FLASHBACK - ORPHANAGE 12 YEARS AGO

Shadow 6 enters the "Leap of Faith" an orphanage located in Los Angeles, California. The building is a tall, red brick building encompassing half a block. Shadow 6 heads towards the reception desk, flashing his ID at the receptionist, and continues down the hallway without missing a beat.

He passes several partitioned offices that resemble a "bull pen" more than an actual orphanage. He is met by the Orphanage's Director, Mrs. Johnson.

Mrs. Johnson: Nice Meeting you Mr. Crown, your office said you would be here in one hour, and here you are.

Shadow 6: Brief me on the girl.

Mrs. Johnson: Well, Alexa is blind from an auto...

Shadow 6: I know all that history. I want to know her behavior, her interactions, and her motivations as you see them.

Mrs. Johnson: She doesn't seem like a blind girl, Mr. Crown, she knows everything, doesn't miss a thing, and for the life of me, I think she is clairvoyant.

Shadow 6: Hmmm.

They both enter a large room where a five year old by the name of Alexa sits patiently and unmoving in the middle of the room.

The walls are covered with wallpaper of Disney characters, Pluto, Mickey, Minnie, Donald Duck, etc. The floor cover resembles those of state of the art Gyms, made of soft black rubber, with a two-foot yellow trimming around the perimeter.

Large windows expose the California sun behind Alexa's chair. Fresh fruit and other food sits on a round table next to her; a large playpen full of toys covers one corner of the room and a bookshelf about four feet tall loaded with coloring and storytelling books extends from one end of one wall to another. Shadow 6 sits on the floor, facing Alexa, in an eastern Sitting Position, legs crossed in front of him. He speaks to Alexa.

Shadow 6: What is your name beautiful girl?

Little Alexa: You are very tall.

Shadow 6: How do you know?

Little Alexa: Your footsteps, they are heavy.

Shadow 6: Couldn't I just be short and very fat?

Little Alexa: No, your steps would sound different. Your voice also comes from high up.

Shadow 6: Is Mrs. Johnson tall or fat?

Little Alexa: She is afraid of you.

Shadow 6: Well, how do you know that?

Little Alexa: She is not being bossy and her breathing is very fast.

Shadow 6: Can you see my hand?

Shadow 6 lifts his hand near Alexa's face and it is immediately grabbed by Alexa's right hand in a defensive fashion.

Little Alexa: No sir, I am blind, I cannot see. I just feel and hear things. You are very strong.

Shadow 6: Alexa, right?

Little Alexa: Yes.

Shadow 6: You don't have to be afraid of me; I am here to make sure you are safe and protected.

Alexa smiles.

Shadow 6: Well then Alexa. Call me Shadow 6. The people that I like, I let them call me Shadow 6. Would you call me that?

Little Alexa: Yes… Shadow 6.

Mrs. Johnson: Well what do you have those you don't like call you?

Shadow 6: Mr. Crown.

Mrs. Johnson stares with embarrassment. Shadow 6 takes her to the side.

Shadow 6: This girl has been abused by you or your staff or both. Her reaction to my movement tells me that. Have all the security tapings of this girl for the past year at my office by 9:00 AM tomorrow morning. If I ever hear of you or anyone in this place abuse any child, I will shut you down and throw you in a place that would make Guantanamo Bay look like a Disneyland ride. Do you understand me?

Mrs. Johnson's hands begin to shake, her unblinking eyes show dying fear as she replies.

Mrs. Johnson: I understand, I understand.

Shadow 6: Get the paperwork ready.

Shadow 6 returns to little Alexa's side and kneels over.

Shadow 6: Young lady, you are a sharp one, I am taking you home with me so you can meet your brothers and sisters.

Little Alexa extends her arms out and hugs Shadow 6.

Little Alexa: I like you Mr. Shadow 6.

END OF FLASHBACK

Back at the school parking lot.

Shadow 6: And that was Alexa then, and she hasn't changed, she is just gotten better.

Ethan: I can't remember a day without her in my life.

Everyone agrees, some of the Warriors teary eyed, either from laughter or melancholy from being taken back to childhood by Shadow 6.

Shadow 6: Everyone in the van, now. In any event, you are through celebrating. You are all in for some severe adjusting. That is not the way a Shadow Warrior behaves, I am taking you all out of that school before you corrupt everyone, including the principal.

Shadow 6 smiles. They all take off for the training camp.

SHADOW 6's QUARTERS

Jimmy: We surely paid for that for weeks of hard training and restriction, but it was worth it, it was so funny.

Carmen: It certainly was. But we got to go to two other high schools after that. I guess it took Shadow 6 some time to figure out that we don't belong there.

Their eyes lock and are about to kiss. As Carmen looks at Jimmy Shadow 6 enters the room.

They are abruptly surprised and disengage.

Shadow 6: A little out of our zone, aren't we? And yes, Carmen, you guys belonged in public schools. You just didn't know how to behave like normal kids then.

Jimmy: define normal.

Carmen looks at Shadow 6 and starts sobbing. She holds the pictures of her parents tightly in her hands.

179

Jimmy: It's OK Carmen. I understand. We are all orphans. We are your family now.

Carmen continues crying as Jimmy holds her in his arms rocking her back and forth. Shadow 6 looks on.

Jimmy: We're so sorry sir...

Shadow 6: I know, I did the same at your age, but you broke a very important rule.

Jimmy: How much trouble are we in – exactly?

Shadow 6: Just get her to her quarters, and make sure this does not happen again.

As Jimmy helps Carmen out, Shadow 6 stares at Carmen's still face.

Jimmy: Thank you sir...

Shadow 6: Out!

Shadow 6 closes the door and removes his invisible suit. A tear rolls down his cheek. He hangs his suit back in the armory. Shadow 6 breathes a sigh, and flops down on his bed. He just closes his eyes when there is a knock on the door.

The door opens.

Shadow 6: (sternly) What?

Eric Stone: Easy now tiger.

Shadow 6: Sorry sir. What's up?

Eric Stone: I was just stopping by on my way to thank you once again for the demonstration earlier. That really flipped the Senator's wig. I owe you one. You know, that

Alexa was great. I know she broke the rules, but she is sure a sharp cookie. I love that girl.

Shadow 6: No problem, Eric.

Eric Stone: You know the word in Washington is that they were thinking of taking the program away from me. That's why they sent Marshall. They figured if I can convince him, well... This is all just one big ass kissing anyway.

Shadow 6: Good, now we're even for the hacker.

Eric shuts the door. Shadow 6 lies back in bed.

Back at the conference room, the elevator takes the room upwards; the sun is blinding and it is another day in California with great weather. Eric is seeing off Senator Marshall, the Senators, Anusha, and Annie Crothers.

Senator Marshall: Thanks again for the tour General. You have a great program here, and I am all for it.

Eric Stone: My pleasure senator and I thank you for your support.

Senator Marshall: Alright then, I've got to get back to Washington, tell them to give you guys some more funding.

Eric Stone: (smiling) that's the idea Senator.

They shake hands as Senator Marshall, Anusha and Annie Crothers get into the military helicopter.

Stone takes the elevator down to the underground complex and as he steps off the elevator and steps on to the dock, a staffer approaches him carrying a brief case.

Staffer: Excuse me, sir, but have you seen our guests?

Eric Stone: They just left. Why?

Staffer Well, I think one of them left their brief case behind.

Suspicion overcomes Eric Stone. He eyes the outside of the brief case.

Eric Stone: Young man, put that down, slowly.

Staffer: What?

Stone carefully opens the brief case.

Eric Stone: It's a bomb! Tell everyone to clear out, now! Get to The Young Warriors! I'll take care of the bomb.

Stone hits the alarm on the wall and goes tearing down the hallway towards the outside to dispose of the bomb.

Outside as the helicopter departs, the blaring sound of the alarm can be heard all around. Senator Marshall sits in the back seat of the chopper with Annie Crothers.

Senator Marshall: (to the pilot) it sounds like something's wrong, stop the chopper.

Annie Crothers pulls a pistol from her purse and shoots the senator in the head. Anusha points a gun at the pilot's head prodding him to take off.

Annie Crothers: Just keep driving, wheel man.

The helicopter takes off, as we see the desert behind them blowing up from underground. Annie tears off her fake nose, and pulls off her wig. We see that she is really Gina Venezie, daughter of the biggest mastermind criminal in current history. She dials out from her cell phone.

Gina: Daddy, it's me. Mission accomplished. I love you too. I'll see you in two days. By the way daddy, I got you 3 *Bracelets*, you'll love them!

Gina hangs up her phone and lets out a maniacal laugh.

Inside the underground facility remains, the flashing lights of ambulances, police bomb squad vehicles and fire engines can be seen blanketing the entire area. From above the underground the facility now looks like one big crater.

Shadow 6 sifts through the ashes and blown out remains of the building as the few surviving staff members are putting out random fires still burning. Shadow 6 finally hears Eric from under the wreckage. He pulls the debris aside to find him badly burned and bloody.

Eric's phone rings. Eric tries to unsuccessfully reach for it. Shadow 6 picks up the phone and answers.

Shadow 6: Hello who is this?

Voice on the other end: Eric?

Shadow 6: No, who is this?

Voice on the other end: Get out of the building, there is a bomb ready to go off, click.

A click is followed by a dial tone. Shadow 6 perplexed but with no time to figure out what just happened, hangs up and tends to Eric.

Shadow 6: Eric, lay still, I'll get you a doctor.

Eric Stone: The kids?

Shadow 6: They're okay...but the senior Warrior team has been wiped out and we are missing three of the *Bracelets*.

MUSLIM MOSQUE

An hour later Anusha enters inside a Muslim Mosque, dressed in a full Muslim Burka. Only her beautiful green eyes are exposed for all to see. She walks up to the Imam of the Mosque and hands him a note written in Arabic which reads:

تم يـ ذلك إن شاء ، الله الله أك بر، الله الـ حمد أك بر، . (ytm dhlk 'in sha' alllahu, alllah 'akbara, alhamd lilh).

"It is done, God willing. God is the Greatest, *All* praise be to God".

HOSPITAL IN LOS ANGELES

Shadow 6 enters the hospital. The large automatic doors give way to the imposing figure of Shadow 6 as he enters the lobby as many enter and exit as well. An information center is located about 30 feet from the front door.

A senior citizen in her seventies, white hair, 5'3" brown eyes, proudly wears the badge of "receptionist". She sits behind the reception desk. She wears heavy makeup in efforts to unsuccessfully smooth the wrinkles on her face. She smiles almost as if she was about to enter a ride at Disneyland. She makes believe she is busy and proficient as she looks through her designer "Dollar Tree" store glasses at the paperwork in her desk. Her nametag reads "Ruth".

Shadow 6 asks for instructions to Eric's room.

Shadow 6: Excuse me, but can you tell me what room is Mr. Eric Stone in?

Ruth: Yes, good morning young man. Let me look that up for you. You know how busy this hospital can get.

She busily shuffles a bunch of papers and looks at her computer screen. She tries to get the mouse to slide on her desk, but her moves are choppy and inconsistent.

Ruth: Well, if this little mouse would just cooperate, I can get you that. Whoever thought of calling this gadget a mouse? I abhor mice; they scare me they are so fast.

And in a whispering voice, she adds.

Ruth: And they poop all over the place.

She picks up the mouse and bangs it on the desktop a couple of times.

Ruth: Oh, there, it just needed some spanking. Let's see here, Mr. Bone...

Shadow 6: Stone, ma'am.

Ruth replies without looking up.

Ruth: Stone Bone...

Shadow 6 replies in a stern voice.

Shadow 6: No Ma'am, Just Stone, Eric Stone!

Ruth looks up at Shadow 6. With a sweet look on her face she says.

Ruth: You know, young man, it's not sunny here, you can take those sunglasses off. You poor boy, no wonder you are so uptight; you probably can't see anything through those glasses. You know I had a neighbor once... Pete, yeah I think that was his name...

Shadow 6 removes his glasses and lowers his face to hers and gives her a stern look.

Shadow 6: The room number, now please!

Ruth: Oh, that is much better, such pretty eyes, you shouldn't hide them. Let's see he is in room... Oh, dear, I have to...

In a whispering voice, placing her hand on the side of her mouth to avoid anyone else from hearing, she waves Shadow 6 close to her and whispers.

Ruth: This is top-secret young man. I have to call security and the head nurse. Hold on.

Shadow 6 just looks at her indignantly.

Ruth dials a number and cups the phone with her hand in a secretive manner.

Ruth: There is a very big young man looking for room 215.

A few seconds later while she is still on the phone, a nurse and a policeman approach Shadow 6.

The policeman in his mid-30's, good shape, 6' dark hair addresses Shadow 6.

Policeman: Do you have identification sir?

Shadow 6 puts his sunglasses back on and answers.

Shadow 6: Xavier Crown, Special Ops director, SOG unit.

> *SOG: a highly classified, multi-service United States special operations unit which conducts covert **unconventional warfare** operations, clandestine agent team activities and psychological operations.*

186

Shadow 6 shows his ID.

Policeman: Very well, I am sorry, but we have to take precautions.

Shadow 6: Understood.

The policeman introduces the nurse to him.

Policeman: This is the Intensive Care Unit Head Nurse, Emilia Gomez.

Emilia Gomez is a heavyset woman in her late 40's, rigid, well groomed, 5'10". She gives an air of knowledge and command as she speaks. She shakes Shadow 6's hand.

Emilia: I was expecting you Mr. Crown, please follow me, Mr. Stone has been asking for you.

They head towards the elevators. They enter and press floor 2.

Ruth, addressing a new visitor to the hospital whispers to her.

Ruth: You know I just talked to a "secret agent". He couldn't see so well, but when I had him take his sunglasses off...

As they exit the elevator, the policeman and Emilia walk Shadow 6 through a long hallway, past a nursing unit located in the center of the patients' rooms in the second floor. The nursing unit is compact in a circular fashion with easy access and view to all the patients' rooms. Two policemen stand guard in front of room 215. Shadow 6 and his escorts enter the room.

Eric lies in his bed and a nurse sits next to him, tending to his needs.

Eric: Son, good to see you.

Shadow 6 addresses the Policeman and Emilia.

Shadow 6: Some privacy please.

Emilia: Of course.

The policeman and Emilia leave the room and close the door behind them.

Eric lays on the bed, severely burned; gauze and casts covering most of his body.

The Nurse: I can only give you a few minutes with him. He's being prepped for surgery within the hour.

Shadow 6: Thank you.

The nurse exits the room.

Eric Stone: Tell me the truth kid, I won't make it will I?

Shadow 6: Eric, I've seen weaker men survive worse.

Eric Stone: I'm getting too old for this.

Shadow 6: Who do think is responsible for this?

Eric Stone: That'll be up to you to find out. I can only give you one name... Gabriel.

Shadow 6: Oh, him.

Eric Stone: He was with the agency, back in the early days when we first started the program. An explosion during a mission left him in a wheel chair for life. He blames me for it to this day. He wants me dead, and obviously you as well.

Shadow 6: Where can I find him?

Eric Stone: I haven't the slightest. But I think he just found you. Be careful. I know this is his work; he's the most devious man I know.

Shadow 6: We'll find him, he'll pay for this.

Eric Stone: I'm sorry...about the rest of your team.

Shadow 6: They were all good men... and women.

Eric Stone: What about the kids?

Shadow 6: Ah, you just asked yesterday after the explosion. (Sighs heavily) Fine. Shaken up, but fine. They're tough kids. The only saving grace was the fact that they made it to the bomb shelter; otherwise they would all have been killed.

Eric Stone: You have to promise me something.

Shadow 6: Anything.

Eric Stone: Take care of them, after this you're the only family they have left.

Shadow 6: The program could be shut down.

Eric Stone: Regardless, take care of those kids. Don't let them get swept up by the system. Whatever happens, they are your responsibility now. I won't make it through the night.

Shadow 6: You have to stop talking like that.

Just then the door opens, and in step two NSA agents.

CHAPTER 12

A PROMISE TO AN OLD FRIEND

NSA HEADQUARTERS LOS ANGELES

Agent Lopez, 5'7" brown hair, blue eyes, well-built, clean shaven, dressed business casual.

Head of the NSA investigative department in "El Robles" New Mexico. An NSA veteran, Lopez wants to make one final big bust and retire to South America.

Agent Green, 5'8" Bold, blue eyes, well-built, dressed business casual.

Being in New Mexico for 3 years as a government advisor and with no hope for a promotion. Agent Green decides to join Agent Lopez with his work and promises for a "Big" future.

Agent Lopez: Shadow 6, I'm Agent Lopez; this is Agent Green, NSA. We need a word with you.

Shadow 6: I don't think so. There is no need for us to chat. Please don't let the door hit you in the back on your way out.

Agent Green: With all due respect agent 6, there has been a major breach in the security of the program as it stands; we must speak to you, now! I don't report to you and I am damn aware of the breach, we do our own investigation.

Shadow 6: Is the breach in your department the reason why my complete team is now dead? By the way, it's Shadow 6... I'm busy right now, so get out.

Agent Lopez: Sir, it is imperative that you...

Shadow 6: Please, I need a few moments with my friend.

Shadow 6, annoyed by the attitude of the two agents at such a delicate time, stands up in anger. The agents back up in fear.

Shadow 6: I told you, I don't report to...

Eric Stone: It's okay Xavier, go with them.

Shadow 6: Are you sure, Eric?

Eric Stone: Go, while the trail is still warm.

Shadow 6 hesitantly starts off with the two agents.

Eric Stone: 6, take care of those kids.

GABRIEL VENEZIE'S MANSION

The full moon gives a clear view of Gabriel Venezie's hidden mansion in the middle of California's more desirable real estate, Beverly Hills, where Jed Clampett and his family of misfits chose to spend their fortune in the 1962 CBS comedy.

As the black Lamborghini pulls up to the front door, Tex is greeted by several armed guard men in military fatigues; Tex steps out, followed by Jeffrey. They are met on the front porch by Gina, sexy as ever, in a slinky black dress and stiletto heels.

Gina : It's about time. Doesn't that car have a gas pedal?

Tex: Funny.

Tex and Gina share a long passionate kiss.

Gina: And how was Puerto Viarta... and the new house?

Tex: It was great, the house is great; you know, I love Mexico, I love the people. So genuine.

Gina squeezes Jeffrey's cheek.

Gina: And how about you, my little genius? Did you miss me?

Jeffrey: (to himself) Not really.

Gina smacks Jeffrey in the face, hard. Jeffrey bends over holding his face in pain.

Tex: Is the "Boss" in?

Gina: Heck no. Your wild freeway chase scared him all the way into the Alps mansion.

Tex: Damn, it's about time he places more confidence in my work.

Gina: Actually he does. He mentioned to me that he should believe more in you that you never let him down. However just in case, he split.

Tex: Well then, pack your stuff; we're taking a little field trip.

NSA OFFICE – LOS ANGELES

The NSA office in Los Angeles, California is a satellite office of the National Security Agency in Fort Meade, Maryland. Tucked away in downtown Los Angeles, the office building is unassuming and unsuspecting to the public.

Inside NSA the LA office Shadow 6 sits across the desk from agents Lopez and Green, they are going over surveillance pictures, mug shots, and criminal dossiers.

Agent Green: What do you know about this woman?

Agent Green shows Shadow 6 a photo of Gina Venezie.

Shadow 6: What should I know? You guys are the "code makers" and "code breakers" of the intelligence community, why come to me for information you should already have?

Agent Lopez: Gina Venezie is now number two on the FBI's most wanted list. She's the acting head of the entire World Crime Syndicate, UNITY, which is a conglomerate of Mafia's, Chinese, Russian, Mexican, Italian, you name it.

Shadow 6: So you know the answer to your very question. Our agency knows who she is, Lopez. FBI code named, the "Panther".

Agent Lopez: So you do know of her. This is not a game. We need to know what you know; in return we'll brief you on everything, however...

Shadow 6: Spare me; you don't need to share information with me. Anything you guys know is old hat to us.

Agent Lopez: I think it's for your own good to share information with us. We don't want to bring down the whole government on you.

Shadow 6: Hey, kid I don't work for you; however my security clearance enables me to do as I please with anything and anyone. And that includes two NSA agents, do we understand each other?

Agent Green: (Standing up) Did I just hear you threaten me?

Shadow 6: (Leans back on his chair remaining calm and poised) Yes. (staring at Agent Green, arms folded, long pause) But don't get your panties in a bunch; I'll listen to what you have to say and formulate an opinion from there (with a smirk on his face).

Agent Green: Look here...

Shadow 6: (Completely ignoring Green, he turns to Lopez) Why don't you tell me what you know, and if I can, I'll fill in the blanks.

Agent Green: Well, she did five years at Chowchilla, from ages 18 to 23 for extortion and money laundering. We haven't been able to pin anything on her since, but the fact is, she's been a part of every major organized criminal act in this country worth over one hundred million dollars in the past five years.

Agent Lopez holds up a photo of the Boss Gabriel Venezie.

Agent Lopez: Her father, Gabriel Venezie, was the first one of two experimental Warriors in 1958 with your mentor, Eric Stone.

Shadow 6: Really?

Agent Green: Well, we know you're familiar with Gina's boyfriend and right hand man... number one on the FBI's most wanted list.

Agent Green holds up a photo of Tex.

Shadow 6: Tex.

Agent Green: I knew that one would ring a bell.

Shadow 6: Childhood friend. He died, years ago.

Agent Green: Not according to the Agency.

Shadow 6: (sarcastically) Wouldn't you know it? Bad Intel you think?

Agent Lopez: Take a look at these photos. They were taken a week ago by a surveillance satellite over the Rockies.

We see a photo of Tex and Gina leaving Community Central Bank.

Shadow 6: Amazing, almost an impossible occurrence.

Agent Green: Well, it seems there are a lot of impossibilities going around these days, especially when it comes to you and your clandestine group of agents.

Agent Lopez: We think Tex was recruited by the Venezie's. His death was a set up.

Shadow 6: Well, thank you for your pearls of wisdom, but I have to go.

Agent Green: I thought you were going to fill us in on what you know?

Shadow 6: Well, I changed my mind. You guys know everything already.

Agent Lopez: Changed your mind?

With an air of superiority and efforts to be funny and degrading Agent Lopez tries to attack Shadow 6's masculinity.

Agent Lopez: Changed your mind? Hey big *"hombre"* you are talking like my wife (he lets out a big laugh).

Shadow 6: So your wife tells you often that she changed her mind? That she has a headache? Well, I am not interested in how many times your wife refuses to have sex with you. I can see that you are not only stupid, but also, sexually repressed and a male chauvinist pig. What you seem to "not know" is that there is a leak in your organization. Somebody is getting his palms greased by Venezie, and everything your department knows, so does the underworld.

Agent Lopez: Look, man, this is no time for games, we must share information. You certainly don't think that one of us is on the take. They hit the facility, because you and your Warriors were the ones commissioned to stop them.

Agent Green: The computer programmer you were sent to recover last night; he's on their payroll.

Shadow 6: I only share information with my employers. And understand this, when just one of your so-called agents goes on the take, it puts doubt on everyone in the department. So deal with it and get me the rat that caused twenty good man and women to die unnecessarily. Then I'll start sharing info. Until then you can consider me NSA – **N**ot **S**haring **A**nything.

Agent Green: Why do you think you were sent in?

Agent Lopez: The hacker has found a way to manipulate every banking system in the world without anyone noticing.

Shadow 6: Well, doesn't the Secret Service have people that can circumvent that sort of problem already?

Agent Lopez: Yes, but they've lost a lot of agents trying. We have Special Operative Reynolds that has been in deep cover for the last year. She's Venezie's personal secretary.

Shadow 6: Then can't she find out when this attack on the Banking system will take place?

Agent Lopez: Negative. She's not involved with that aspect of Venezie's business. But she can tell you who to follow and who to watch.

Shadow 6: Okay, even if I said yes, I can't do it alone. I work with a team, each one of us has a very specific function. That's why it works.

Agent Lopez: Let me level with you Shadow 6. You don't have a choice. But you won't be alone.

Shadow 6: How do you figure? My team is dead, and I'm not going to slap together some dirty dozen made up of a bunch of suits or men in black or whatever. Then we'll definitely end up dead.

Agent Green: I was hoping you'd get on-board. There is one other option. Another Shadow Warrior unit ready for full commission.

Shadow 6: Who? You mean the kids? You can't be serious.

Agent Lopez: Yes we are.

Shadow 6: They're not ready.

Agent Lopez: Those kids have been in training since they were toddlers, that's more training than all US military special operations combined.

The phone rings, Agent Lopez steps out of the office to handle the call.

Agent Lopez: Yes, who is this?

The response from the other end of the phone is inaudible.

Agent Lopez: This is not good, thank you for the call... this is not good.

Agent Lopez walks back into the office. He stares at Shadow 6; he seems a little shook up.

Shadow 6: But they don't have the field experience!

Agent Green: Well, then you better get cracking and teach them what field-ops is all about...

Agent Lopez: Your program is changing 6. You either go with it, or get left behind.

Shadow 6: You send those kids after *Tex* and *Unity*, and they're done for!

Agent Green: We don't have a choice. The way things stand right now the Shadow Warriors go with or without your leadership. Orders from above.

Shadow 6: What do you mean by that, I need to talk to Eric.

Agent Lopez: That's my point. You can't.

Shadow 6: Why not?

Agent Lopez: That call I just handled, was the hospital. Eric Stone just passed away.

Lopez looks at his watch.

Agent Lopez: Ten minutes ago. I am sorry; we'll give you till the morning to think it over.

Shadow 6 is in shock by the news, his foster father, his mentor, his best friend just passed away with the blink of an eye.

Shadow 6: Get out; get out of my sight right now.

Shadow 6 stands up.

Agent Lopez: The information Shadow 6, we need it.

Shadow 6: This information still remains classified Gentlemen... time to leave.

The agents stand up in fear and quickly leave the room. Shadow 6 sits down, hits his fist down on the desk, feeling the loss of his mentor.

As the two Agents walk down the hallway to leave, Lopez speaks with Green. Lopez is quite shook up by Shadow 6.

Agent Lopez: That guy is dangerous.

Agent Green: Just stay clear of him and don't piss him off, hate to have to shoot him before it's time.

EXTERNAL - ITALIAN AIRPORT - ENTRANCE - DAY

Gina, Tex and Jeffrey arrive at the Milano airport, met by the Boss in the back of his limo.

Gina: Hello father.

The Boss: Hello princess.

Gina kisses the Boss on the cheek. They all get into the limo.

ERIC STONE'S OFFICE

Shadow 6 sits in Eric's old office going over some of his things; he finds pictures of Eric with him as a boy.

FLASHBACK - 35 years ago...

In the training camp of the Argentinean Pampas two children ages 5-7, Xavier, and SIMON practice Kenjutsu, the art of the sword, as Eric Stone supervises. Xavier takes a cheap shot and knocks Simon to the ground. Tex, Xavier's best friend watches, along with several assistant Lin Kuei instructors from China.

Eric Stone: Good work Xavier. But remember the way of kuji-Kiri; you should feel your opponent rather than see him.

Simon: But sir, that was a cheap shot.

Eric Stone: This isn't a sport son. This isn't a game. Cheap shots, as you call it, can win in combat, remember that. It's a mindset Simon; it's about survival.

Simon: Yes sir.

Tex: (to Eric Stone) Mr. Stone. I think I could have ducked. I can be good at this. I want to train too.

Eric Stone: That's a tall order young man. I admire your spirit. Xavier was carefully selected for this training, but if you like you can help and be his sparring partner. I will tell Master Lee.

Tex: Thank you sir! I'll do good, you'll see.

END FLASHBACK.

Back at Eric Stone's office, Shadow 6 puts the picture of Eric, Tex and him into a box. Sarah passes by the office carrying her things.

Sarah: Sir?

Shadow 6: What is it Sarah?

Sarah: Will you be coming with us to the new facility?

Shadow 6: Absolutely. I can't wait to get you guys back into training...fast.

Sarah: Sir, we won't let you down.

Shadow 6: I'm sure you'll all manage just fine.

Sarah: Thank you sir for your confidence in us. I'm sorry for your loss; I know this transition must be hard for you. Just know that we're here for you too. We are the only family left.

Shadow 6: Thanks Sarah.

Sarah: You know sir, I have spent every moment of happiness and excitement since I can remember with you and the rest of the Warriors in training, even when things didn't make sense.

Shadow 6: Like the mystery murders on the ship?

They both laugh

Sarah: Oh, my god I was so scared, I didn't think I could pull it off!

Sarah gets a flashback of the incident...

FLASHBACK

On a hidden road exposing the ups and downs of a twisted path in Malibu Canyon, dust bellows and pebbles quickly roll down the trail attempting to escape the inevitable crush of the wheels of an SUV attempting to conquer the road ahead. As if from an apparition right out of a fairy tale, the path that the road marks begins to cut into a thick forest, willow trees wave at the SUV as stern oak trees stand in vigilance of the intruders, pine trees shed small tears, maple birch trees lend a sweet sensitive smile. The SUV reaches a rusted old gate guarding a "haunted" looking mansion. The gate creaks as it opens, swallowing the SUV whole into its steel jaws.

The ground attempts to desperately breathe through the deep bed of dead leaves on the ground. As the SUV approaches the front of the majestic structure, the leaves seem to scatter in fear of being crushed under the rubber and steel monster rolling towards the front door, giving the ground a much-needed shot of oxygen and view of the sky.

The driver of the SUV brings the vehicle to a complete stop, jumps out of the car and walks towards the large, heavy, dark brown wooden door dressed with twists and turns of rod iron decorations. The door slowly opens as he enters and greets the occupants.

There, nine teenagers, a staff of four military personnel and Shadow 6 reside temporarily. The inside of the mansion is eerie, with tall ceilings; held by thick, robust columns, heavy oak furniture decorates throughout. A large staircase swings its way to the upper floors, carrying with it its dark detailed carved railings. A chill is felt when walking from room to room; dark and light brown curtains defend the interior against the possible attack of a persistent sunray. The face of the man that entered the mansion is hidden by the shadows and darkness of the ambiance. He delivers a package to Shadow 6 and proceeds to exit.

The "Shadow Warrior" training program focuses on the trainees adapting to civilian life and the everyday way of life. This part of the program is essential in perfecting their skills in body language, common "tells", common sense, and the diverse manipulation that takes place from those that seem trustworthy and those that walk on the "dark side". For that purpose the mansion is set-up near the city where all the nine trainees can live and experience interaction with the outside world.

Jimmy: How do we experience the life of the common folks, when this house is like Frankenstein's retreat? And that is if you can even find it, in the first place.

Ethan: Can you imagine inviting some high school kids here? They would think that they entered the "Texas Chainsaw Massacre" home.

Carmen: Ha, ha, ha... You are so right you guys.

A daily mission is given to every "Warrior" in training to mingle with the public and experience the everyday life outside the Warrior's hideout and without their masks of combat.

The siblings, Max and Sarah are texting to each other. Max is in the living room watching TV and Sarah is in the den on her computer.

Sarah: (TEXT) Will you cook your vegetarian lasagna tonight? LY (Love You).

Max: (TEXT) CID (consider it done)

Inside the living room's mansion, Shadow 6 calls everyone to attention.

Shadow 6: Sarah and Max, your mission today is go to downtown LA and window shop at the LA Mall, interact with the population, act like real kids. Report back to me and tell me what you observed.

Max: We are real kids.

Mike: You are a geek living in Boris Karloff's mansion.

Tom: Bring some victims, I mean friends over so we can burn them at stake.

William: Hey, steak sounds great about now.

Everyone laughs.

Shadow 6: Alright, all of you. Sarah, Max, on your way. You can take the Hummer.

Sarah and Max leave the mansion through the back door that connects to the garage. A fleet of cars are housed in the ten car garage, each one altered with hidden weapons and ultra-sophisticated electronic counsels. Max and Sarah hop into the Hummer; Max drives as Sarah sets up the GPS.

Sarah: We are on our way.

GPS: You are on the quickest route to your destination. The traffic is light as usual...

Sarah and Max: IN LA????

GPS: You should arrive at your destination by 2:30 PM.

Max takes the winding roads of the canyon at top speed with the expertise of a racecar driver. He avoids the vehicle catapulting into the air and dropping off the one hundred foot drops of the canyon on every turn. They both scream at every bend and twist, and then laugh incessantly.

GPS: There is a slowdown on Topanga canyon that will cause a 20-minute delay. You are still on the fastest route to your destination.

Sarah and Max laugh and let out a howling shout.

Forty-five minutes later Sarah and Max Park at the LA Mall and head for the entrance. As they approach the long cement path to the front door they spot well-dressed man in his 40's, dark hair, medium built laying on the ground asking for help.

Injured Man: Please help me get inside I think my leg is broken.

Max: We'll call 911.

Injured man: No, there is no need, my brother in law works in the first store near the entrance of the mall; he can take me to my private doctor. I phoned my doctor's office already and they are waiting for me. Please help me get up and I can hop to the mall entrance.

Sarah: Why isn't your brother in law out here helping you?

Injured Man: He went to the underground garage to get his car and he'll take me to the car down the mall elevator.

Sarah and Max help the man up and each one wraps one of his arms around their shoulders and carry him as he hops along to the mall entrance. After a few steps, the man suddenly with a quick, snapping move releases his wrists from Sarah and Max, turns and sprays their face with a chemical substance that shoots out from under the sleeves of his jacket. Both Sarah and Max faint from the sprayed chemical.

SEVERAL HOURS LATER

Sarah and Max's voice can be heard darting out of a pitch black surrounding.

Sarah: Are you here? Where are we?

Max: I don't know. I am a little dizzy. This whole place is moving. Are there lights anywhere?

Sarah: It's too dark. Wait I have my cell here. I have a flashlight app.

Sarah turns on her flashlight and scans what seems to be a hotel room. Blood covers the walls, the couch, and the broken coffee table. The bodies of two dead people lay on the ground. One male about 6 feet tall, blond hair, dressed casual with blood pouring out of the nose and ears, dry blood around his eyes, his throat is cut. One female, about 5'7" dark wavy hair, dry blood covers her low cut white evening dress. A bullet hole seems to have entered her chest at heart level. Her throat is also cut.

Max: Who are they?

Sarah: I don't know, I can't remember a thing. Just that man by the mall... Max, there is blood on your face and shirt.

Max grabs Sarah's phone and points the flashlight at Sarah's face.

Max: You are bloody too. Did we kill them?

206

Sarah: I don't know. I don't think so, but it doesn't matter what happened, we'll get blamed. How in God's name did we get here?

Max: We need to clean up and get the hell out of here.

Max stands up and struggles to keep his balance.

Max: Are we on a boat?

Sarah works her way over to the room's curtains and slides them open.

Sarah: We are not on a boat, we are on a ship. A big mother for what I can tell.

Light penetrates the room from the outside sun. Sarah and Max can now see the whole room. Chairs busted, a bloody knife laying on the floor, a busted coffee table, blood all over the room. Two dead bodies lay motionless on the floor with their throats cut.

Sarah and Max look at each other in a daze.

Max: Ok, let's think this out. We need to get out of here.

Sarah: Remove all fingerprints

Max: Wash up and change clothing. Look in the closets; see if we have clothes there. I'll check the dressers.

Sarah: Don't touch anything, get some towels from the bathroom and use them as gloves so we don't leave any more prints.

They both desperately go through every inch of the room wiping off any fingerprints and to see if they can find any spare clothing. They find nothing.

Max: I have nothing here

Sarah: Me neither. Ideas Max?

Max: Yes.

Max begins stripping down to his underwear.

Sarah: What are you doing? Are you going nuts?

Max: I have my towel here, my briefs look like a bathing suit, so I am going to walk this ship and break into every empty room till I find something for both of us to wear. Finish cleaning here, I'll be right back.

Max looks at the room number he just exited, it reads 126. He desperately walks the corridors of the ship. The hallway is empty and after unsuccessfully trying to open a few room doors he sees the "kitchen" sign. He sneaks past the busy cooks, chef, and servers. Plates clang on the counters, the steam blows out of the dishwasher as it operates at full force, an array of lunch dishes cover half the kitchen as waiters grab their orders and exit through the swinging doors.

Max stumbles into a dressing room off the kitchen where maids, servers, and cook uniforms hang neatly in a large closet. Max grabs a couple of uniforms and sneaks back out of the room, into the kitchen and out the hallway.

Max goes back to room 126.

Max: I got some clothes for us.

Sarah: Oh, now we are hired help?

Max: Better than "naked help".

Sarah: You are weird... but effective. Let's get out of here.

Both Max and Sarah walk out into the hallway dressed in white uniforms and carrying sets of towels in their hands as if going for a room delivery. Max carries a trash bag with their bloody clothes.

Max: We need to find an incinerator to get ready of these clothes.

Sarah: Maybe the ocean will serve as good.

Max: Whichever comes first.

As they pass the kitchen door two men with guns drawn intercept their path. Max and Sarah toss the towels in their face and break out running through the kitchen. Bullets fly in every direction from the pursuers guns.

Max runs into a waiter carrying a *flambé recently lit and a bottle of 80-proof liquor in his hand.*

Max: Perfect!

Max, followed by Sarah sets the bag of bloody clothes on the flaming flambé, as he takes the bottle of liquor away from the waiter and strikes it against the metal counter, breaking off the bottle's head. With a quick jump on the counter Max extends his arm and pours the liquor on the burning clothes causing a vicious flare of fire to hit the ceiling and set the kitchen on fire.

Sarah: You are setting the ship on fire! We are all going to drown.

Max: I doubt it, follow me.

Max does a "turnaround" back down the hallway to room 126. Max and Sarah are followed by the armed pursuers. Max breaks down room 126's door with a flying kick and both Max and Sarah enter the room as the two corpses are getting off the ground and cleaning up.

Sarah: What gives?

Max: Say hello to the undead.

Sarah: What is going on Max?

Max: Maybe you should ask Shadow 6.

As he finishes his sentence Shadow 6 and two Operatives enter the room.

Shadow 6: Good work Max, cleverly done.

Sarah: How did you know it was a test?

Max: The first clue was the room number, 126. I am Shadow 1, "The Eagle", you are shadow 2, "The Viper", and of course 6 is our mentor's calling card number. The wood behind the numbers was discolored as if a different number had been there before.

The second clue was the closet full of uniforms. There were too many uniforms and everyone I noticed in the kitchen was overweight, the cooks, the servers, the dishwasher... So why the skinny outfits?

Then I started thinking why would someone be shot and have their throat cut at the same time, isn't that overkill?

I was not completely sure until we got shot at and I followed the trajectory of the bullet that hit the ceiling and didn't leave a hole; I then knew then, they were blanks. So I thought setting the kitchen on fire would be a lesson for trying to trick us.

Sarah: Not us Max, you. Very impressive. Shadow 6 was right by telling me that you would figure it out rather quickly. He had faith in you. Sir, I owe you five bucks.

Shadow 6: No problem, we'll go double or nothing next time.

Max: What? You were in on this? And you bet against me? I am disowning you! You are no longer my sister, I could have been killed!

Sarah: With what? Blanks?

Max: Well, no, but burned alive by a flambé!

They all burst out laughing.

Shadow 6: The test was for both of you. For Sarah, to test her ability to trick others, friends as well as foes, that she was on their side. Maybe one day she will need to make a terrorist group believe that she jumped ship, no pun intended, and is now a criminal, who knows. She passed with flying colors, making her brother think she was also a victim.

Max: Totally, I didn't see that coming.

Shadow 6: For you Max, the test was to see if you could decipher clues in a dangerous emergency situation that would take you to safety. You passed with flying colors too.

Sarah goes over to max and hugs him.

Sarah: Oh, my little brother is such a clever genius.

Sarah plants a kiss on Max's cheek.

END OF FLASHBACK

Sarah walks off. Shadow 6 looks down to the 6 *Bracelets* he has in a special case.

Shadow 6: Sarah, you're right, we're family. Hey, listen; I tell you what, to celebrate our new facility I am going to give you guys tomorrow off. Tell the others. Go have some fun.

Sarah gets a big grin on her face over the good news. Agent Green enters the room.

Agent Green: I'll handle those kids; they'll be taking orders from me from now on.

Shadow 6: No dice.

Agent Green: What?

Shadow 6: I'm coming with you. I don't think you can be trusted with my team.

Agent Green: But I thought...

Shadow 6: Just carrying out a promise to a dying friend, Agent Green.

Shadow 6 walks past Agent Green and out the door...

CHAPTER 13

DISRESPECT CAN GET YOU DEAD

THE UNITED STATES LOS ANGELES NATIONAL CEMETERY

A Military Ceremony takes place at the cemetery honoring "Those Who Served". Ten caskets line up in a reserved area of the cemetery. US flags are draped over the ten caskets, nine of the caskets for the fallen Shadow Warriors and one for their leader and mentor Eric Stone.

A priest and a rabbi give sermons before the final burial. The playing of "Taps' is played by a lone bugler. The folding and presenting of the flag takes place. Each of the individual flags is presented to each of the spouses of the fallen Shadow Warriors.

Shadow 6 and the young warriors are in attendance. There isn't a dry eye in the house. A folded flag from Eric Stone's casket is presented to Shadow 6.

Fighter jets in "missing man formation" by the United States Air Force perform an aerial flyover. The formation of a rifle party consisting of 7 service members, fire a **three-volley salute**. A "**Final Salute**" is given. The caskets enter the ground.

Shadow 6: From dust to dust. I will forever miss you my dear friend.

Tears roll down Shadow 6's face.

VENICE BEACH, CALIFORNIA

The young Warriors gather in Venice Beach with their skateboards and bicycles.

Venice beach was originally a haven for the hippie generation of poets, painters, and artists. Venice today stands out as a vibrant, cultural, circus-like atmosphere neighborhood in LA. Famous for its boardwalk, graffiti art, surfing, skateboarding, cycling, and bohemian lifestyle, Venice's authenticity and eccentric flavor is what gives it an edge over the Santa Monica neighboring community.

Venice is a beach city full of character, individuality, giving its visitors an upbeat and creative vibe with a dose of alternative culture, as well as access to local, independent shops and cafes with a style all of their own.

As the Young Warriors, all in street clothes, play with their skateboards and bicycles, we can see the vibrant murals along the Boardwalk, alleyways, and side shops while people get approached by vendors and singing hopefuls and artists with their wears and cd's.

They skaters pass a group of kids break-dancing, people demonstrating broken glass walking, sword swallowing, fire breathers, mimes, musicians, jugglers, jesters, and everything in between. The Warriors laugh and joke as they argue as to whether they should have their "fortune" read, get a temporary tattoo or have their name written on a grain of rice.

Unique arts and crafts, odds and ends and one of kind's only obtainable wears, paintings, photos, rocks of various sorts and sculptures and more are offered to the Warriors as they skate pass the Venice Beach corridor. They rummage through every sort of t-shirt under the sun, from the politically motivated to sexually charged to the plain old Venice Beach t-shirt.

They window shop through tattoo and piercing stores, skate and surf shops, medical marijuana dispensaries, sun glasses shops, beer stands and shoe stores.

They pass "Muscle Beach" as they playfully interact with each other and others on the street. Muscle Beach was the exclusive Santa Monica location that marked the birthplace of the physical fitness boom in the US during the 20th century. It started in 1934 with predominantly gymnastics activities on the south side of the Santa Monica Pier.

Today *Muscle Beach Venice* is the contemporary title of the outdoor weightlifting platform constructed in Venice, 18 years after Muscle Beach was established.

The Warriors skate their skateboards on ramps and perform jumps, while others do wheelies on their bikes. Some talk to strangers they meet. Tom *(The Leopard)* gets on the skating ramp and continues to go around and around the ramp gaining incredible speed. Everyone clears the ramps watching in amazement with the feeling that something really unusual is about to happen.

Tom reaches a top speed and is catapulted twenty feet in the air, he is separated from his skateboard as he performs "air summersaults", and he finishes with an incredible "split". He lands back on the skateboard and back on the ramp. The crowd goes wild, cheering, and applauding. The rest of the Warriors are shaking their heads and motioning for Tom not to show off, but their warnings come too late.

People chase Tom to talk to him and congratulate him, but joined by the Young Warriors they make a quick getaway from the Boardwalk, hop into the Hummers and leave the beach.

THE BOSSES' MANSION

Several limousines, all windows tinted, all keeping close space behind another carry some of the most dangerous "Capo" criminals in the world as they pass through Vipiteno, a beautiful Italian town as it displays a long main road lined with pastel-colored buildings from different eras. The buildings in the town are converted into shops, hotels and restaurants. The road of the town is divided into two parts, the Old Town and the New Town, by a tall clock tower called Zwolferturm.

The residents of the town out on the streets cheerfully wave to the limousines as if they were greeting the President, a movie star or a high government official.

The limousines continue out of town into and up the Alps through winding treacherous roads. The limousines reach a mansion well-hidden and extremely well-guarded. They pass the checkpoint; they stop as they reach a gigantic circular driveway. The passengers start exiting their respective limousines. The crisp cold air and the radiant sun make it for a perfect day in the Alps.

Entering Gabriel Venezie's (The Boss) mansion, the group of criminals are met by a solid marble and gold entryway, twenty foot ceilings with an enormous crystal chandelier resembling the Zenith in Palazzo Morando, trimmed with expensive crystals and diamonds, with light reflecting perfectly through the cut-to-sheer fiery diamonds and crystals and its intricate craftsmanship.

The chandelier hangs boldly and majestically over the center of the entryway embraced by two breathtaking stairways on each side of the 60-foot hallway. A gold elevator sits between the stairways.

The "guests" are ushered to a conference room with a 20-foot marble table. As all the guests arrive the giant conference table fills up with representatives from all the major crime syndicates around the world. They comprise UNITY, the largest united crime organization in the world.

From a grand double door enters the "Boss", mid-60's in a wheelchair, he's being wheeled by his daughter Gina. She wheels the Boss to the head of the table and parks his chair. The Boss whispers to Gina, she then addresses the room. As she speaks, electronic translator units convey her words in the respective languages used around the room.

Gina: There should be many familiar faces as you look around the room, some old friends, some old enemies, and again we would like to thank you all for putting aside your past differences to unite in this project, which will in the end, be beneficial to each and every one of you.

We can see the scary faces of each of the "Capos" or bosses from each part of the world that composes "UNITY" as Gina introduces them.

Gina: From Tokyo, the Yakuza family's Mr. Taka Onotsu; from Saudi Arabia Sheik Muhammad Ri-Ule; Alihamad, from Beijing, Hang Li Kan of the Kan family dynasty; Ukraine's Mr. Viktor Katsov of the Katstov family; from Israel, Hyman Weiss, and his associates; from Ireland, the infamous Sean O'Roscoe, led by the; from Sicily, and the Americas, Don Francesco Cataldo the "Il *Capo dei Capi*".

The Boss whispers to Gina again.

Sean O'Roscoe: Pardon me lady, but before we get to the meat and potatoes of this, why the hell are you addressing us? I'm the head of my family. I demand respect, a fact that might of escaped that pretty little empty head of yours. The Boss should be addressing us.

The Boss looks up at Sean O'Roscoe, leader of the Irish Mob. Fear succumbs the room, there is a brief pause that seems to last for hours, Gina gives him a look of contempt and continues speaking, totally ignoring O'Roscoe's comment.

Gina: As I was saying...

Sean O'Roscoe: Lady, I don't like being ignored.

As the Boss takes a sip from his glass of water, he calmly takes a 9-millimeter automatic and without missing a beat he squeezes the trigger. One swift shot in the forehead, O'Roscoe collapses. Two bodyguards hurry behind O'Roscoe's seat.

The Boss takes another sip of water from his glass and peacefully continues.

The Boss: Lets' go on then. No more interruptions please.

Sean's thugs scramble around O'Roscoe's limp body.

Daniel O'leary (40's) dark hair, O'Roscoe's second in command, speaks.

Daniel: He is dead.

The Boss: Well, unfortunately, a bullet to the head will do that...

Daniel: But...

The Boss: Quiet, take his seat. Now you're the new Boss of the Irish Family. Welcome.

Sean's men remove the body.

The Boss: (To the Daniel) I trust you will respect the new responsibility bestowed upon you.

The Boss without waiting for a reply, motions to Gina.

The Boss: Go ahead sweetheart.

A holographic image of the Center of operations for the secret "HUB", *"The World Bank"* Headquarters in Geneva appears floating over the table.

The *World Bank* is an international financial institution that provides loans to developing countries for capital programs. It comprises two institutions:

The International Bank for Reconstruction and Development (IBRD), and

The International Development Association (IDA).

The World Bank is a component of the *World Bank Group*, which is part of the United Nations system.

The World Bank's official goal is the reduction of poverty. However, according to its Articles of Agreement, all its decisions must be guided by a commitment to the promotion of foreign investment and international trade and to the facilitation of Capital investment.

Geneva is a city in Switzerland that lies at the southern tip of expansive Lac Léman (Lake Geneva). Headquarters of Europe's United Nations and the Red Cross, it's a global hub for diplomacy and banking. French influence is widespread, from the language to gastronomy and bohemian districts like Carouge.

Currently an estimated one-third of all worldwide funds held outside their country of origin (sometimes called "**offshore**" funds) are kept in Switzerland. In 2001, Swiss banks managed US $2.6 trillion. The following year they handled US $400 billion less which has been attributed to both a **bear market** and stricter regulations on Swiss banking. By 2007 this figure has risen to roughly US$ 2.7 trillion, a record amount. All those funds electronic as well as "hard cash", gold, silver, and precious stones are transferred in secret to a hidden location called the "HUB" or "Center of Operations for The World Bank".

Gina: Gentlemen, you are looking at what we call the "HUB", the well-hidden and extremely protected World Bank Headquarters in Geneva. We will begin there.

We see Agent Maggie Reynolds, 30 years old, 5'7" hair down to her shoulders, sparkling green eyes, beautiful face and figure, posing as a secretary, bringing in another glass of water for the Boss. She takes a good look at the bank holograph, studying it for her report.

Agent Maggie Reynolds

Her vibrant young beauty makes the young agent mesmerizing to the eyes of those around her. Maggie's specialty for the CIA is undercover work. For a year she has been infiltrating the Unity organization and has worked her way to a position as Gabriel Venezie's (The Boss) personal secretary. She is a Harvard Law graduate. This is her third undercover operation. She is strictly a "by the book agent".

Gina (continuing) This is the greatest secret banking institution in the world, but not for long. Gentlemen, in five days, we will be the only financial institution left. There isn't anything or anyone that could possibly stop us. With your help we will make sure that "*Candy*" is migrated into every banking mainframe in the world. You all received private instructions in writing prior to your arrival. The envelope with further instructions is sitting in front of you. Please read them in confidence now.

All the crime lords open up their envelopes. Each one of them finds a sheet of clear hard plastic with a one-inch circle on the right hand corner.

Gina: Please place your right thumb in the circle gentlemen.

As the group follows the instructions we see large letters appear across the plastic. They read "AUTHORIZED". The letters fade and the instructions slowly appear in its place.

The "Boss" motions to one of his bodyguards by slightly tilting his head to the left, towards the door. With his right hand he makes a sawing motion over his left thumb. The bodyguard leaves the room and comes back with O'Roscoe's thumb. He places it on the conference table in front of *O'leary*.

The Boss smiles at O'Leary and nods. O'leary picks up the thumb and uses it on the clear hard plastic.

221

The criminals read their individual instructions: "Japan Crime Lord, Insert disk into Yahoo headquarters, Tokyo. *Unity* will blow the main HUB"; Mexican Crime Lord, "insert disk into AT&T headquarters, Mexico city. *Unity* will blow the main HUB".

Each Crime Lord reads their instructions. *The Boss* hands his plastic card to his secretary. As he presses the circle with his thumb, it reads: *"Insert the "Candy" disk with the "virus" into the HUB'S mainframe. The password is "deceit".*

The letters on the plastic begin to disappear slowly.

Gina (continuing) You all know what to do when you reach your assigned destination. Let's get to work gentlemen. Meeting adjourned.

The Boss: (directing his comments to Daniel) any comments or objections from you Daniel?

Everyone in the room sits silently.

The Boss (continued) Bravo then, (clapping his hands) I see we're all in accordance, so let's carry on.

UNDERCOVER FACILITY-LOS ANGELES

Outside the new undercover facility downtown Los Angeles in the middle of the night, a black Suburban arrives at a dark alley. Two bums are sitting by a lone doorway. As the SUV approaches, Agent Green, who is driving the SUV, flashes his badge for identification. The bums acknowledge and quickly open the overhead door. The SUV drives inside.

Agent Green: (to agent Lopez) those overrated kids will flip when they see how high tech this facility is.

VENEZIE'S MANSION

Inside the Boss' mansion, the dining room reveals a lavish setting with a 20-foot dining table; Van Gogh's hanging on the walls, silk curtains with gold decorations. Silver and gold candelabras and solid oak chairs surround the lavish table.

The Boss is eating his dinner; a slightly sizzled steak. Tex enters the room.

The Boss: What is it?

Tex: These so-called crime lords are common thieves. They're nothing more than morons in nice clothes.

The Boss: Your point?

Tex: Why do we need them?

The Boss: No man stands alone Tex.

Tex: But you're not alone, you have Gina, myself, and a small army at your command. I don't see how bringing together all these street thugs and drug dealers is going to help our cause.

The Boss: There are many things you don't see Tex.

Tex: Maybe I choose to have people believe that.

The Boss: The virus has to enter into each selected bank at the source. How do you propose we do this? Are you going to be the one breaking into fifty heavily fortified buildings all over the world at precisely the same time?

Tex : No. Our own men could. We don't need to share with scum.

The Boss: Just keep your ill thoughts to yourself. I'm the Boss for a reason, Tex.

Tex: No offense intended. I wasn't doubting you; I am just protecting what is rightfully ours.

The Boss: Forget about it Tex. It is your tenacity and character that will make you my perfect successor. Tomorrow at midnight, it begins. In two days the virus will be circulating through every system in the world.

Tex: So what's next?

The Boss: Clean up the mess my daughter left of the Shadow unit.

Tex: But the only survivors were the kids, sir.

The Boss: No matter. Don't underestimate this particular unit, besides, there was one more survivor left from the old crew, their leader, Shadow 6. Go after him, as I know for sure he's planning to come after us.

Tex: It'll take him years to be effective with this new team.

The Boss: First, underestimating the enemy is a crime in any situation. Second kids through history have always been the real warriors.

Tex: I'm not underestimating Shadow 6, sir. He is overrated, always was. He doesn't have the edge, the guts, (with a smirk on his face and raising one eyebrow)...or my talent.

Tex begins to walk away.

The Boss: Tex, overconfidence may be your downfall one day. Do as I suggest and when you are done bring me those *wrist bands* too; they're important in fulfilling our plan.

Tex: *Bracelets.*

The Boss: Whatever Tex, just get them to me.

We see three of the Warrior's Bracelets in a display cabinet on the Boss's desk.

The Boss: It's time I complete my collection. Nine is the magic number.

Tex looks at the bracelet on his wrist.

The Boss: And Tex, make sure that bastard, Stone, is dead. I'm in this chair because of him. Keep your eye on the ball. I want the *wrist bands*...all of them and a member of their unit. It'll be good insurance.

Tex: Did you try them on, the bracelets?

The Boss: Oh, no. I am not making that mistake. I need them all, and then we'll figure out how we can wear them without harm.

The Boss bangs his fists on the armrests of the chairs.

Tex: Yes, sir. By the way, Stone is already dead, courtesy of our friends from the land of black gold.

In a violent rage, The Boss screams to the top of his lungs.

The Boss: If he's dead, then bring me his corpse. I want the proof.

Tex looks back with a smirk on his face. He exits.

As Tex and the Boss speak, Maggie Reynolds peeks into the room from a crack in the doorway, where she has been eavesdropping the whole time. She slowly backs away. She enters the bathroom, locking the door behind her. She opens up a compact from her purse. The compact converts into a communication device. She speaks into it.

Agent Maggie Reynolds: They're planning a break-in of secret location of The World Bank Headquarters in Geneva, requesting instructions.

She closes the compact as somebody knocks on the door.

Agent Maggie Reynolds: I'll be right out.

Maggie turns on the faucet, wets her hands, then dries them. When she opens the door, she is met by VICTOR, 40's, 6'7" thick and muscular, who holds up a pistol pointing it at Maggie.

Victor: Hello dearie, spying is dirty work, isn't it? But I see you remembered to wash your hands. Victor points to the ceiling, where a tiny eye of a camera can be seen, camouflaged by the bathroom decor.

Victor (continuing) We have them all over the house, audio and video. I know what you're thinking; a camera in the bathroom, that's highly invasive, maybe even immoral! Well, you see... bottom line, Agent Sweet Cheeks, we are... hmmm...criminals!

UNDERCOVER FACILITY-LOS ANGELES

At night time inside the new undercover facility Shadow 6 and the kids are walking through, checking things out.

Jimmy: Wow, would you look at all this stuff. This place must have cost a fortune.

Agent Lopez Half a billion dollars to round it off, so don't touch anything.

Jimmy scoffs at this. Max finds the computer network center.

Max enters the computer center mesmerized.

Max: Oh my god, this is the most sophisticated computer Network I've ever seen. I could... I could, well; there isn't anything I couldn't do with a network like this.

Agent Lopez: Good, that's what I want to hear.

Shadow 6 walks into his new office. He places the picture of Tex, Eric, and him on the desk as Ethan enters the room.

Ethan: Is that you with General Stone?

Shadow 6: A long time ago.

Ethan: Who's the other kid?

Shadow 6: His name is Tex Murphy. He was a childhood friend. He went on to be an accomplished SOG operative.

*Special Operations Group (SOG) is the department within SAD (Special Activities Division) responsible for operations that include high threat military or covert operations with which the **U.S. government** does not wish to be overtly associated.*

As such, members of the unit (called Paramilitary Operations Officers and Specialized Skills Officers) normally do not carry any objects or clothing (e.g., military uniforms) that would associate them with the United States *government. If they are compromised during a mission, the United States government may **deny all knowledge**.*

SOG is generally considered the most secretive special operations force in the United States.

Ethan: Special Operations Group. What happened to him?

Shadow 6: Yes Ethan, a CIA Black Ops unit, real bad guys. They're bred and trained for only one thing. He wasn't the loyal type, and he could never handle being part of a team. He had the lone wolf syndrome.

Ethan: So he quit?

Shadow 6: He faked his death and became a mercenary. A gun for hire. He sells to the highest bidder, sometimes making millions for a single hit.

Ethan: Must be loaded.

Shadow 6: And now he's using that money for evil purposes.

Ethan: Wow, Darth Vader.

Shadow 6: You're not far from the truth. He had his team build the most innovative and cutting edge weapons that money can buy. We can't underestimate his group of Mercenaries – they're the best in the world.

Ethan: I'd like to meet him and take him down.

Shadow 6: No you wouldn't, that I can guarantee you.

Agent Green enters the room.

Agent Green: We just got word from our agent in Milan; they're going after the HUB in Geneva. We fly in four hours.

Shadow 6: If any of our Young Warriors gets killed I am personally coming after you.

Agent Green: You got your orders, just follow them. Agent Green leaves the room.

Ethan: What should we do?

Shadow 6: We follow rule number one.

Ethan: We do as we're told?

Shadow 6: Correct. Go get the others, meet me in the training center.

Darkness falls, several box trucks pull up in front of the House of International Banking building. Dozens of armed men jump out of the backs of the trucks and storm into the bank.

CHAPTER 14

CANDY MURDER & ROCK AND ROLL

TRAINING FACILITY

Night slowly falls upon the city. An exact replica of the old *Training Hall* was now built in the new facility. Inside the *Training Hall* of the new facility, the room is lit with candles. As nine Young Warriors sit around in a circle, silent, Shadow 6 stands before them.

Shadow 6: This will be your first mission. Some of you, if not all, might have to kill or be killed. Sometimes we don't have a choice in these matters. We are missing three *Bracelets* and some of you won't be able to effectively communicate with the rest of the group.

As you know for security reasons, we can't use the standard agents' communication system, so all of you must be extra cautious on this mission. Tom, Mike, Will. Any concerns? Tell me now so we can deal with it.

Tom And Mike: No problem with us, sir.

Will: I am in, sir.

Shadow 6: Tom, Mike, Will, we need your skills, but we are missing your *Bracelets*. Warriors, they'll be running a great risk without their *Bracelets*. They won't have visual or audio of your locations; therefore, you must make sure you never allow them to detach themselves from the unit.

Without those three *Bracelets* they will only have limited communication with the group. Use Sign Language whenever you can and always be within eye contact of one of them. Understood?

The Warriors: Yes, sir.

Tom Mike and Will: We won't let you down, sir.

Shadow 6: Okay then. You have now completed your journey, but the training will never end. You will find that as you wear these sacred *Bracelets* your thirst for knowledge will constantly increase. Your awareness of each other, as well as your knowledge of each other's thinking pattern and behavior will increase as if they were your own.

You will become one mind, one body, and one soul that can be in nine different places at the same time. Your powers and the knowledge of your fighting techniques will automatically transfer to the rest of the group as long as you are wearing the *Bracelets*. Make me proud. I believe in you. You're now the new "Shadow Warriors". When in doubt "Let the Darkness be your friend"...and "remember the way... our way".

Agent green is standing in the corner. He walks over to Shadow 6 and stands in front of him.

Agent Green: This is boring. Let's go, we still have to brief you guys before we leave.

Shadow 6: Students, rise.

Agent Green: C'mon, time is money.

Shadow 6: (with solemn calm) Students, agent Green needs a quick explanation of the riddle of the "Kyoki".

Kyoki: Japanese meaning: Sobbing, weeping.

231

The Riddle of The Kyoki is put forth by sorcerers casting a spell through Arcane cards spell, representing the magic woven by kami (Great Spirits), the art typically depicts mortals getting enlightened or influenced by the spirits. The Riddle of the Kyoki is the Eater of Minds, Corrupter of Thoughts, Bringer of Madness, Lord of Fear.

Shadow 6 places the back of his hand on Agent Green's chest and rotates his hand over, striking Agent Green with his palm. Green flies through the door and lands in the hallway from the impact.

Shadow 6: (walking up to Green, as he lays on the ground and kneels over him) I trust you will never disrespect me, us, or what we stand for, ever again. You don't know me Green; don't underestimate what you don't know. I am looking forward to your next interruption, perhaps in the middle of our flight. The "Kyoki" has many riddles and works even better 30,000 feet up in the air.

Kyoki is the Mad Devil, mad Ghost. The riddles of the Kyoki is a series of "play on words" riddles.

Agent Green lays on the ground in shock.

Shadow 6 (continuing): (to the warriors) Everyone get ready, I have to say "good-bye" to an old friend. I'll catch up to you.

LOS ANGELES NATIONAL CEMETERY

The Los Angeles National Cemetery is a United States National Cemetery in Sawtelle, an unincorporated West Los Angeles community in Los Angeles County, California. The cemetery was dedicated on May 22, 1889. It is directly connected to the central Veterans Home facilities by Constitution Avenue's underpass below freeway.

At the Los Angeles National Cemetery, of West Los Angeles, Shadow 6 salutes his nine fallen Warriors and stands over the fresh grave of Eric Stone. He lays a single black rose upon it.

Shadow 6: Rest in peace, my friend.

HOUSE OF INTERNATIONAL BANKING

Inside the House of International Banking Lobby, several guards on the night watch gather on the front desk going over the supervisor's instructions for their shift as the fortified front door of the Bank gives way to a powerful blast of a large C4 charge.

Pieces of glass and torn steel fly in every direction. The sound is deafening; the guards attempt to take cover and draw their weapons to no avail. The intruders are too quick, too well organized, and with the element of surprise they are too much to handle by the unsuspecting guards.

All the guards are shot down quickly by the dozens of armed men led by Gina Venezie charging thorough the blown entrance of the building where the doors once kept the interior of the bank safe and protected. From the dark shadows of the night the ever-imposing figure of Tex enters the bank.

Gina: Let's go! We're on a schedule!

CARGO JET

The young Warriors are tightening up their gear inside the cargo jet. The freighter displays a wide/tall fuselage cross-section, a **high-wing** to allow the cargo area to sit near the ground, a large number of wheels to allow it to land at unprepared locations, and a high-mounted tail to allow cargo to be driven directly into and off the aircraft. The inside carries only the Young Warriors, Shadow 6, Elisa, and Agent Lopez. Shadow 6 and agent Lopez go over some photos.

Agent Lopez: Now, here are the blue prints of the HUB.

Shadow 6: The place looks like Fort Knox.

Agent Lopez: This place makes Fort Knox look like a guard shack. Every international banking transaction in the world goes through here. They keep it locked up tight and secure.

Shadow 6: Call the Swiss Authorities and their security to handle this.

Agent Lopez: We can't risk a leak. Anyone could be on *Unity's* payroll, as you mentioned, many times. *Unity* will be bringing a hacker inside the building, so he can access the Closed Network System. It's the only way to send their virus online to every bank on earth at the same time.

Shadow 6: Then someone on each individual bank has to open the contents so the virus is spread correct?

Agent Lopez: Correct.

Shadow 6: That means that Unity has men in every banking institution headquarters right now, all at the same time waiting for the virus so they can activate it.

Agent Lopez: You are right again, hard to stop that, it would take too much Federal manpower.

Shadow 6: Then we can't allow that main HUB to get infected.

Agent Lopez: Right again, we can't allow that.

Shadow 6: So where do we come in?

Agent Lopez: You'll rendezvous with our insider, special agent Reynolds, who will be waiting for you in the building.

Shadow 6: Then what?

Agent Lopez: Stop the bad guys! Do I have to hold your hand through all this? I thought you were a professional.

Shadow 6: Right. So you don't have a plan. You're either way stupid, or you play ball for the other team. I can see why they don't let you do any meaningful work.

Agent Lopez stares at Shadow 6, he starts to get the impression that Shadow 6 knows more than he leads on. Agent Lopez turns away and speaks to the Young Warriors.

Agent Lopez: Everyone get ready, we're getting close to our target.

The large rear cargo door opens slowly.

Shadow 6: (to the warriors) Warriors, when you clear the craft, pull the red cord. Once you hit "Terra Firma" it's too late.

Max: Oh, my lord, our leader made a joke, ha, ha, ha…

Sarah: Yes, but you won't be laughing when you splat on the ground.

Ethan: Hmmm, sassy.

Carmen: He is so adorable when he jokes around.

Jimmy: He never joked around before, how can you tell?

Mike: Warriors pay attention; he said hit the ground then pull the red cord!

Tom: Ha, ha...

William: I don't know this group; I take no responsibility for the dead here. Alexa, did you get that?

Alexa: Yes, I am blind, not deaf... my red cord is in Brail... ha...ha...ha...

Alexa jumps off the plane.

Shadow 6: Alexa wait!!!

Shadow 6 hands each of the Warriors instructions.

Shadow 6: Hurry, these are your instructions. Fill in Alexa if she doesn't kill herself out there. I will have the pilot loop back around before you jump so we don't lose Alexa.

Jimmy: Sir, she is the last one I would worry about.

Shadow 6: I agree son, I agree.

They open the envelopes and read them. "Rendezvous point, Rêve d'O Club, 19 Rue de la Coulouvrenière, Geneva. Target, Hanz Freedman, white male, 6'2", 310 Lbs. courier for "Candy". Hand off Wolfgang Schmitt, private room in club Rêve d'O. Transportation, motorbikes; cover dress, punk-rock disguise.

Mike: Punk Rockers?

Sarah: Motorcycles?

Shadow 6: Just follow them EXACTLY as I instructed.

Shadow 6 walks past Agent Green on his way to his seat.

Shadow 6: How's the chest? The rear door is open and you have no chute, should we resolve another riddle?

Shadow 6 winks. Agent Green gives him a dirty Look.

The Warriors jump out. Minutes later Shadow 6 and Elisa exit the plane.

The eight Warriors fall from the sky directing their parachutes to the designated meeting spot as the sun starts settling in the horizon. Alexa is sitting on the ground in a yoga position.

They land on the arranged location; they hide their parachutes in the brushes nearby and hop on to the main road. Crossing over the road, they spot an old deserted barn. They enter the barn to find nine Ducati 1098's. Each bike has a backpack strapped to the side of it.

Carmen examines the motorcycles carefully.

Carmen: Guys, these have L-Twin Cylinder Engines. Hmm, 4 valves per cylinder, desmodromic, and liquid cooled. Awesome!

William: Really? Who cares about the mumbo jumbo? Can they go fast?

Carmen: Well, Their top speed is about 169 mph – about 271 kilometers per hour.

Ethan: What are we waiting for? Let's test these puppies at top speed!

Alexa: I will ride dead center; I can sense my path by the noise of the bikes, the wind pressure, and your stupid jokes.

They all laugh admiring Alexa's guts and abilities even with her handicap.

OUTSIDE THE BARN – MAIN ROAD

The Young Warriors travel in a *Delta Formation* taking on the twists and curves of the road, quickly approaching the bikes' top speed.

Two Young Warriors as wingmen on each side of the leader, one Warrior bringing up the rear and followed by the last three of the nine Warriors traveling in "V" form behind them. They wear state of the art Communicator helmets and full protection gear.

Birds fly away in fear, grazing animals on each side of the road run for cover, the sound of the outdoors is completely drowned by the deafening sound of the nine bikes traveling in unison.

Nighttime overtakes the Young Warriors. They now all travel wearing night vision goggles, for the exception of Alexa of course.

GENEVA RÊVE D'O NIGHTCLUB - Night Time

The club is built of an exposed-metal interior converted from an old riverfront warehouse that vibrates nightly to hardcore techno, with occasional forays into drum'n bass and triphop.

The Young Warriors all dressed in punked-out leather, spikes and chains, ride up outside the club on their newly inherited motorbikes. Their ultra high performance bikes look like a dealership display, all black, all shiny, all brand new.

The Warriors remove their helmets and night vision goggles and smile at each other while listening to the music blaring from inside the club.

Will: This is the place.

Outside a group of girls greet the warriors.

French Girl: Nous y voilà!!! Le jour J'est enfin arrivé après des semaines de préparations ...

Y attendons nombreux ce soir soirée de folie.

Jimmy: We are Americans! Good to meet you.

French Girl: We, I love Americans. Welcome with us.

Jimmy: Ok, thanks

Warriors: What's up?

Jimmy speaks with a thick French accent.

Jimmy: They jave been preparing foo weeks for thiiis krazy party, it's going to ve wild, and ve can shoin them if ve vant.

Mike: That is way cool.

Jimmy: Fjrench giurls love us, aha.

The Young Warriors laugh. They get off their bikes and enter the club; all eyes are on them. At the door they all receive a mask as part of the annual carnival party.

BACK ON THE ROAD

Shadow 6 drives the SUV through the pitch-black roads of Geneva. Elisa rides shotgun.

Elisa: 6, where's this nightclub? It's supposed to be along this road. You sure we got the right coordinates?

Shadow 6: I'm positive.

They notice a group of motorcycles parked outside a nightclub.

Elisa: (sarcastically) I have a feeling we found the children dear.

They stop and park.

INSIDE THE RÈVE D'O NIGHTCLUB

Inside the Rêve d'o nightclub club the nine Warriors wear carnival type masks, in all colored leather outfits, with blue, green, and red dye in their hair as they join the costume party.

The room is semi dark, Inflatable LED stars of every color hang from the 40' ceiling of the warehouse club. A full color disco party nightclub ceiling decoration lights up the warehouse ceiling.

Loud rock music blasts throughout the warehouse, state of the art sound-activated LED stage and DJ ceiling disco nightclub lights go on and off with the beat of every song. The club is crowded to the max and teens start to line up outside the club's door as security prevents them from entering until some of the patrons leave the club and the masses thin out.

CLUB OFFICE

Sitting in the night club managers' office, Agent Lopez and Green are in a heated conversation with *Wolfgang Schmitt,*

(40's) dark hair, well built, member of the *Blackwater Mercenary Team*. Wolfgang sits in a chair behind a large mahogany desk.

Agent Green: (directing his conversation to *Wolfgang*) This is a great opportunity. The agents from SI-9 are arriving here to get the 'disk'; we can overpower them and remove their *Bracelets* and "The Boss" will have what he wants.

Wolfgang: Where is the disk now?

DANCE FLOOR

Back at the dancing floor, the Warriors follow someone who fits the description of Hanz Freedman throughout the club. The "pack" of Warriors encircles Freedman as they begin the "hunt", closing in on their prey.

Carmen passes Freedman and sprays a mist on his face that temporarily blinds and disorients him. He coughs and gags.

CLUB OFFICE

In the clubs office the conversation with Agent Lopez and the member of the Blackwater Mercenary Team continues.

Agent Lopez: Some guy by the name of Hanz has it and is scheduled to deliver it to you here...about now.

Wolfgang: What? Hanz? That man is an idiot, I should know, he's my half-brother. Those kids will take the 'disk' from him. Get out there, make sure he makes it here, and the 'disk' is unharmed.

Green and Lopez head towards the dance floor when they spot the 'Warriors'.

Agent Lopez: (stopping Green by the arm) We can't go out there, we'll be compromised.

Reaching under the desk, Wolfgang pulls out two automatic weapons.

Wolfgang: Get out there now, or die in this office. Better compromised than dead...you think?

The agents hurry out to the dance floor, seeking cover behind the patrons so the Warriors won't spot them. Wolfgang follows looking for his brother and the Warriors.

In the dance floor Hanz stumbles and falls unto Jimmy, who skillfully and unnoticed grabs the disk out of Hanz's pocket and passes it to Will. Will then passes it to Tom who hands it off to Sarah as she dances away.

Freedman slowly comes to and notices that the "Candy" disk is gone as Wolfgang's bodyguards approach him to take him to the private office.

Hanz Freedman: (Yelling in desperation in a French accent) Ze disk! Ze disk is gone!

Hanz Freedman points to Jimmy.

Hanz Freedman: He picked my pocket, he has it!

Bullets fly from the office and everyone scatters to safety.

The bodyguards go after Jimmy. The Warriors form a circle of protection around him. The biggest of the bodyguards steps forward and rushes Jimmy. The circle opens up to let him through and Jimmy engages him, Hitting him with such force that he crashes through the second floor window.

As bullets start flying from the gangster's guns, everyone rushes out of the club through any means possible. Agents

242

Green and Lopez sneak out the building through a side door.

Outside a mosh pit of young partygoers are waiting to get in to the club as they dance and jump to the music heard from inside which muffles the sounds of the bullets. They hear the glass shattering from above as broken pieces fall on them. The crowd looks up to see the bodyguard flying out the window.

Hundreds of hands rise as if to catch him, and then suddenly they all move away as the bodyguard hits the ground with a deep bellowing thud. Hundreds of people rush out through the front door and windows.

Shadow 6 and Elisa watch from the suburban.

Shadow 6: Hmmm.

Elisa: We found our children... Hey?

Shadow 6: (In a low voice) We sure have. (Raising his voice) We better get them; we have a mission to finish.

Elisa: Let me get them, it'll only be a second.

Elisa jumps out of the SUV as the last of the patrons run out.

Elisa, cautiously walks into the bar with a sexy walk. She finds the Warriors standing back-to-back in a circle, warding off twenty of the Blackwater Mercenaries. The music has stopped and there's a hush throughout the entire club. No one moves.

Elisa: Kids, come to mama, its' time for dinner.

Thug #4: Mama, why don't you leave the kids to get the spanking they deserve and you and I can go in the back room and have some fun.

Thug 3 puts the barrel of his Glock 19" under Elisa's chin. Elisa steps to the side and with her right hand pushes the barrel of the gun to her left away from danger. She holds on to the barrel. With her right knee she strikes the thug in the chest and as he flies back, Elisa extends her leg and strikes the thug in the throat with a front kick.

As the thug falls to the ground Elisa holds his weapon, she releases the magazine with her thumb, the magazine hits the floor, she pulls down both sides of the slide lock lever and pushes the slide forward separating it from the gun. She throws the pieces to the ground – they fall as if in slow motion, bouncing off the nightclub floor.

Rapidly spinning, Elisa releases a rapid-fire succession of nine Shuriken (throwing stars). The Shuriken hit each of nine Blackwater Mercenaries in specific targeted, but non-lethal parts of their bodies. Most of the thugs scatter; a couple stay behind frozen in fear. The Young Warriors start to walk out of the club slowly and carefully.

The Young Warriors turn to insure that they are all making it out safely. Wolfgang runs after a girl on the floor. Mistakenly, Wolfgang shoots down a girl dressed in the same outfit as Sarah.

Wolfgang: Damn SI-9, I will kill you all...

Wolfgang then turns the gun in Elisa's direction.

Max: (Grabbing Sarah's arm) Sarah, that girl was dressed just like you. She was murdered because they thought it was you.

Sarah: Oh, my God.

Tom: These are the merciless killers Shadow 6 warned us against. We'll meet again... On our terms and teach them a lesson they won't forget.

All of the Young Warriors make it safely out of the club. Sarah walks up to Shadow 6 and hands him the disk. Elisa spots Wolfgang pointing a gun at the Young Warriors, ready to fire. Elisa draws her weapon and fires', hitting Wolfgang as his gun goes off and the bullet barely misses Elisa's head. Wolfgang hits the ground dead.

Elisa: (Staring down the remaining thugs) Who's next?

No one dares. Elisa leaves the club.

Shadow 6: (to Elisa as she enters the SUV) A new rock group?

Elisa says nothing.

Shadow 6: Hey, what's eating you?

Elisa: They killed an innocent girl, 6. Just because she was dressed like Sarah.

Shadow 6: You avenged her, even though that won't give her back her life. That is all you could do.

Elisa: You are right Shadow 6, you are right.

Shadow 6: OK then, move on, and let it go. I need you alert.

Shadow 6 and Elisa leave in their Suburban. They are followed by nine motorcycles. Shadow 6 inserts the disc into his laptop and confirms that it contains the anti-virus to "Candy".

Shadow 6: We're being played here. The warehouse, the nightclub and I bet you anything that the bank is also a set-up. I told Eric there was a mole, now I know who it is. We need to get to the World central bank immediately.

Shadow 6 speaks into his *Bracelet*.

Shadow 6: Warriors, follow me to *Credit Europe Bank*, the address is Rue du Mont-Blanc 12, 1201. The HUB is underground within their walls.

Shadow 6 and Elisa race along the dark road followed by the Young Warriors on their motorcycles. Unexpectedly, the night traffic slows down.

Shadow 6: This slowdown is uncharacteristic of late night traffic, something is up.

Shadow 6 and Elisa spot a roadblock up ahead. Five *men in masks*, accompanied by *Local Police* with shotguns and semiautomatic weapons block the road with their vehicles, inspecting everyone in line.

Shadow 6: Hmmm, masked men and fake police? (Speaking into his wrist band) Warriors, trouble ahead. Take evasive action. I think this roadblock is in our honor.

Ethan: (Into His *Bracelet*) Copy that, sir.

Shadow 6: (to the group through his *Bracelet*) Warriors, break off.

The Young Warriors drive off into the woods and dismount from their bikes.

Shadow 6: I think someone is looking for us.

The search gets to the vehicle in front of Shadow 6's Suburban.

Shadow 6: Elisa, handle this. It seems like *Unity's* tentacles reach much further than I realized. This has been a set up from the very beginning. Let's get through this roadblock and get to the bank. We still need to follow orders. And Elisa, please, no more wild exhibitions.

Elisa: You have my word on it. I was just having some fun, but then it quickly turned ugly. I learned my lesson; I won't make that mistake again.

Shadow 6: We need discipline with the team or we'll get them all killed. They are really young and they will easily follow anything that is fun without thinking of the consequences.

Elisa: You got it 6. I am sorry.

The door opens and Elisa walks out with the disposition of a mentally challenged individual. She walks up to the thugs and engages them in conversation.

Nine Warriors masked, wearing all colored leather outfits, slowly approach the roadblock from the wooded area, surveying the situation, as they stealthily position themselves around the perimeter where they can have quick access to the thugs and the armed police.

Distracted by Elisa's crippled mannerism the armed villains let their guard down. Two of them come close enough to

Elisa giving her the opportunity to break into full attack mode.

Elisa throws a flying spinning kick at the head of one of the armed villains and using his falling body as support, she spins again striking the second villain in the solar plexus. Both of them lay knocked down on the side of the road, Elisa strips them of their weapons. The Warriors engage the rest of the Mercenaries disarming them. An all-out battle ensues. The Warriors overcome the thugs and the crooked cops.

"Poise of the Leopard"

The stoic stature of confidence and poise of the Leopard strikes multiple times with incredible agility and unmatched power leaving no room for retaliation from the enemy. His steadfast, skillful, and unforgiving blows are impossible to counter.

Elisa walks away from the scene with a very sexy walk, turns and winks at the Warriors.

The statuesque figure of Shadow 6 looks on, as his team nullifies the threat posed by the thugs.

Shadow 6 walks towards the automobiles. Smoke and dust cover the air. He taps on the side of the cars motioning them to get moving. Shadow 6 and Elisa get back in their truck. The Warriors get back on their bikes and continue following Shadow 6.

Jimmy does a wheelie and pulls next to Ethan. He attempts to smack Ethan in the back of the helmet; Ethan extends his arm with lightning speed and punches Jimmy. Jimmy equally quick blocks the punch. They both laugh.

Shadow 6: (into his *Bracelet*) Stop it! Behave like professionals, or I'll have you turn back.

Alexa: (into her *Bracelet)* They're not professionals, they're children. Get them diapers and a pacifier.

Shadow 6: (into his *Bracelet*) Under my command disobeying a direct order is an act of treason. Do you know what we do to traitors?

Max: (into his Bracelet) What sir?

Shadow 6: (snickering out the window at Carmen) Ban them from playing video games for life.

All the Young Warriors shout at once into their *Bracelets*.

No way!

The "Young Warriors" stop playing around understanding Shadow 6's implication which is much more serious than restricting them from video games.

The Suburban enters the main streets. The group passes Geneva's Red Light District situated in the heart of Pâquis, not far from Gare Cornavin, Gare Routiere, and lakeside on *Rue de Berne Street.*

The streets are very busy and lively, full of exotic restaurants and cafés. People stand outdoors chilling, smoking shisha (tobacco often soaked in molasses or honey and mixed with fruit) and hanging out. Ladies in tights and high heels looking for paying customers are watched from a distance by their bodyguards.

Shadow 6 and the Young Warriors race through, Rue Pellegrino-Rossi, and Rue Docteur-Alfred-Vincent streets. They are now speeding through the center of Geneva's Red

Light District, four minutes away from their Bank destination. Women in red and purple neon windows show themselves off awaiting company. Hookers stand on the corners making their nightly hunt for johns in need.

Shadow 6 and the Young Warriors speed past many sex shops and some nightclubs that make up the unique atmosphere of the Geneva's Quartier Rouge.

CHAPTER 15

BLOWING UP A TRAIN

Moving forward at high speeds, Shadow 6 and The Young Warriors pull to a stop in a dark alley. Shadow 6 jumps out, the "Young Warriors" park their bikes; they all carry the backpacks that were fastened to their bikes.

Elisa waits in the Suburban behind the wheel, monitoring for signs of trouble approaching.

Sarah: Is this it?

Shadow 6: it's half a block over.

Shadow 6 gives out commands.

Shadow 6: Jimmy and Ethan, get on the roof of the bank for surveillance. Carmen and Alexa, across the street on back up. Elisa, you are the wheelman...well, person, keep the car running. Max, on close circuit camera. Alright, everybody knows what to do?

The Young Warriors acknowledge.

Elisa: All set.

Shadow 6: Let's move. As soon as you reach your destination, change into your gear. Remember why we're here; insert the anti-virus at all costs.

Shadow 6 heads to the *Credit Europe Bank building*, as we see the Young Warriors changing into their outfits and start doing their jobs around the building. Shadow 6 looks in a window and sees that the guards at the desk are dead. He walks around to the front of the bank finding the front door blown off. Nobody seems to be around.

Shadow 6: (to himself) We got trouble here, where's my contact?

Shadow 6 carefully walks in through the front door, looking around.

Inside the Bank Shadow 6 investigates, but sees nothing.

Shadow 6: (whispering to himself) Hello, anybody home?

Shadow 6 goes deeper into the bank's lobby looking around, but there isn't a soul in sight.

Shadow 6: (into his *Bracelet*) Warriors, we have trouble here. The front door is blown to bits and there's no security, no cops around. Any visuals?

From the roof of the bank Jimmy replies.

Jimmy: (into his *Bracelet*) Nothing from up here, sir.

Carmen responds from the back of the bank.

Carmen: (into her *Bracelet*) Copy that sir, nothing from down here either.

Unsuspectingly, *Unity's* special unit of hired mercenaries moves in silently toward the Suburban. They surround it, they move swiftly, gassing Elisa. She's out in seconds. The mercenaries remove her from the SUV. She's gone.

Shadow 6: (into his *Bracelet*) Max?

Max looks at his laptop showing the image of the bank. He switches his computer screen to thermal imaging.

Max: (into his *Bracelet*) I've got you on screen. No Thermal temperature changes. Wait-hold on a second, I've got something, lower level, in the basement, one person, looks to be sitting down.

Shadow 6: That's got to be our computer nerd.

Max: (on his *Bracelet*) Yeap.

Shadow 6: (on his *Bracelet*) No offense Max, but do you see it moving?

Max: No sir.

Shadow 6: Make that a dead computer nerd then.

Shadow 6 makes his way through the building, to the basement of the bank. He cautiously creeps around the corner, he hears muffled screams. Upon closer inspection he finds a woman, tied up in a chair with duct tape over her mouth. Shadow 6 tears the tape off her mouth.

Tied Up Woman: Ouch! Easy you jerk!

Shadow 6 stares at the woman as if in a trance. He can't take his eyes off of her. Flashbacks of the Crown's car parked at the old bridge, the shooting, and his parent's faces pass through his mind. Shadow 6 can't believe the incredible similarity of this woman's features to his mother.

Tied Up Woman: Hey! Are you ok? What is wrong with you?

Shadow 6: (showing his badge) Hum, oh…identify yourself.

Agent Maggie Reynolds: Special Agent Reynolds.

Shadow 6: Reynolds?

Agent Maggie Reynolds: Untie me now; the place is wired for demolition. It will implode in a few minutes.

Shadow looks around and spots several sticks of dynamite wrapped together strategically positioned on the main supporting beams.

Shadow 6: (into his *Bracelet*) Ethan, Jimmy, get off the roof.

Jimmy: (into his *Bracelet*) Sir...

Shadow 6: (into his *Bracelet*): Now. Warriors! Code Red! Code Red!

The Warriors start scrambling to gather their things and get off the building. Shadow 6 quickly unties agent Reynolds.

Shadow 6: (under his breath) I hope you can run better than you can spy.

Shadow 6 unties Agent Reynolds.

Agent Maggie Reynolds: I heard that!

The building starts imploding as they flee.

Agent Reynolds and Shadow 6 run for their lives out the front door.

The building implodes as the Young Warriors run towards the Suburban. They all climb in, Shadow 6 jumps into the passenger seat, thinking Elisa is ready to drive off. She's not there. Everyone goes silent. Something has gone horribly wrong. Shadow 6 motions for Sarah to get into the driver's side. She screeches out of the area.

Max: They took her, 6. They killed her?

Shadow 6: (pounding on the dash) No, if they had, her body would be in the car. Damn! If they even think of harming her...

Agent Maggie Reynolds: They took what, whom? The driver?

Everyone goes silent. Sarah continues speeding out of the area.

Agent Maggie Reynolds (continued): Who are ...

Shadow 6: I'm the guy who just saved your life, buckle-up!

Jimmy: The bikes.

Shadow 6: Forget them, there is no time now.

The Young Warriors take off their masks, Reynolds flips.

Agent Maggie Reynolds: They're kids?

Alexa: Who's this chick?

Agent Maggie Reynolds: Are you guys even with the agency?

Shadow 6: SI-9, we're The Shadow unit.

Agent Maggie Reynolds: Bull, stop the truck right now!

Jimmy: Somebody get this lady a drink.

Shadow 6: Jimmy, shut up.

Agent Maggie Reynolds: I call for an extraction and this is what I get? I know about SI-9 and its Warriors, and they're not kids!

Shadow 6: Get something straight right now, these kids, as you refer to them, just pulled you out of the grave, so you could at least show some respect, not to mention one of our senior members has just disappeared.

Agent Maggie Reynolds: The driver.

Shadow 6: Max, contact headquarters, have them give us the coordinates on her tracking device.

Max: Yes sir. Right away, sir. It won't be long before we have a lock on her position.

Agent Maggie Reynolds: My apologies, you're right. It's just...

Shadow 6: Firstly, why did they demolish the bank? Second why were you set to go with it?

Agent Maggie Reynolds: My cover was blown. There must have been a leak in the agency, and I'm not sure why they blew up the bank. Up until tonight, I was under the impression they were going inside to put a virus on the computer system. Guess I was wrong.

Sarah: Where to now, sir?

Shadow 6: Where are their headquarters?

Agent Maggie Reynolds: The Alps past a town named Vipiteno.

Shadow 6: Back to the airport, Sarah.

Agent Maggie Reynolds: Negative. I don't do planes.

Shadow 6: Did you say you were a Federal agent?

Agent Maggie Reynolds: How do you feel about trains?

VENEZIE'S MANSION

Inside Venezie's Mansion in the Italian Alps, the Boss sits at his desk shuffling paperwork and working on his computer. Gina enters the room.

Gina: Father, it's almost 11 PM, you should stop working.

The Boss: I am almost done sweetheart.

Gina: I have good news.

The Boss: Yes?

Gina: The HUB has been destroyed, and we've captured the head of their intelligence unit. We're ready for the next step.

The Boss: Splendid. And my lovely secretary? Miss undercover agent?

Gina: Ashes and dust.

The Boss: Get word to all the families to go ahead with phase three. Get the team together; we're heading to the 'Sanctuary'. Have them take the captured agent there. We'll be on our turf and well protected. They can't get to us there. By the way, we have been informed that the Shadow Warrior Unit will be traveling by train to visit us. Make sure that we leave a present for them on the train.

Gina: Sure dad, right away.

The Boss: And Gina, make sure that it will be the last present they will ever experience in this lifetime, please.

Gina: Absolutely.

The Boss: You make me very proud to be your father Gina.

Gina: Thank you, father.

Gina smiles to herself as she walks away.

THE TRAIN

From his boxcar Max raises Shadow 6 on his *Bracelet*. We hear Max over Shadow 6's bracelet.

Max: Elisa's tracking is live and locked sir. They're on the move.

Shadow 6: Acknowledged. Max, make sure all bracelets are stowed back in the case, we don't want to expose any of your identities.

Max: They're all tucked in sir; I'm on my way to secure mine. Over and out.

In the dining car as the train speeds through the countryside, Shadow 6 and Agent Maggie Reynolds sit on the train eating dinner.

Maggie Reynolds: How's the lasagna?

Shadow 6: (under his breath, staring into space) She better be alive... (out of his trance) I'm sorry, still frozen. What about the Salisbury steak?

Maggie Reynolds: Well it's definitely Salisbury. I don't know how much of it is steak.

Shadow 6: Scary.

Agent Maggie Reynolds: Do you think the kids will be alright back there alone?

Shadow 6 smiles for a second.

Shadow 6: They can take care of themselves

Agent Maggie Reynolds: Are you sure?

Shadow 6: Trust me.

Agent Maggie Reynolds: I just thought that...

Shadow 6: Listen, these kids, as everyone insists on putting it, are highly trained Government agents. If I have to worry about them every second, I rather not have them on a mission with me.

Agent Maggie Reynolds: I suppose you're right. I'm sorry...

Shadow 6: (smiling) Yes, you are. But I'm kind and I forgive you.

Maggie Reynolds: Well Mr. Kind, I'd like to thank you, for saving my life back there.

Shadow 6: It's nothing.

Agent Maggie Reynolds: It definitely was a lot to me.

Shadow 6: Well, you're welcome then, I guess.

Agent Maggie Reynolds: Shadow 6...

Shadow 6: Call me Xavier please.

Agent Maggie Reynolds: Ok, Xavier. At the bank, when you came to rescue me, you just stood there frozen looking at me, what was going on? In your mind I mean.

Shadow 6: Well, this is hard. When I was four years old my parents were both murdered in front of my eyes.

Agent Maggie Reynolds: Xavier I am so sorry.

Shadow 6: Their faces are burned in my mind and I surely miss them both. And when I saw you...

Agent Maggie Reynolds: With all due respect, what does that have to do with me, or the bank...

Shadow 6: With the bank, nothing. With you... well maybe it would be better for me to show you.

Shadow 6 pulls out his cell phone and shows Agent Reynolds a picture of his parents.

Agent Maggie Reynolds: Oh, my... Your mom, it's that your mom?

Shadow 6: Yes it is.

Agent Maggie Reynolds: She...she... is a spitting image of me with blonde hair!

Shadow 6: So you can see how that took me by surprise, Agent Reynolds.

Agent Maggie Reynolds: Please call me Maggie.

Shadow 6: Ok Maggie, that is the reason I froze. Seeing you took me back to my childhood. It was as if I was seeing things and my mother was sending me some message.

Agent Maggie Reynolds: I can assure you I am not your mom.

Shadow 6: Well if you are, you are the youngest looking woman in your 60's that I have ever seen. Where are you from Maggie? Where are your parents from?

Agent Maggie Reynolds: Xavier, I can also assure you that we are not related.

They both laugh.

Agent Maggie Reynolds: My father was from the Ukraine, an exchange student and my mom from Colombia. She moved to the US as a child with her parents. My parents met at Harvard University in their freshman year. They lived the American dream, they wanted me to be a doctor, I wanted to join the FBI and save the world. So I went to Penn State University, graduated, applied with the Bureau, and got accepted.

Shadow 6: Well, there we have something in common; we both want to help the world stay free and get rid of the bad guys.

Agent Maggie Reynolds: Is that what you wanted to grow up to be? What college did you attend?

Shadow 6: Hmmm... in a way... it's a long story, better left for another time.

YOUNG WARRIORS PASSENGER CAR

In the Young Warriors passenger car, Jimmy and Ethan are playing cards while Max is typing on his laptop. Tom, Mike and Will calibrate their weapons and adjust their outfits.

Ethan: So what do you guys think about agent Reynolds?

Jimmy: I think you don't have a chance.

Ethan: Shut up, Jimmy.

Max: She's beautiful, smart, independent, a career girl, with real upward mobility. Yeah, Ethan you don't have a chance.

Ethan tosses a pillow up at Max.

Ethan: Okay, I take it back. Maybe if she was blind, and it was 20 years from now, and...

Jimmy: And she just got out of prison, and was horribly deformed.

They all laugh.

Ethan: I wonder what her first name is.

Tom: Too old, her first name is "Too old for Ethan" lol...

Mike: She could be your mother.

Will: Her first name is Agent, Ethan. Repeat after me... A.g.e.n.t.

ALEXA, SARAH, AND CARMEN - PASSENGER CAR

In the second passenger car Alexa, Sarah and Carmen are relaxing. Alexa is getting her ear pierced by Carmen for the fourth time while Sarah is painting her nails.

Carmen: Now just hold still. I'm almost done.

Sarah: You know we might have to actually kill someone on this mission.

Carmen: Well, only in self-defense. It doesn't make it any better, but the people we are after are ruthless criminals. You saw how that mercenary killed that innocent girl thinking it was you, Sarah.

Sarah: Regardless I don't like the feeling of being an assassin.

Alexa: Killing in self-defense does not make you an assassin.

Sarah: I know but we are after them, so they are defending themselves.

Alexa: We are after them because they are ruthless criminals trying to destroy our way of life, not to mention kill us all.

Sarah: I know, I know...

Alexa: Don't kill anyone then, just let them kill you. When we meet up with Tex, or Gina, I'll let them know how you feel. I'll tell them to make it quick and painless.

Carmen: Incredible, Alexa! You don't have to put it that way.

Alexa: I do Carmen. It is our job. We are government agents defending the probable collapse of our country's financial system as we know it. We are going to be acting in self-defense. We aren't going after traffic violators. The ruthless killers that we're after want to destroy our country, our friends, our family.

Sarah: And us, as you say, I guess.

Carmen: There's no guessing in that, they murdered the whole senior Warrior team. That mercenary killed an innocent girl in cold blood. In their minds, we're next.

Alexa gets frustrated with Carmen and Sarah's soft attitude.

Alexa: Great, so act like government agents, not nurses aids at a retirement home debating whether we should kill some old folks or not because they refused a deep enema.

They all burst out laughing at Alexa's comment.

Sarah: You are a trip Alexa. But you are right, let's give them plenty of reasons to try to eliminate us.

Alexa: People like this murdered my parents. They need to be stopped.

Sarah: You're right, we need to be strong, too many lives and our freedom, and the freedom of America depend on us.

Carmen: We know how you feel inside Sarah, but you have to overcome those feelings or they'll get all of us killed. We were chosen; we can't let our country down.

Alexa uncomfortable with the conversation and trying to avoid getting more worked up walks out of the room.

As the train keeps on gobbling mile after mile of beautiful nighttime countryside, Alexa walks down the hall to the bathroom, as she is about to close the door behind her, *Four Assassins* creep down the hall towards the *Young Warriors* rooms.

Another group of assassins break into Shadow 6's room and begin rummaging through his things. They find the brief case with the *Bracelets* in it.

Assassin One: Bingo! I got the hardware, now, let's get those kids.

Out of the bathroom now, Alexa walks back to her room. As she opens the door, she walks into a deafening silence. She senses the change in the atmosphere. A negative, dark energy is emitted by the assassins who are holding Sarah and Carmen at gunpoint. She freezes, assesses the environment, assumes a stance to secure her footing then adopts the Toh position of Kuji Kiri and addresses the evil within the room.

TOH: A state of harmony which one maintains with tolerance, humility and a spirit of forceless adaptation. A state readiness with calm and easiness to flow with the aggression of a foe and use its force against him to defeat him.

Alexa: (in an eerie whisper) I... hear... you... breathing...

With lightning speed Alexa spins on one leg and strikes the assassin behind the door killing him instantly. She then assumes the Pyō position of Kuji Kiri, hands clasped in front of her chest and feet together.

Pyō, or the seal of the great thunderbolt, enables a ninja to direct his energy. When fully charged, the ninja can quite easily crush a skull with one hand or rip the beating heart from an adult panda. The seal of Pyō is a particularly complex one.

She then speaks again...

Alexa (continued): In darkness there's sin... (inhales) in darkness there's death... (inhales) sin negates spirit and the killing of you all here today without spirit... can only be looked on as an act of charity.

She then smiles. Tom, Mike and Will walk into the room, see the commotion and join in to help. Alexa springs into action, as do the other girls and a battle begins.

"The Ghost in the Darkness"

She can't see nor can she be seen. Her senses are able to detect things that the average human eye cannot. Her twists, turns and spins as she strikes frustrate and instills fear in her attackers... The Ghost cannot be engaged, those who dare try, pay with their lives.

Back in the boy's passenger car Max is still typing, Jimmy and Ethan still playing cards. They hear a thumping sound.

Max: Did you guys hear that?

Jimmy notices that two men with machine guns have repelled outside their window and are hanging there ready to fire. He yells out.

Jimmy: Get down!

The room erupts in gunfire from outside the window and the boys duck as not to be hit. The shooting finally stops. The gunmen start reloading.

Ethan: Max, go warn Shadow 6! Get everyone to suit up.

Jimmy and Ethan dive out the window at the two gunmen, as Max runs out of the room. Jimmy strikes his target in the throat with a punch as he grasps the rope. Ethan with the force of a "Tiger" slashes away at his opponent in midair. The two gunmen fall to their death. Ethan and Jimmy come swinging back through the broken windows.

As Max exits the room, running through the train's corridor, he finds himself in a gauntlet of assassins. Max, 'The Eagle' flies into action, kicking and striking his way through them.

"Talons of the Eagle"

Majestically and with vicious intent, the Eagle claws through its opponents, each becoming a trophy of death as their bodies hit the ground gasping for their last breath. Its power, relentless striking, and pride are complemented by an unyielding barrage of commanding and mighty slices from its wings, making it one of the most feared animals of the Lin Kuei System.

DINING CAR

In the dining area Maggie Reynolds is pouring cream in her coffee; the dining room is quiet and only the sounds of the train grinding its way through the tracks can be heard. Agent Reynolds thinks she heard a strange noise and questions Shadow 6.

Agent Maggie Reynolds: Did you hear something?

Shadow 6: Train sounds.

Agent Maggie Reynolds: I love trains. Planes have always given me the chills, with all the things that can go wrong up in the air, storms, mechanical failure, human error...

TRAIN CART

In the last train cart of the running train, Tex waits as the assassin with the *Bracelets* arrives. The assassin opens the case for him.

Assassin: Six Bracelets.

Tex: Very good. Now activate the relays, blow the train, and let's get out of here.

Suddenly six Warriors in full gear enter the cart where Tex and his assassins are about to exit.

Alexa: Now that is so rude, trying to leave us with a bang. And not saying goodbye?

Carmen: The Ghost is right; you're not supposed to leave without saying goodbye.

Tex looks up at them and smiles.

Tex: As you wish.

A half dozen more assassins enter the room from the front of the train.

Jimmy: I think we outnumber them...

Tex: Goodbye...

Another fight begins:

"Strike of the Cobra"

It's victims fall blinded by the venom of the Cobra. As the Cobra strikes, the smell of terror from its attackers fills the air. Panic can be seen in the eyes of the villains just before the Cobra injects its powerful venom that strikes them dead. Those that dare swiftly and regretfully realize that they've walked into the final duel of their existence. One by one the cobra strikes, one by one the enemy falls.

Tex ducks out the back door. The Young Warriors overcome the thugs, tossing guys out the windows left and right. Carmen tears the lid off a wooden crate to strike an assassin in the head with it. As she strikes him and follows with a heel kick that tosses him off the train, she notices that the crate is full of explosives. A timer counts down as the explosives are about to go off. She smashes another one of the assassins as she speaks.

Carmen: Guys...we got a problem!

Jimmy looks inside and sees the bomb.

Jimmy: Holy shit guys!

Max : Throw it out the back door!

Ethan: (pulling on the box) we can't! It's bolted down!

Jimmy: Hold on I have seen this before while searching through documented criminal news and mug shots.

The numbers on the LED display of the explosives rapidly count down, 3 minutes, 2:59, 2:58.

Alexa: Let's get outta here!

Jimmy: This is a relay bomb system H431, when it goes off it sets off the timer of the next bomb, and that one does the same. There has to be at least four more of these on the train.

Alexa: One in each train car?

Jimmy: That's right

Alexa: Then there could be more of them than four...

Jimmy: Yeap, a lot more...

Carmen: Can you defuse it?

Jimmy: They all carry the same defusing code, I could try, there is twelve numbers to this code, and if I fail at least I can get some of the numbers and try the explosive readout in the next car. Then keep on going until I get all twelve numbers.

Ethan: Jimmy you try to diffuse that thing, but be careful. I'm going after Tex

Carmen: Ethan, I'm coming with you!

Jimmy: You guys go ahead.

The LED Read out now reads .59, .58, .57 seconds. Jimmy is able to decode four numbers on the explosive. Jimmy jumps off the caboose to the next train car yelling.

Jimmy: 7943! Wow!!!

Kaboom! The bomb goes off.

The rest of the Warriors fled the caboose just in time, and head towards the dining cart. As Ethan and Carmen climb out the back door Tex stands in front of them. He addresses Ethan and Carmen with a smirk on his face.

Tex: My ride is a few minutes late, but don't despair, it will be here shortly.

Above the roof of the caboose, a helicopter flies within a few feet of the train. They send down a rope for Tex, and as he goes for it, Ethan and Carmen attack him.

Ethan: I don't think you know who you're messing with Mr...

As Tex fights them off, he replies.

Tex: Stupid children, correct?

The helicopter moves away from the train towards the front train cars, Tex follows jumping from car to car. Ethan and Carmen keep hot on his trail. (

An explosion goes off blowing another train car to smithereens.

A fight begins between the three,.

"The Cobra Whips its Tail"

Revenge and the pursuit of justice drive the Cobra to her enemy's destruction. As she defiantly coils, twists, turns and moves away, she unleashes every strike, with such unequaled power, strength and intensity that the enemy simply falls where he stands.

Carmen strikes Tex. Tex loses his footing and falls off the train. Ethan yanks the brief case from Tex's grip as Tex falls from the train. Tex drops and rolls on the ground at a rapid speed from the moving train. As the battle comes to an end Ethan stands on the roof of the train cart with the brief case carrying the six bracelets.

THE DINING CAR - THE EXPLOSION

Inside the dining car Shadow 6 is paying the waiter for their dinner bill.

Shadow 6: Keep the change.

Agent Maggie Reynolds: Thanks for dinner; I'll get the next one.

Shadow 6: Hopefully not on a train.

There is a succession of loud booms, the sound of the bombs going off at each train car.

Agent Maggie Reynolds: Shadow... The sound trains make?

Shadow 6: No, that's the sound bombs make. I don't get it. There's got to be a mole in headquarters, or we're dealing with psychics.

They try to run towards the passenger cars but pandemonium breaks out all over the room. People scream in terror, they trample each other in efforts to reach the exit. Several passengers' crash through the doors, some fall to their death. Shadow 6 and Agent Reynolds are stuck in the dinner cart trying to restore calmness.

Several explosions light up the night sky. On the roof of the train the vibrations from the explosions shake the train cars and Carmen slips off the train as Ethan grabs her and pulls her back on.

Meanwhile Jimmy drops inside the surviving cars that have not exploded yet and tries to decode the detonator for the explosives. He works on another bomb, this time he gets four more numbers and jumps on the top of the next cart yelling.

Jimmy: 79438106... Wow... Wee!!!

Max and Mike enter the dinner cart yelling.

Max: The bomb... in a crate! Look for the crate!

Mike: Jimmy is trying to figure out the decoding number before the other bombs go off!

Shadow 6 and Agent Reynolds rip the dinner cart apart looking for the crate. Max and Mike help.

On the top of the surviving carts, Carmen and Ethan chase the rest of the villains.

Carmen: Let's go!

Ethan: Wait Carmen, I don't know... Are we doing the right thing? We are now attacking, not defending...

Carmen: Remember the Hannah-Shin-Kyo, it is the oath you took, "In darkness there's sin, in darkness there's death, sin negates spirit and the killing of beings without spirit shall only be looked on as an act of charity." These evil men killed the senior Warrior team!

Carmen puts her arm around Ethan and they make a diving jump from one train cart to the next.

Jimmy enters another cart in mad search for the crate with explosives in it.

Carmen: We are Warriors, we're that good, and today we won, fair and square.

Ethan: Thanks, Carmen.

Carmen: That Tex-guy, you think he let me win?

Ethan: Nah... You kicked ass girl, you're bad!

Just as one of the cars is blown to bits, a fireball engulfs the helicopter. It crashes into the next cart. The explosion triggers several train cars to blow in succession.

On the roof of the train, Ethan and Carmen jump from car to car barely outrunning each explosion by inches.

Jimmy decodes the last four numbers of the bombs 794381062591. The bomb in that car does not go off; however an explosion is heard outside from another car.

Jimmy: Oh, shit, this was not the brain of the relay. I need to get to the dinner car, like now!

Jimmy exits the car and runs on the roof of the train from car to car and dives into the dinner cart through the broken doors yelling.

Jimmy: 794381062591, 794381062591, 794381062591.

Shadow 6 finds the crate with the explosives behind the bar. The LED readout reads 30 seconds. Jimmy keeps on yelling the code out loud as he slides on the floor of the dinner car. 794381062591, 794381062591, 794381062591.

Shadow 6 inserts the code. All explosions cease.

The explosions stop short of the car that Max, Sarah, and Alexa are. The back wall of their car is completely exposed, blown off. Max, Sarah and Alexa are breathing hard, shaken up. Shadow 6 arrives with agent Reynolds, whose gun is drawn.

Shadow 6: Two questions.

Ethan: Yes sir?

Shadow 6: Number one, where are Ethan and Carmen?

Just then Ethan and Carmen climb down from the roof, Ethan with the briefcase, he hands it to Shadow 6.

Alexa: What's the second question?

Shadow 6: Where's the rest of the train?

Jimmy: What are you talking about?

Sarah: Yeah, we didn't even notice.

The Young warriors all give sarcastic smiles in relief. From afar we see three train cars at the rear of the train engulfed in flames and smoke as the train speeds along the track.

Shadow 6: Grab your gear; we're getting off the next chance we get.

Agent Maggie Reynolds: I believe you're right, 6; there is a leak at the bureau.

Jimmy: Duh!!

Agent Maggie Reynolds: And I thought plane rides were dangerous...

CHAPTER 16

THE YOUNG WARRIORS GO TO WAR

THE BOSSES MANSION

Inside the Grand Hall of the Boss's mansion as the sunset disappears from the sky, all the crime Bosses sit around the table once again, Gina is at the head. They are celebrating their success by throwing a gigantic party at the Mansion. Hundreds of underworld figures walk, talk, and dance to the music in the huge ballroom next to the Grand Hall.

Gina: Gentlemen, have the preparations been made?

Everyone nods.

Gina: Alright, in three, two, one...

The clock on the wall chimes midnight.

Gina: Let's make some noise.

Views of banks all over the world being broken into, by all the underlings of the crime families can be seen on a gigantic screen. Each time it is a violent entry, where teams of men move to the bank's computer mainframe and a disk is put into the drive, downloaded, and taken back, as they quickly rush out, leaving behind the most deadly virus to date, *code name "Candy"*.

Each break-in ends with a phone call to the respective Boss.

Inside the Grand Hall Daniel O'leary hangs up the phone, as Gina and the rest of the crime Bosses wait patiently.

Daniel: It's done.

Gina: That's the last one.

Gina breathes a sigh of relief.

Gina: Father is going to be very happy.

Gina starts to leave the room.

Daniel: Wait!

Gina: Yes?

Daniel: What about us? We did our part, now where's our money? You promised us cash up front.

Gina: Daniel, you must have more faith in your partners. Let me be the first one to say thanks to each of you for all your help. As promised, Tex will take care of you.

She kisses Daniel on the forehead and exits. Tex enters the room with a machine gun. He opens fire on the room, hitting everyone point blank. All the Bosses fly off their chairs, hitting the ground and taking cover. To their amazement, no one seems to be hurt.

Tex: Bang, bang, you're all dead. Don't forget this day; I was under orders to kill you, yet you live.

Tex turns around and leaves the room before anyone asks any questions. Everyone is left in shock.

THE EISACK RIVER

The **Eisack** River, the second largest river in **South Tyrol, Italy** whose source begins near the **Brenner Pass**, at an altitude of about 1990 meters above **sea level**. It borders small villages and desolated homes for many miles. At one point the river flows through the medieval town **of** Vipiteno.   Shadow 6, agent Reynolds and the Young

Warriors travel the river in three speedboats cruising at top speed to reach their destination.

Shadow 6: Okay, where am I going here?

Agent Maggie Reynolds: About a mile up. It's a huge estate, right off the water, and up the mountains. We are almost there.

Shadow 6: I hope so, time is of the essence. Did you inform the authorities and requested transportation?

Agent Maggie Reynolds: Sure did. We should have vehicles waiting for us at the dock.

The boats reach their destination and Shadow 6 ties up the boat to a pier as Agent Reynolds and the Warriors are getting off. The Warriors tie up their respective boat. Max keeps an eye on his GPS-PDA, tracking Elisa.

Agent Maggie Reynolds: So what's the plan?

Shadow 6: We're walking right in through the front door.

Agent Maggie Reynolds: What?

Shadow 6: Why not, your cover's blown. What do you have to lose?

Agent Maggie Reynolds: Nothing, everything, I... this is not how things are done.

Shadow 6: They are when I'm running the show.

Agent Maggie Reynolds: But...

Shadow 6: Well, wait here if you want.

Agent Maggie Reynolds: No. I'm coming with.

They all leave the boats. The Young Warriors are dressed for battle, full armor, and masks on. Shadow 6 carries a garment bag with him. They get into a couple of SUV's left there by the local police for their use and head towards the mountains.

On their way to Venezie's mansion, Shadow 6 receives a call on his cell from the Center of Technical Operations Headquarters. Shadow 6 answers.

Shadow 6: Yes this is he. How can I be of help? Really? Are you positive? Understood, we are on it.

Shadow 6 hangs up the phone and bangs his fist on the dashboard.

Shadow 6: Damn!

Agent Maggie Reynolds: What is it 6?

Shadow 6: That was the Center of Technical Operations Headquarters. They deciphered the code on the "Candy Disk" containing the anti-virus and found out that that disk is missing the "Closing Code" to activate the "anti-virus". There has to be another disk with that code.

Agent Maggie Reynolds: How do we find it?

Shadow 6: Well, we are heading into the middle of the "wasp's nest", let's pray it's there, if not all has been for nothing.

They travel twenty minutes up the mountain and they arrive at the gates of the Boss' Mansion.

Shadow 6: I'll be walking in the front door. I want all of you to enter the mansion through the rear and side doors.

Agent Maggie Reynolds: You're going to crash the party?

Shadow 6 unzips his bag and pulls out a tuxedo.

Shadow 6: You could say that.

Agent Maggie Reynolds: Invitation?

Shadow 6: (Exposing an invitation in the inside pocket of the tux) You have to ask?

Max lifts his left wrist exposing the *Bracelet*.

Max: We'll be on the air, waiting for your orders.

Carmen: Let's do it.

Shadow 6 goes into the wooded area to change. The Warriors suit up, Agent Reynolds heads with the group of Warriors to the back side of the Mansion.

In the Ball Room of the crime Boss's Mansion the "Mothers Against Crime" Charity event cocktail party is in full force.

Shadow 6 enters the event and is greeted by some of the most influential politicians in existence.

Prime Minister John Howard of Australia, French Prime minister Dominique de Villepin, King Abdullah II of the Hashemite Kingdom of Jordan, King Harald V and Queen Sonja of Norway, Chancellor Angela Merkel of Germany. The list is endless.

Agent Reynolds and the Warriors enter the mansion through the back and side door and head for Grand Hall in 'force concentration' mode.

Force concentration is the practice of concentrating a military force so as to bring to bear such overwhelming force against a portion of an enemy force that the disparity between the two forces alone acts as a force multiplier in

280

favor of the concentrated forces. It is aimed to cause disproportionate losses on the enemy and therefore destroy the enemy's ability to fight.

The Grand Hall room is encased by floor to ceiling glass doors. Elaborate draperies cover them. Oversized candles, two feet in diameter rise six feet from floor to wick. The fire from the lit candles gives the room a warm exotic feeling.

Shadow 6 carefully avoids the crowd and makes his way to the Grand Hall. Tex stands on the landing of the stairs looking down on them. Tex claps his hands slowly.

Tex: Well look at you. I see you brought the high school band with ya. Long time no see. You finally made top dog. Bow wow. Good to see you've kept your girly figure.

Shadow 6: You don't look so bad yourself for a dead man. Nice try at trying to fool the authorities. It didn't work; they had pictures and video of you after your death. Go figure.

Tex: You're right; maybe the Gods had other plans for me. Should we invite the guests in the Ball Room so they can enjoy your performance? I tell you what; if you get a "10" from the judges on your performance I will personally give you this.

Tex reaches into his coat pocket and pulls out a disk marked "Candy Closing Code".

Tex: (Continuing) that's right band leader, you forgot to pick up the second disk on your last rock and roll club performance. I would of love to have been a fly on the wall when operations cracked the code on disk number one... and got nothing!

Tex lets out a maniacal laugh.

Shadow 6: Let's cut to the chase Tex, make this easier on yourself, just hand over Elisa and the Candy.

Tex: (with a smirk) Aw, come on Xavier you know me better than to make it easier for myself. Besides, you and the high school band? You have to play me a song first. I must reiterate... some of our guests in the Ball room would enjoy the added entertainment.

Just then, from downstairs, Gina Venezie sneaks up behind the group. She puts her pistol to the back of Maggie's head.

Gina: Lose the weapon.

Agent Maggie Reynolds: (Under her breath) Shit...

Maggie tosses her gun and puts her hands up.

Gina: (smiling) Need I say more.

Gina shoves Maggie forward and motions to the others to move towards Tex.

Alexa: Elisa...I feel Elisa.

The group looks around.

Ethan: (pointing to the outside) There she is!

Gina: What you brought a psychic with you? That will sure add to the entertainment.

The group spots Elisa being taken from the back of the house towards the forest by a group of mercenaries.

Instinctively the 'Young Warriors' run towards the glass windows disregarding Gina's threat. Agent Reynolds spins around and knocks Gina into one of the large candles. The weapon goes off in the direction of Alexa who angles her body, avoiding the bullet's path.

Gina's fall topples one of the large candles, setting fire to the drapes. Within seconds the room is engulfed in a raging fire. Everyone scrambles to safety. The Young Warriors rush to the outside of the mansion. Tex makes himself scarce in the confusion.

As people reach the front door, fire engulfs the entire house. Everyone in the Charity event is quickly ushered outside to avoid injury. The young Warriors make it to the outside where everyone stares in disbelief. The Warriors are met by a group of Mercenaries armed to the teeth.

"The Way of the Snowtiger"

The Combat is fierce and savage as the Shadow Warriors morph into all the animals of the Snowtiger attacking the enemy quickly and mercilessly with careless abandon, crippling and killing with dispassionate intent.

Inside the mansion, there's fire everywhere, beams falling, walls crumbling. Still inside, Shadow 6 picks a path between the flames. He spots a weapons room and heads for a cabinet. He opens it and looks for a moment.

Pondering, he strips off his tuxedo, revealing his combat clothes. He pulls out weapons -- a "Savage" sniper rifle, two combat knives, two fully automatic pistols, three other rifles, and a long-bladed knife.

He puts on his war mask, then ducks and slips into a closet, opens a trunk and takes out the *"Kukri"...An Ancient and Deadly Blade used by The Lin Kuei.*

Shadow 6 dumps all the weapons in a box sitting in the corner. He pulls smoke powder packets and ammunition cartridges from the shelves and puts it all in the box. Lifting the box, he quickly heads towards the exit before the building starts to fall on him.

Shadow 6 walks *Out Of the Burning Mansion* carrying the box on his shoulders. The Warriors finish overcoming the small group of mercenaries. Without breaking stride, Shadow 6 throws rifles and knives to Max, Jimmy, and Carmen. They catch the weapons, ready to put them to use.

Shadow 6: Maggie, take Alexa to the river trail and head up to the clearing. Stay there. Check with headquarters. Let them know our position. If you don't hear from us within the hour, go upriver to the rendezvous point. Headquarters will give you the coordinates. There you'll meet the SAS agents. They'll take you to the USS Eisenhower. Max, Jimmy, and I are going to get Elisa.

The rest of you...shadow us.

Maggie: But what about the disc?

Shadow 6: Forget about it for now. We will get it in time. Take care of Alexa.

Alexa: I don't need to be taken care of; I can take care of myself. I can...

Shadow 6: This is no time for pride, Alexa. Do what's right. Go with Maggie and make me proud. Think of Elisa.

Alexa surrenders to his logic and command. She bows her head in respect to him. He puts his hand on her forehead. Shadow 6 turns to the rest of the group as they all mask themselves.

Shadow 6: They took Eric Stone from us. He was our most revered. Now they aim to take... Elisa. Warriors (pause) ...this will not happen. Move!

Shadow 6 repeats himself.

Shadow 6: Warriors (pause)...this will not happen! Let's go!

Shadow 6 turns and runs off toward the forest, Max, Carmen and Jimmy follow. The other Shadow Warriors spread out in formation. They are well trained. It shows. They shadow their mentor and brothers in blood.

Maggie hesitates, then shepherds Alexa toward the river. The Mansion and its contents are savagely mauled by the ferocious breath of the fire which grows in strength and size by the minute gobbling everything in sight.

It is now dusk, and Shadow 6 runs through the wooded path, his endurance is that of a young Warrior, keeping a punishing, steady pace. The thin air takes its toll on his lungs, but he forges forward with the determination of a madman. Max, Carmen and Jimmy run behind, less winded than their mentor at this time. Shadow 6 pushes forward with bold fury ignoring the diminishing performance of his lungs from the thin and cold air.

Alexa stops on her tracks and speaks to Maggie.

Alexa: Maggie, go on and follow Shadow 6's instructions, I am going to double back and see where I can help.

Agent Maggie Reynolds: But Alexa, you could get hurt, you know you can't...

Alexa: Maggie, I did not volunteer for this job, I was adopted, recruited and put as part of a team dedicated and sworn to protect the American way of life. I wasn't recruited to be a pet or to be put on a shelf.

Agent Maggie Reynolds: The forest is treacherous, and you need your eyes...

Alexa: Maggie, I can see just fine, not through my eyes, but my senses can see sharper and clearer than anyone I know in any situation.

Agent Maggie Reynolds: But...

Alexa: Maggie, can you see those bluebirds by that tall tree in front of us? Can you see the running stream of water ahead of us; can you see the drop on the ground approximately 25 feet from here on the west side?

Agent Maggie Reynolds: How can?...

Alexa: But most of all can you see those two Blackwater Mercenaries heading in our direction about 50 feet east of us?

Agent Maggie Reynolds: Alexa, unbelievable...

Alexa: Whether or not you see them, we either hide or fight... or die.

Agent Maggie Reynolds: In the bushes Alexa. Get down.

They both hide in the brush and let the Mercenaries go by without altercation. Agent Reynolds is in total awe and shock over Alexa's power of her senses.

Agent Maggie Reynolds: Ok, Alexa, you proved your point, but in your place I would be scared to death. I am sorry for doubting you.

Alexa: No problem, all is good. I like freaking people out. I'll see you again when this is over.

They both smile and part ways.

In the wooded hillside, Max keeps an eye on his PDA, making sure they're on track. Shadow 6 keeps looking back for his lead in direction. Shadow 6 runs up to the crest of a wooded hill. He slows and crawls the last few feet. Max, Carmen, and Jimmy just behind him look over the hillside.

A path runs through a gully, about eighty feet below. Shadow 6's eyes dart, absorbing the terrain, looking for advantage. He points.

Shadow 6: Max, there. Jimmy, there. Carmen, there. Go. Now.

Shadow 6 has the Young Warriors covering all angles - The young warriors go where they're told.

Shadow 6: I'll fire first. Max, you terminate whoever is closest to Elisa. Carmen, kill those on the flanks. Jimmy, kill the last man in the line. Remember; kill those with the highest rank first.

The young Warriors are frozen under the significance of his commands. Shadow 6 notices it and continues on.

Shadow 6: After that, Jimmy, Max, Carmen, load for each other. *Do Not Hesitate.* If something happens to me, leave no trace. Run, fast, that way, downhill. Make your way back, get to the others and go to the rendezvous point.

The young warriors hesitate. Shadow 6 looks at them firmly.

Shadow 6: Warriors... steady.

Max, Carmen & Jimmy: Yes, sir.

Shadow 6 listens. He can hear *Unity* Mercenaries approaching with Elisa. Shadow 6 disappears into the underbrush. The other Shadow Warriors can be seen flanking him, shadowing his moves, but keeping a good distance. They move totally unseen. They blend completely with the forest.

Down the path, two dozen *Unity* Mercenaries approach. They are the most dangerous and effective guns for hire group of assassins answering to the name of *"The Blackwater Mercenaries"*. They lead Elisa rapidly down the path with a rope around her neck and hands tied in front of her.

Deeper into the narrow path, ahead of the *Blackwater Mercenaries* Shadow 6 waits in the thick undergrowth. He sees the *Mercenaries*, sees Elisa, but doesn't see Tex or Gabriel Venezie. He ponders this.

On the hillside, Max, Carmen, and Jimmy grip their rifles and exchange an anxious look; distressed, restless.

The Blackwater Mercenaries enter a gully. Shadow 6 waits... and waits. Then, picking the right moment, he *fires*, killing the Blackwater Mercenary deputy-leader with a shot to the head.

Max, Carmen, and Jimmy *instantly fire,* dropping another mercenary, plus the last Blackwater Mercenary in the line and the one holding Elisa's rope.

288

The Blackwater Mercenaries STOP in confusion, some scatter...taking cover behind nearby tree trunks, taking ready-fire positions.

Elisa kneels, out of the line of fire. Six *Mercenaries* encircle Elisa. The Blackwater Mercenary *Leader* takes command.

Blackwater Leader: (Shouting to the top of his lungs) Combat Command! Hollow Square Formation! Steady men... Steady! Lines...Ready yourself! Get ready to f...

BANG!

Shadow 6 KILLS the '*Leader*' with a shot to the back of the head... Jimmy finishes reloading, swaps rifles with Carmen who *fires, dropping another Blackwater Mercenary.* They look at each other in proud amazement.

The other Shadow Warriors, moving like ghosts within the forest, start their onslaught. It is skilled, deadly, and silent. They use shuriken; dipped in doku [an ancient poison that paralyses before it kills].

They climb trees, burrow into the leaves on the ground; anything to blend with their surroundings. Shuriken, blow darts and shaken blades fly. No sound. *Blackwater Mercenaries* drop.

Blackwater Mercenaries seeing their comrades are falling all around them, without hearing a gunshot, realize they are in over their heads. Are these the ghost warriors of the forest they all heard of, *The 'Forest Demons'?*

In combat formation, the Blackwater Assassins look, upward, all around them, in the trees, down the gully to no avail.

Blackwater Assassin: (Taking command he shouts) Ready...

Before the Mercenary can complete his command, Shadow 6 FIRES, killing the Assassin, the last man of rank...

Shadow 6 ducks to the side as a *Barrage of Blackwater Rifle and Shotgun Fire* tears into the area marked by Shadow 6's rifle smoke...

From This Moment On, Shadow 6 Never Stops Moving. He strides rather than runs, staying just inside the brush, offering only glimpses of himself. Now his breathing has somehow become steady and calm.

He changes his pace and direction repeatedly, ducking and weaving, firing and loading while moving. He never gives the Blackwater Mercenaries a stationary target. He is hidden by the billowing smoke from his smokescreens [dropping smoke bombs along the way]. An ancient Lin Kuei tactic. It works.

The Blackwater Mercenaries *Track Him with Their Barrels*, about to fire... Shadow 6 suddenly *Stops Dead, Reverses Direction*, several Blackwater Mercenaries *Fire and Miss. He Moves Like A Phantom... A Ghost.*

Suddenly the sounds of wild, vicious animals could be heard emanating from deep within the forest. The Blackwater Mercenaries freeze. Ten Blackwater Mercenaries are left. Some preparing to fire, some reloading, others realizing their last moments. A Blackwater Mercenary draws a bead on Shadow 6, who drops to the ground and... *Fires*, killing him.

Another Blackwater Mercenary aims at Shadow 6. *Elisa Bulls into Him,* causing his shot to go awry...

As the Blackwater Mercenary turns on Elisa, he puts a blade to her throat;

Blackwater Mercenary: You want her? Here is her head!

Shadow 6 kills shoots with the perfection of an expert marksman; the bullet misses Elisa by one inch and penetrates the Mercenary's head. He falls dead behind his kidnapped victim.

The Shadow Warriors move in. The Blackwater Mercenaries hear the sounds of the wild animals again, this time coming closer.

Jimmy, still in shock as he loads, hands a loaded sniper rifle to Max who FIRES...

The Blackwater Mercenaries turn their attention to *the spot marked by max's muzzle fire...*

Shadow 6 *Sees* Blackwater Mercenaries *aiming toward the young* Shadow Warriors. He instantly *strides out into the open*, drawing the Blackwater Mercenaries' attention from his young protégés...

Shadow 6, running toward the group of mercenaries, *fires both of his fully automatic pistols*, killing two Blackwater Mercenaries...*then killing some more.* His movement is uncanny and hard to predict.

One Blackwater Mercenary finishes reloading... Alexa steps out of the brush and rushes him, with blinding blows to the Mercenary's collar bone forces him to drop his weapons, and *slams* him in the face with her elbow [bull attack]...

Shadow 6 is stunned to see Alexa, but his focus keeps him viciously attacking and destroying his enemies. This is a *Ferocious, Savage Shadow 6*, killing with the same stunning brutality seen in the sequence when he was a boy of just fifteen. The other Shadow Warriors, preparing to move in, stop and watch, also shocked to see Alexa in action.

As the mercenary drops to the ground from Alexa's blows, Shadow 6 *catches* the Blackwater Mercenary's *loaded rifle* before it hits the ground, shoves that rifle into another Blackwater Mercenary's abdomen and *Fires...*

Several Blackwater Mercenaries are left, some reloading, others finished loading, some taking off with Elisa...

Alexa moves back into the brush after other Mercenaries. Shadow 6 *charges*, drawing his *Kukri*, ignores a *glancing machete wound* to the neck, HACKS a Blackwater Mercenary open... He's splattered with *blood...*

CHAPTER 17

THE FINAL SHOWDOWN

*Kukri: A **Nepalese** knife with an inwardly curved blade, similar to a **machete**, used as both a tool and as a weapon in **Nepal** and some neighboring countries of South Asia.*

Another Blackwater Mercenary, an athletic young man, tries to slip into the woods but Alexa leaps in front of him, blocking his path.

Alexa: You don't want to go in there. They're worse than I am.

Shadow 6's students, all with spent weapons, watch as the young Mercenary grabs a dropped *machete* and squares off with Alexa who is armed only with a *Kukri*.

The young Mercenary *slashes towards Alexa*... Alexa evades the blow, ducks under another *slash* and in an unusual but practiced motion, *strikes upward with her knife*, nearly severing the *Mercenary's* arm.

Then, without pausing to take a breath, Alexa strikes the Mercenary with a flying kick to the chest. The *Mercenary's* body flies in the direction of Shadow 6. Shadow 6 raises his *Kukri* and butchers the *Mercenary* with a quick series of hacking blows.

Shadow 6's young students are stunned at what they are witnessing. Carmen, Jimmy, tears rolling down their face, normally pretty tough kids, are now stunned. Shadow 6, battle-focused, checks the Mercenaries bodies, unaware of his students' eyes on him.

The other Shadow Warriors slowly emerge from the brush and trees, moving with uncertainty.

The other Blackwater Mercenaries have gotten away with Elisa as Shadow 6 was busy focusing on the last victim in his midst. Alexa is quickly on her way following Elisa's kidnappers. She is focused, determined, and as quick and stealthy as a *Ghost*.

This Mercenary team was a decoy. The rest of the Mercenaries head up the path, increasing their pace as they try to meet up with the main Mercenary team that is heading to Gabriel Venezie "backup" mountain hideaway, to meet and protect the 'War Lord'.

It is now dusk, in a forest gully, Shadow 6 and his warrior protégés convene. He's tired; covered in blood. He stays focused. His orders are quick, concise and deliberate, "*Get Venezie, Recover Elisa*". They move.

Shadow 6 and the Warriors pound across the pasture towards the Blackwater Mercenary's path, who have now taken the route along a cliff bordering the mountains.

Shadow 6 and his team of young warriors continue their relentless pursuit that leads them half-way up the rock face – a short-cut to cut off the enemy's path. They approach an overhang. They climb with reckless desperation.

Jimmy reaches the cliff overhang first. The overhang sticks out about ten feet from the face.

Jimmy's hand jams into a crack in the rock face; he forms a fist and twists, making a wedge. He swings out, dangling in space by the hand wedged into the rock. His right hand reaches out and up, searching the vertical face for... a ledge... a rock flake, an indentation. Anything. His fingers find a diagonal crevice and...

Jimmy swings out, now hanging by the vertical face above the overhang. His features are distorted with determination. Nothing will stop him. His right hand grabs another rock. His arms snap him up. Then push. He's on the ledge. Moving fast ... all the other warriors follow him. Shadow 6, taking up the rear, is impressed with his team's astounding performance.

On point and with precision excellence the Blackwater Mercenaries approach the path above the Cliff. Five *Burmese Gurkha* warriors accompany them and are ahead of Tex; ten Blackwater Mercenaries are behind him. A Mercenary literally drags Elisa. They all run at a punishing pace. Gabriel, "The Boss" has made sure to hire the best.

Jimmy, on the parallel ledge above, runs past the group of Mercenaries. He's above them. He swings down...

A *Gurkha* starts up the narrow path. Suddenly, Jimmy slams him off the rock with a grappling hook wedged into the rock face, the rope wrapped around his forearm; the *Kukri* in his other hand, leading his swing.

Three Mercenaries pointing at Jimmy quickly approach him. Jimmy swings, *cuts one of them in the throat be*fore falling. As he is about to get shot, Jimmy *throws his Kukri* with all his might striking the assailant between the eyes. Jimmy lunges and rolls, picking up the dead Mercenary's rifle and shooting the third attacker. He yanks his Kukri from the dead man's face.

A Fourth Mercenary fires, misses, and swings his rifle at Jimmy. Jimmy slips the swung rifle, but it catches his elbow. Jimmy's rifle falls. Before it hits the ground his Kukri , if ok) is out and hacks his attacker and sends him with a flying kick over the edge.

Tex, running forward past one of his Mercenaries comes to help. He confronts Jimmy head on. Tex is incredibly fast. Jimmy's three *Kukri* swings are dodged by Tex whose own blade streaks like silver flashes. Jimmy, gashed on both arms and chest, feints right and slams Tex with an elbow, closes in; he grapples him and the men are intertwined steel and muscle.

Tex throws Jimmy, holding on to him. They tumble together as Tex rolls off Jimmy, his knife slashes into Jimmy's armpit, rendering his right arm useless. Jimmy, despite the searing pain, scrambles up. Next to the expertise of a mature 'warrior' like Tex, Jimmy's raw, young determination may not be enough. He is totally surprised by Tex's skill, unaware of his opponent's latent abilities.

Shadow 6, witnessing the encounter between Jimmy and Tex, freezes momentarily, then...Moves. Fast. Toward Jimmy's rescue. Alexa follows.

Jimmy, closing, swings. Tex moves inside, stabs at Jimmy twice, misses, grabs his hair, turns him to face the edge, jerking his head left to expose the right underside of his throat. Tex's knife arm punches forward. Jimmy deflects it, slips, and falls over the edge. Tex lunges forward, almost off the cliff himself, in attempts to grab him, he catches Jimmy's sleeve and takes to him.

Tex: Young man, don't look down, look at me. Slowly turn your hand and grab mine. Below you there's a small ledge. If we fail at this attempt take that knife in your belt and with all your might stab at the ground and hold tight. Do you understand?

Confused by Tex's actions, Jimmy just hangs there in a trance. He starts to slip and quickly regains his senses.

Jimmy: Yes, sir.

Tex: Slowly turn your hand.

Jimmy attempts the move, but falls short of Tex's hand. As he falls, Jimmy draws the knife from his belt and follows Tex's instructions. The knife strikes the ground on the small ledge. The ground is soft enough to allow the blade to penetrate, but strong enough to hold Jimmy, who now dangles from the edge, attempting to pull himself on to the ledge.

The shock of it all takes its toll. Carmen collapses to her knees on the ground and her face falls forward into her hands...

Shadow 6, seeing his student appear to be killed, *Cries* out [bellows] and charges up the path, Max and the other Shadow Warriors follow. They shoot and cut their way through the Blackwater Mercenaries in their path with ease and violence. Their intent is relentless, their goal obvious.

Elisa backs toward the edge. Tex moves on Elisa. His knife is low, about to strike. She stares at him. Her calm and almost innocent eyes, open, captivating, seem to stop Tex...

Tex inexplicably drops his knife hand. He's captivated by her. But there's a glimmer of something else in him. He appears to have humanity, but for this one brief moment.

297

He reaches out with his other hand to offer her safety, to bring her back from the edge...

Elisa looks down at Jimmy's, her favorite student. Jimmy managed to pull himself on to the rocks below, but lays unconscious from the ordeal. She turns to Tex with enigmatic calm. Her eyes seem to see into him. He seems mesmerized by her. She slips her hands out of the ropes, drops a blinding powder packet into her hand from a concealed pouch inside her shirtsleeve, and brings her hand up to her face. She blows as Tex gets just close enough.

Some of the powder hits its target as most is blown away from the windy cliff. She advances on Tex but stops immediately as she realizes that he isn't fazed by the powder. She steps back, closer to the edge. Turns and jumps.

Tex looks over the edge. It's too dark to see. She's gone.

Tex: Oh, no...

Blackwater Mercenary warriors run down the path to intercept Shadow 6 who's charging uphill, fueled with a Warrior's rage. Max follows. One Blackwater Mercenary aims at the center of Shadow 6's chest...

Max *Fires* past his mentor's side. The Blackwater Mercenary is blown off the path as the bullet penetrates his throat. Max races to reload on the run...

From the edge of the cliff Tex look up and sees the approach of Shadow 6.

Blackwater Mercenary warriors are an irrelevance. Shadow 6 slams one Mercenary aside with a Bull rush. He throws an elbow to the chest knocking the wind out of another Mercenary. Cuts another with the *Kukri*.

Max *Fires* again, a Blackwater Mercenary with a machete, about to blind-side Shadow 6, is shot down. Alexa fights of two other Mercenaries, making quick work of them.

Tex charges Shadow 6.

The two men, like vicious, wild animals, race to collide at the center of the cliff. The other Warriors fall back. It's a one-on-one, *Mano a Mano Combat.*

Max slows ...

Tex shows extreme confidence, adrenaline shoots throughout his body...he knows he is in a life or death fight. Tex feints with his left; his *Short Sword* appears in his right hand as he throws a sweeping backhand. He throws his blade to his left hand as he completes a jamming motion to Shadow 6's gut. The blade completes its move, except as if by magic, Shadow 6 is not there.

Shadow 6 rolls on one knee with his back to Tex, his arm slams rearward. The ancient Lin Kuei war blade crashes into Tex's back.

Tex stunned, turns to cut Shadow 6 with his sword. Shadow 6 rapidly stands towering over Tex and slams the back of the Kukri knife breaking Tex's arm and derailing Tex's assault.

Shadow 6, keeping his momentum, spins, jumping into the air landing a strike that cripples Tex's left side and crushes part of his chest.

Another blow is rapidly directed to Tex's shoulder. With the sleekness and poise of a cat, Tex avoids the fatal blow.

Shadow 6 without missing a beat rips the pouch hanging from Tex's neck carrying the "Candy Anti-Virus" disk.

Tex stares in amazement. His body is broken and crippled, but he still stands. He looks into the eyes of the last true student of the ancient LIN KUEI masters.

SHADOW 6 yells out, NINPO IKKAN!!!

Shadow 6 spins and swings, the blade side of the war blade is directed into Tex's chest. Tex manages to block the blow. Four Blackwater Mercenaries rush Shadow 6 as Tex falls to his knees from the force of Shadow 6's blow and his injuries. Shadow 6 is forced to turn and defend against the Mercenaries assault.

Tex is helped up by one of his mercenary assassins and is moved away into the forest, unnoticed in the turmoil.

Max watching Shadow 6 heaving back from the onslaught of the four Mercenaries moves in to help. He is passed by the other Shadow Warriors. They engage the four Blackwater Mercenaries with violent disregard. The Young Warriors overcome the danger and dispose of the evil Mercenaries. The *Battle* is over.

Carmen sits alone, kneeling in the pasture. Her eyes downcast, tears streaming down her face...

Shadow 6 and his team of young warriors gathered on the cliff, looking below to see if there is any way to rescue Jimmy. Two Warriors repel down to the body of their fallen comrade, his vital signs show he's still barely alive, but fading fast. They radio for help to get a Civil Defense Protection Unit to send a helicopter with an EMT team.

On the radio they get a reply from the S.A.S. with helicopters already on their way to help.

The sounds of the S.A.S helicopters can be heard in the distance with Maggie aboard. The British Army helicopter lands. The Warriors take cover while pointing their weapons at the helicopter.

Shadow 6: Stand down Warriors.

Shadow 6 approaches the chopper, the Warriors follow.

Shadow 6: Just some old friends of mine in the Special Air Services, commonly known as SAS.

British Pilot: Fancy meeting you here, old boy!

Shadow 6: We need to move fast one of our 'Warriors' is fatally injured. And on a second note I need to get this disk to the NSA so they can install the "Candy" Anti-Virus into every banking system before the economy as we know it collapses.

British Pilot: Understood Sir. We are on it. Nothing will go "pear shaped sir", you can count on that.

Shadow 6 gives the pilot a strange look and replies.

Shadow 6: "That's smashing old mate"

The British pilot laughs.

Everyone gets aboard the helicopters. Expert medical help is aboard. Shadow 6 and the Young Warriors gaze in amazement of the Brits' weapons and gear.

British Officer: (pointing at the gear carried in the copter) They're exact replicas of your outfits and weaponry.

Complements of Uncle Sam, held in reserve by the Queens' Army in a case of an emergency.

Shadow 6: Hmm. Good to know.

British Officer: You Yanks are drafting them younger every year, huh?

Shadow 6: Yep. Taking a page from your book of war heroes.

Above them is a banner, the motto of the SAS it reads:

"He Who Dares Wins"

British Officer: What happened down there?

Shadow 6: Evil pushed too far and fell under the sword of the righteous.

Young Warriors: Amen.

Shadow 6 turns and faces Alexa.

Shadow 6: You disobeyed a direct order young lady.

Alexa: Well, I thought you mistook me from the club's mascot, so I had to ignore it.

Shadow 6: I can truly say that I am glad you disobeyed me this time.

Alexa: Sir, you selected me as part of the team because you were sure I could do the job, blind or not. I need you to treat me the same as everyone else and if I fall in my attempt to do good, then I will be falling doing my duty, and dying with a calm and satisfied soul.

Shadow 6: I understand Alexa, my apologies, it will never happen again. And thank you, you did an excellent job out there.

Alexa: My senses can see far deeper and more clearly than the human eye sir.

Alexa smiles and salutes Shadow 6.

LOS ANGELES AIR FORCE BASE HOSPITAL - 483 N. AVIATION BOULEVARD BUILDING #210 EL SEGUNDO, CALIFORNIA

The entire Warrior team waits in the Los Angeles Air force Base Hospital lounge as the doctors operate on Jimmy. His injuries were bad and he made it to the hospital in critical condition. As their friend lies unconscious, each warrior goes through his and her own anguish. The pain can be seen on their faces.

The lead surgeon walks into the waiting area. His 'poker face' shows no sign of the outcome of the operations.

Surgeon: Who is in charge?

Shadow 6: I am sir. What's the prognosis?

Surgeon: He's going to be fine. His wounds should heal fast; he is a strong young man. A few weeks of rest then a few weeks of rehabilitation and he'll be back in the field again. Best behind a desk for a while. He is asking for you.

Shadow 6: He is awake?

Surgeon: Yes, but you only have about five minutes, and then you'll have to leave. Rest right now will make the difference between full recuperation or not.

Shadow 6: I understand, I won't be long.

Shadow 6 is buzzed into the intensive care unit of the hospital. He enters Jimmy's room. He stands next to Jimmy's bed. Tubes are connected to Jimmy's arms, he receives medicine intravenously, and the heart monitor beeps with every thump of his heart.

Shadow 6: I am glad you are doing fine, but you should rest, your condition is delicate. We can discuss things when you are out of here.

Jimmy: I know sir. I just needed to tell you that he tried to save me.

Shadow 6: Who the doctor?

Jimmy: No sir, Tex. Why would he fight me then try to save my life. He held me by my sleeve when I fell down the cliff; he told me how to survive the fall. I don't understand...

Shadow 6: I wish I had an answer for you Jimmy, but I don't. Sometimes people do things out of instinct, and this must be one of those times. We are lucky you survived, let's be thankful for that.

Shadow 6 looks over at Jimmy, who is holding tightly to his hand and notices that he is fast asleep now. Shadow 6 exits the room with a pensive look on his face. He joins the rest of the Young warriors.

All the warriors sigh in relief. Smiles appear in all their faces.

LOS ANGELES CEMETERY

At the Los Angeles National Cemetery, of West Los Angeles Shadow 6 puts the last shovelfuls of dirt on Elisa's grave.

They never found her body [maybe the river took her], but they had a ceremony in her honor. Near tears and unsure of what to do next, he turns to Eric Stone's gravestone. He walks right behind Stone's grave and again salutes his former Shadow warrior team. The soft wind blows.

As he walks back he sees his warrior team looking at him. With an extreme effort of will, he holds in his own tears. He gathers the young warriors around him, allowing them to cry.

SIX MONTHS LATER

Inside the Ceremonial Hall in the SI-9 Center, a secret ritual takes place as nine Young Warriors receive their certification as members to the new SOG special Undercover Unit of Shadow Warriors. The SI-9 badge is pinned on each one of them by a 4-star general.

Shadow 6 stands on the side proudly witnessing the affair. Agent Reynolds stands next to Shadow six. Her face shows excitement and pride for the Young Warriors

Shadow 6: Those are my Warriors...

Agent Reynolds holds on to Shadow 6's arm.

Agent Reynolds: You are so proud of them Xavier, and so am I.

EXTERIOR - DESERT ROAD - NIGHT

A black Lamborghini at a demon's speed heads towards Mexico. The CHP vehicle Tex passed on the way to the warehouse several days ago sits on the side of the road.

The digital counter on the CHP'S speed gun reads 250 mph and suddenly drops to zero as the Lamborghini stops. The roaring of an engine can be heard by the police officer right across from him. It's another pitch-black night out.

The CHP stares out the window but can't see anything. The Lamborghini sits idle on the road across the lane from him, all lights off. Tex stares at the cop through his night vision glasses and pulls out an electrical jamming device from his glove compartment activating it. The CHP tries to put his lights on, his siren, his horn, his radio...all dead.

From inside his car, Tex smiles and looks out the window at the CHP.

The CHP steps out of the car and slowly walks across the road. Tex waits until the CHP gets close and floors the car taking off at blinding speed. The CHP is stunned by the noise and the sound of the speed. The Lamborghini stops and does a 360 without stopping about 200 yards from the CHP.

For a split second the CHP gets a glimpse of what seems to be some brake lights from a vehicle. He slowly un-holsters his weapon. The Lamborghini takes off at top speed towards the CHP the speedometer reads 145 MPH. The Lamborghini barely misses the CHP as it passes him. The force of the wind created by the speed of the car tosses the CHP to the ground. He rolls around helplessly. His gun goes off, shooting a bullet through his patrol car's left rear tire.

The CHP gets up and takes a hard look at his vehicle.

CHP: Damn! What in God's name was that? Now look at what you made me do, I am going to have to change that tire. Where the hell's the wife when you need her?

As the CHP stands up close to his car he senses the same force heading towards him again. He turns and aims the gun at the road and repeatedly fires. The Lamborghini speeds towards the CHP, this time the speedometer reads 220 MPH. The Lamborghini barely misses the CHP once again tossing him to the ground. His weapon goes off again the bullet penetrates his left front tire and continues through to perforate the right one.

The CHP gets up aiming at one side of the road then the other; still not sure of what happened. He runs into his car and calls headquarters. His radio works now.

The CHP stands outside his car speaking to headquarters.

CHP: Car 72 to headquarters, can you read me?

Operator (HEAVY SOUTHERN ACCENT): Come on in Harold, we read you loud and clear.

CHP: Betty, I need back up, a roadblock, and night vision goggles at the Oak Creek Crossing.

Operator: Harold that is in the middle of nowhere. What exactly is your problem?

CHP: I...I was attacked sort of by this thing, that caused a lot of wind...maybe a UFO, but a ground one, because this thing wasn't, flying, but … it was flying. Now wait one second, well it was flying, ha, but right down on the ground...

Operator: Harold, are you drinking on the job again?

CHP: Betty, no I am not, I shot three of my tires and I only have one spare. I was attacked and tossed on the ground and lost control of my weapon.

Operator: Attacked by whom Harold?

CHP: This huge wind...ahem...thingamachigger... This is the second time this happens, the first time I kept quit, but no more.

Harold pulls off his hat and scratches his head.

Operator : Sure Harold, stay put for a second, I have to put you on hold.

Inside the Oak Creek Police Department, the operator turns over to the police sergeant *Billy Joe*, 45, 6' feet, dark hair.

Operator: Billy Joe, have someone pick up *Harold* By the Oak Creek Crossing. I think he's drinking again...he shot three of his tires because he thought they were a UFO.

Billy Joe lifts his eyebrows and slowly speaks.

Billy: OK, nothing wrong with that. (He smirks).

DESOLATED AREA- OPEN ROAD - IN SIDE TEX'S AUTO

As the Lamborghini speeds through the desolated area, inside Tex's car we see through Tex's night vision goggles the speedometer and the road as Tex enters Mexican territory at 220 MPH.

Tex lets out a loud and hearty laugh.

The End

I want to thank our men in the United States Armed Forces who help protect and safeguard our way of life. You have my respect, my admiration and my full support. May God be with you and keep you safe till your return home.

Shadow 6

Special Ops director,
SI-9 - SOG unit

www.ingramcontent.com/pod-product-compliance
Lightning Source LLC
Chambersburg PA
CBHW070219260626
47160CB00002B/609